Something al[l] had changed

A tall redhead, Heather seemed to fill the tiny room. She was wearing jeans today. Tight ones. They looked about the size of Addy's jeans, but Heather filled them out a whole lot different.

"Bet you could use a little relaxation after work, huh?" she said softly.

After work. The houseful of kids came immediately to mind. Bickering and squealing and splashing water all over the bathroom. Another mountain of dirty jeans and T-shirts Addy would have somehow found the time to turn into neatly folded stacks of sweet-smelling clothes.

"I have a wife and family. I like to get home to them after work." Something in his traitorous head gave a big *harumph* at that one.

She smiled with something bold shining in her baby blues. "That doesn't mean you have to quit having fun, does it?"

Now Danny was beginning to get it. Heather Yates was trying to…well, she was acting downright… well, what she had in mind was…

Nah. That was the craziest thing he'd ever come up with. Wait till he told Addy that one!

Dear Reader,

My heart has never left Sweetbranch, Alabama, I guess.

Sweetbranch, the setting for my 1993 Superromance *Late Bloomer,* is a composite of a number of small Southern towns that I knew as I was growing up in Alabama. When I close my eyes and think about the diner and the beauty shop and the men in overalls walking the sidewalks of Main Street, I feel myself going home to the places of my childhood.

So when I thought of doing a trilogy about homecomings, there could be only one place for me to take my characters home—to Sweetbranch.

In my **3 Weddings & A Secret** trilogy, you'll find out what's happened to Rose and Ben since the final pages of *Late Bloomer.* Plus, you'll meet four other very special couples who find the kind of love that says we're truly home. In D*ouble Wedding Ring, Addy's Angels* and *Queen of the Dixie Drive-In,* you'll experience first loves, lost loves and even the kind of love that can endure seven problem children—and if that's not love, I don't know what is.

I truly hope you enjoy your visit to Sweetbranch as much as I have.

Wishing you love,

Peg Sutherland

Peg Sutherland

ADDY'S ANGELS

Harlequin Books

TORONTO • NEW YORK • LONDON
AMSTERDAM • PARIS • SYDNEY • HAMBURG
STOCKHOLM • ATHENS • TOKYO • MILAN
MADRID • WARSAW • BUDAPEST • AUCKLAND

ISBN 0-373-70675-8

ADDY'S ANGELS

ABOUT THE AUTHOR

Peg Sutherland, who now lives in North Carolina with her husband, Mike, is originally from Alabama. She grew up in a series of towns she has transformed into the fictional setting of Sweetbranch, Alabama, where her riveting trilogy takes place. Peg knows each character, each building, each house intimately, since for her—like the protagonists—visiting Sweetbranch is like coming home.

Peg, a critically acclaimed author, has created perhaps her strongest body of work here. The trilogy begins with *Double Wedding Ring*, which is followed by *Addy's Angels*, and *Queen of the Dixie Drive-In* (available in February). Don't miss them!

Books by Peg Sutherland

HARLEQUIN SUPERROMANCE

398—BEHIND EVERY CLOUD
428—ALONG FOR THE RIDE
473—ABRACADABRA
525—RENEGADE
553—LATE BLOOMER
580—SIMPLY IRRESISTIBLE
599—PIRATE MOON
620—SAFEKEEPING
630—THE GOOD FATHER
673—DOUBLE WEDDING RING

HARLEQUIN TEMPTATION

414—TALLAHASSEE LASSIE

PROLOGUE

She sat on the wooden merry-go-round in the park where she'd been told to wait. Her feet, in their tiny pink sneakers, didn't reach the ground, so she couldn't make the old-fashioned contraption go round and round.

Still, the little girl smiled. She liked this park. Tall trees gathered around the playground, their limbs spreading and touching. They looked, to her five-year-old eyes, as if they were holding hands, playing ring-around-the-rosy with her and the swings and the see-saw and the sandbox with its bright buckets and shovels.

The birds were here, too, talking to her. And all the squirrels came out of hiding to stare. She smiled at them and they smiled back.

She smoothed the skirt of her white dress. It was snowy white, except for the pink threads on the collar that spelled out her name and matched her shoes and the ribbon in her hair. She didn't want a smudge on the dress when she was found, so she stayed very still, the way you were supposed to sit at church on Sunday morning.

She didn't know how long she would have to wait, but she liked watching the sun come up while she pretended to soar on the swings and spin on the merry-go-round. The sky was growing pink, and she looked up to watch the magic.

When the sun came up, she once again pointed her toes toward the ground. But her chubby legs were still too short to reach the dirt. So she waited quietly, and soon the merry-go-round began to spin. She laughed as the world revolved around her.

CHAPTER ONE

ADDY STIRRED. The morning sun wasn't yet peeping through the dotted swiss ruffles on the windows, but she felt a wake-up call pressing against her.

She smiled, her eyes still heavy with sleep, and arched her backside to bring it into more intimate contact with Danny's morning arousal. Addy sneaked her hand between them, felt the fuzzy warmth of Danny's hard belly against her palm. She sought lower, closed her hand around the reminder that another morning had arrived.

Danny groaned softly against the back of her neck.

"I've warned you what would happen if you keep waking me up like this," she whispered.

"No," he murmured, his voice heavy with sleep. "Please don't."

"I've been lenient up till now." She wriggled around to face him and kissed his chin, running her teeth over scratchy whiskers.

"I'll be good," he vowed, his voice gruff with sleep and something more. "I promise."

"You'd better be."

She moved her bare, smooth thighs against his rough ones and felt the tightness in her breasts, the softening between her legs.

"How long are you going to torture me?" he finally groaned.

"Until you learn your lesson."

As she spoke, she took both her hands and pushed his shoulders back against the feather mattress. She rolled with him, drawing her knees up around his waist. Astride him, she untied the ribbon at the front of her chaste eyelet gown and drew it away from her breasts. Danny grinned the devilish, sleepy grin that always turned her bones to jelly, and she lowered herself, taking him into her, feeling his fullness and his heat.

"I love you, Danny Mayfield."

"And I love you, Addy Mayfield."

They moved together, celebrating the new day.

AFTERGLOW WAS SHORT-LIVED at 619 Mimosa Lane.

"Bacon!" Addy called out from the scratch-and-dent stove they'd bought a year ago to replace the one with which they'd started housekeeping. "Get your red-hot bacon!"

The thunder of a dozen sneakers on hardwood floors greeted her words, rumbling from the back of the house toward the kitchen. She smiled at Danny, whose expression was more of a grimace as he emptied a carton of orange juice into six plastic tumblers emblazoned with cartoon characters.

"The Gates of Inferno rise once again," Danny said, "and all the little devils run free."

Addy didn't even have time to register her protest at his less-than-flattering portrayal of the children.

David, nine, hit the kitchen first, snatched a plate from the stack on the scarred picnic table and bounded up to the stove, plate extended. He was followed, in quick succession, by Terrell, eight; Brook, six; and Reno, eleven, holding seven-year-old Casey and five-year-old Elisabeth by their hands.

"Did you comb your hair?" Addy asked as she dished bacon, eggs, grits and biscuit onto David's plate. She knew the answer, of course, from the way his carrot-colored mop stood on end.

Nevertheless, David looked up at her with his wide blue eyes and his ear-to-ear, gap-toothed grin and nodded. Addy chuckled. "Get your fanny into a chair. We'll do it again after breakfast."

Terrell's straight blond hair was combed, but he had forgotten his glasses again and squinted as he watched her heap food on his plate. He grimaced. "Oatmeal?"

"Grits, Four-eyes," David retorted from the table.

"Hey, hey, hey! No derogatory comments about intellectual types who wear glasses," Addy called out, wondering where she'd left hers last night.

"And don't talk with your mouth full," Reno added, scooting her two shy charges forward in the mess-hall line.

"Hey, Tubbo—" David started to say.

"She's right," Danny said as he placed juice beside the boy's plate. "Keep your mouth closed while you eat and don't call people mean names."

David never lost his impish grin. "How'm I s'posed to eat if my mouth is closed?"

Then he pursed his lips tightly together and poked at them with a forkful of scrambled eggs. Terrell giggled and so did Brook, although she glanced at Danny to make sure it was okay. Brook had been with them since she was six months old and was the only one of the crew who belonged to them officially by adoption.

Addy had tried to count up the number of temporary siblings Brook had known in her six years, but always got distracted around number thirteen. She worried sometimes that the steady parade of itinerant siblings might bother Brook. But her neighbor, Rose McKenzie, said kids were more resilient than folks knew and not to worry. Addy set great store by Rose's advice, so she mostly didn't worry about the gangly girl with the olive complexion and the shiny dark hair.

While the six children and Danny ate a boisterous breakfast, Addy lined up seven lunch boxes on the kitchen counter and packed them. Six peanut-butter-and-jelly sandwiches; ham and Swiss for Danny, along with a salad. Six apples and one orange, the last for Casey, who had fed his apple to a neighbor dog on the way home every day his first month with the Mayfields rather than admit he hated apples. Three sandwich bags of carrot sticks for Elisabeth, Brook and Reno. Girls, Addy had learned, were more cooperative about eating the things they'd been told were good for them. Four granola bars for the men in her life. Six juices with little attached straws and a thermos of iced tea for Danny.

Over her shoulder, the chaos escalated.

"...Brought two snakes into class yesterday and set them loose in the back of the room," Reno was saying. The young girl's maternal instincts would not be squelched, although Addy sometimes wondered where Reno had learned all that mothering. Reno had barely been out of diapers when her own mother had left her in the care of a mean-tempered father and an older half sister. Even the half sister hadn't hung around long—she ran off as a teenager, leaving Reno alone with her stinker of a father. Plenty had thought the little girl was better off when he died a year ago. "Even the teacher ran out screaming."

"Is this true, David?" asked Danny, whose tone implied he had certainly never been involved in anything nearly so disorderly. Addy smiled at that little bit of parental deception, for she remembered otherwise.

"Yeah, but..."

"That's my biscuit!" Casey said loudly, in a rare outburst.

"Is not!"

A squeal. Danny's authoritative bellow. A moment of silence. A very *brief* moment.

Addy tried to review the day she had planned, but it was hard to keep her mind on another washer load of denim and whether or not she had enough quilting thread to finish the place mats she'd started. The youngsters kept intruding.

She wouldn't have had it any other way.

"...Pushed me down and..."

"Did not!"

"Did, too!"

"...So if I just had a computer, I could probably figure out how to..."

"I want to take Dolly to school today. Okay?"

"Yuck! I hate grits!"

"Swap my eggs for your grits."

Few things gave Addy the pleasure she got from knowing these six kids had a happy, stable home, even if only for a while. Chronic runaways, abandoned kids, orphans, all of them were troubled in one way or another. All of them, and all the ones who'd come before them, had felt the sting of being ignored or abandoned—or worse—by a society that no longer seemed to have time for all its children.

And throughout the county, everyone knew exactly what to do when a child needed a temporary home, whether it was for one month or one year. Why, you saw to it that Addy Mayfield knew about it, of course.

"Don't fret. Addy'll take 'em in."

And she did. Cheerfully.

She started at the touch of Danny's hands on her shoulders. "Wish you'd sit down and eat with the rest of us," he said, whispering against her ear, warming her with the memory of their lovemaking less than an hour earlier.

"I'll grab a bite later," she said, snapping the last of the lunch boxes shut.

"No, you won't. You'll get caught up in one of your projects and it'll be lunchtime before you think of it again, and before you can get in here to make a sandwich the school will call and somebody will have an earache and you'll go running up to the schoolhouse and..."

Addy laughed and gave him a kiss as she shoved his lunch box against his chest. She'd always thought Danny's lips must be softer than any baby's cheek she'd ever kissed. "How do you think I keep my girlish figure at my advanced age?"

"You're only thirty-two, and you're not going to change the subject again. Addy, you're running yourself ragged. Don't you think—"

She knew what he was about to say, and she didn't want to hear it. She didn't want any of her little ones, who were still bickering across the picnic table, to overhear it, either. "Now, Danny, what else can we do?"

"Addy, we're not the only family in Sweetbranch. Don't you think six is a little much?"

She gave him a big smack on the lips. "I think six is perfect. And so are you. Now, skedaddle. You've got people to boss around."

Danny sighed and took the old tin lunch box. "I wish you were one of them."

"No, you don't."

She watched through the window over the sink as he went out to his truck, the echoes of six different "Bye, Daddies" following him out the door and down the back walk. He might complain because he worried about her, but Addy knew Danny understood about the kids. He'd been where they were when she first met him. He knew how important it was for kids to have someone who believed in them. She'd believed in *him* when nobody else did. When he didn't even believe in himself. And look how he'd turned out.

Danny stopped to squat beside Barney, the big mutt who'd adopted them four years ago. He rubbed the dog's sandy-colored head and mumbled some kind of man-and-his-dog endearment, then stood and got into his pickup.

Just watching him made Addy's heart swell, even after all these years. Fourteen married years in a little over a month. And two years as sweethearts before that. Danny didn't have the broadest shoulders in town, and he wasn't the tallest man in Sweetbranch. And his thick brown hair had a few gray strands behind his ears that she hadn't mentioned to him yet. But he had a smile that could disarm a nuclear warhead. Danny was tender and funny and dependable, and he was her whole world. Even after all this time.

She swallowed the lump in her throat as the old pickup came to life and reminded herself that, luckiest woman in the world or not, she still had six youngsters to get out the door and on their way to school in the next twenty minutes.

"Okay, troops," she said, clapping her hands and turning away from the window. "Toothbrushing drill in two minutes! Let's make it march!"

DANNY FELT THE RELIEF as soon as he was safely locked in the cab of his pickup. He punched in a tape and nudged the volume up. For the next ten minutes, the only noise in his life would be the sound of a little country rock.

He could forget the big sheet of blue plastic covering the hole in the back wall of his house, a hole he was responsible for turning into a two-bedroom, one-bath addition. He could forget the state of his bank account and the telltale grind whenever he changed gears on the old truck. He could forget the crew waiting for him at the other end of this too-short journey and the production schedule he had privately labeled "The Impossible Dream." And he definitely would not think about the six children who were making his life financially and emotionally precarious. Especially not David, a front-runner for Young Delinquent of the Year.

But try to tell that to Addy.

Addy. He wouldn't think of Addy, either. Sweet Adeline, he called her when he wanted to get a rise out of her. He smiled, knowing it didn't take much more than that to get his wife's back up. He loved her lickety-split temper and her cinnamon-and-nutmeg hair when it tumbled in his face and the big, round glasses that made her eyes look larger than usual when she remembered to wear them.

What he didn't love was her compulsion to take in every stray kid in the county and what it was doing to their life. This morning's magic was long gone, vanished in the ruckus of getting six troublesome kids out of bed and into jeans and at the table in time to beat the school bell. It had been like that for longer than he cared to remember.

Danny was bone-tired and brain-weary.

He eased along Main Street and waved at Tag Hutchins. Tag looked pleased with himself, staring up at the new striped awning over the Lawn & Garden. Once the town's prodigal son, now Tag was engaged to his high school sweetheart. Not a blessed thing had tied Tag down for half his life, yet here he was, looking cheerful and content at the prospect of becoming a father, a grandfather and the husband of a woman who still spent some of her time in a wheelchair.

Danny shook his head. He wouldn't dream of telling Addy there were times—more of them every day, it seemed—when he saw a certain appeal in Tag's once-aimless life trailing after every dirt-track motorcycle race and third-rate rodeo in the Southeast.

If he could only convince Addy to go along, Danny sometimes thought he'd like to do precisely that himself. Run away. Hit the road. Leave all the headaches behind.

But he knew as soon as he parked his pickup and walked through the back door at the paper mill that his headaches had caught up with him. The silence told him the shredder was down again. *Damn!* Escaping his headaches was just as much an impossible dream as meeting the production schedule for which he was solely responsible.

Danny gave one last, longing thought to the lure of the open road, sighed and settled in to shoulder the burden for another day.

CHAPTER TWO

BY THE TIME BUMP FINLEY walked Krissy to school, he was plumb worn out hanging on to young Jake's hand. His three-year-old namesake—what in tarnation kind of name was Jacob Ebeneezer to saddle a young 'un with?—had a mite of a control problem.

"Gonna get you a leash," he threatened.

Jake just laughed. Goldarned tyke didn't have the common sense to quake at the sound of his great-uncle's voice.

"Unka Bunk, park! Wanna swing!"

Bump weighed the suggestion and decided it was a good alternative to going back home and spending the next two hours trying to keep the little boy out of the tree house in the backyard. Just yesterday, Jake had figured out what the wooden slats going up the trunk of the old oak were for and made it halfway up before he lost his adventurous spirit. Bump had had to call Johnsie Wooten's niece from Memphis over to go up after the boy.

Anyway, tearing around the park for an hour or so might slow the boy down a tad.

Bump had learned these things in self-defense, when everybody kept saying a man his age couldn't handle seein' after a young 'un like Jake. Bump had a few choice words for the busybodies, but his niece wouldn't let him say 'em around the house anymore. Not with two little ones with big ears running around, Rose said.

Bump never did cipher out how hearing a little earthy language hurt none. But when it came to the young 'uns, Rose was the boss.

Jake hit the ground at a tear when they reached the edge of the park, and Bump let go of his pudgy little fist. The boy looked like his half sister Krissy, who had been purt' near that age when Ben first brought her to Sweetbranch. Dark hair and big dark eyes, both young 'uns had, though Jake also had Rose's heart-shaped face and dimpled chin.

The boy also had his mama's disposition. Rose never had been content. Always gave her own mama a fit. Though he had to admit, Rose seemed content now. Getting hitched and mothering two young 'uns, and even that business about college studying, all of it seemed to agree with her. Mellowed out, she was now.

"Like her old uncle," he muttered, chuckling to himself.

Taking his creaky knees off the sidewalk and down the path into the park, Bump looked ahead after Jake. He was surprised to see the boy standing stark still by the merry-go-round. There on the merry-go-round sat a little girl, staring back at Jake, all dimples and Shirley Temple curls.

Bump looked around for another adult, but didn't see who the child was with. From this distance, he didn't recognize her, but he imagined he would by the time he drew closer. Weren't many folks in Sweet-branch he didn't know.

"Howdy there, missy," he said as he approached.

She kept smiling. Looked to be about five, and all decked out in a white dress with pink stitching on the collar. She didn't say a word, just stared at him with those eyes as big as the inside of his favorite coffee mug.

"Unka Bunk, pwease to meet Gabwiew," Jake said with as much solemn formality as Bump had ever heard from the boy.

"Gabrielle, huh? Nice to meet you, Gabby." Uncle Bump would have squatted to talk to the children, but his seventy-six-year-old knees wouldn't allow it. If he once got down there, he'd be down there till kingdom come.

She didn't say a word, just sat there with that bright-as-sun smile.

"Where's your ma? Or your pa?"

Still not a peep from the girl. Jake tugged on Bump's trousers.

"Her mommy not here, Unka Bunk."

Bump squinted down at Jake. "Now, how in tarnation do you know that?"

"Her tode me."

"Now, I ain't heard her say a dang thing, son."

Jake simply nodded. "Her tode me."

Beginning to feel uneasy and, therefore, more than a mite exasperated, Bump looked back at the little girl. "S'pose you tell Uncle Bump where you belong, missy. Y'ought not be out here in the park all by your lonesome like this."

Her only reply was to crawl down from the merry-go-round, take Jake by the hand and lead him to the swings, where she proceeded to give him a push.

Feeling crankier by the minute, Bump muttered a few of his favorite swear words under his breath and hobbled over to a bench. He sat and watched the children. He never could tell that they exchanged a word, and Bump knew his hearing wasn't *that* bad. Didn't seem to make a hoot in hell's worth of difference to 'em, though. They ran and played and had a high old time.

Bump kept thinking the little girl's ma or pa would show up. But time for his favorite midmorning talk show came and went and there was still no sign of anyone coming for the girl. Bump knew he couldn't go off and leave a young 'un alone like that, even in Sweetbranch. So he pondered on it for a while and could figure only one thing to do.

Yep, that was just the ticket. He'd take her to Addy Mayfield.

ADDY'S STOMACH RUMBLED, and she glanced up from her work to check the time. Oops. After eleven. Too late for the breakfast she'd forgotten.

"Right again, Danny," she said into the empty house.

As she stood to stretch her back and study the work she'd done that morning, she realized that she seldom took the time to appreciate these long periods of peace and quiet the school day afforded her.

Some days she loaded up a tote bag and took it down the street to sit on the porch and visit with Susan Hovis while she worked. The company was good for Addy. They talked about Susan's progress in recovering from the injuries she'd suffered in an auto accident last fall. They talked about the town's shock when Susan's daughter, Malorie, had announced right before her Christmas wedding that the little boy everyone had believed to be her baby brother was actually her own son. They talked about Susan's mother's bitter reaction to all the changes, and the mild stroke that everybody in town believed Betsy Foster had brought on herself with her meanness. And sometimes they talked about Susan's impending wedding, which she had already put off more than once—"to give Mother a chance to recover," although no one could see any permanent effects from Betsy's stroke.

Most days, however, Addy worked away in solitude, turning out dolls, appliquéd aprons and place mats and pot holders and cradle quilts, most of them done in the design people called Addy's Angels.

"Do some more of those angel things, Addy," Bunny had said to her about three years ago. "Everybody likes them best of all." That's when Bunny had suggested Addy branch out into stuffed dolls.

So Addy had turned out more angels. They were her favorites, anyway. And before long the angels were outselling everything else, even the homemade preserves and pickled okra that had been Addy's first offerings at the little shop Bunny opened when she left The Picture Perfect. Swapping bouffants for boutiques was the way Bunny put it. About a year ago, people started driving to Bunny's Country Bumpkin

Boutique for the sole purpose of buying another of Addy's Angels.

"Honey, we've got a certified retail phenomenon going here. We've got to play it up for all it's worth. These angels could be the next Cabbage Patch Kids. Why, folks come in here tellin' me they have, well, you know..."

Bunny got a pinched, pursed-lip look on her face.

"No. Telling you they have what?" Addy wasn't one to spare people discomfort. She saw it as her contribution to their personal growth.

"You know. Powers. Like they bring people blessings and junk like that."

"Well, of course they do," Addy had said. "You mean folks are just now figuring that out?"

Addy smiled, remembering that day. Remembering that electric instant. She'd made her little joke, but Bunny's revelation had startled her, given her a chill along her spine, not unlike the ones Danny gave her when he sneaked up from behind and trailed a kiss up the back of her neck.

But right now, her tummy was rumbling, and all the gingham-and-calico angels in the world—supernatural powers or not—weren't going to do a darned thing about it. If she didn't feed herself, she'd end up losing five more pounds before school was out. And Danny wouldn't like that one whit. He was already complaining about the last five.

"If you dry up and blow away and leave me here with these kids to manage all by myself, I'll haunt you," he'd threatened when he realized she'd cinched in her belt and bunched up the waist of her size-six jeans yet again.

"If I dry up and blow away, you'd *better* manage these kids all by yourself," she had retorted. "I'm not having another woman moving into *my* house, turning *my* sewing room into her mean old mother's bedroom. You want to talk about haunting, I'd be all over your hide like ugly on a june bug, Danny Mayfield."

Chuckling at the memory, Addy shoved her glasses to the top of her head and fished around under her chair for her shoes. She didn't find them and decided she'd been barefoot all morning; eating lunch that way wouldn't be the end of the world.

Once in the kitchen, she discovered there was no more grown-up food in the house and was putting the finishing touches on a peanut-butter-and-jelly sandwich when Barney jumped up from his guard post at the end of the driveway and started wagging his tail and woofing. Addy always figured one reason crime wasn't a problem on Mimosa Lane was because Barney used his tail to knock all the would-be burglars to their knees. Then he licked them into submission.

Sucking apple jelly off the side of one finger, Addy left her sandwich on the counter and followed Barney outside and up the driveway toward the front of the house. Visitors! Grown-ups! What a treat!

Actually, she saw right away that observation wasn't a hundred percent accurate. At the end of the driveway, Bump Finley was overseeing the procedure as his great-nephew, Jake, tried to climb onto Barney's back for a ride. Holding on to Bump's other hand was another child.

For an instant, Addy thought she knew the child, but realized she was mistaken. Still, her eyes remained riveted on the little girl, who wore a white embroidered dress that was almost old-fashioned by today's standards. A riot of corkscrew curls bounced in all directions, but the child's smile overshadowed everything else; it filled her eyes, made her skin glow.

"Howdy, Addy."

"Morning, Mr. Finley. You've got your hands full today, looks like."

The half-moon of snow white hair encircling Bump's head quivered in the April sunshine. Bump Finley still couldn't manage to tame his hair, but darn if the rest of him wasn't downright domesticated. A bit of a scamp in his younger days, Bump had turned into a querulous old coot over the years. Known for his grumpy disposition, his rarely shaved chin and overalls that looked perpetually slept in, Bump had long been one of Sweetbranch's eccentrics.

Then Krissy McKenzie had come into his life and Bump Finley was a changed man.

You might say Krissy had married into the family. Her father had come to Sweetbranch four years ago and swept Rose Finley, Bump's niece, off her feet. Then Ben became the entire town's hero when he built the paper mill and revived the dying town's economy.

Thanks to Ben McKenzie, people like Danny had good jobs and a good future once again; Rose was no longer front-runner for Spinster of the Year; and Bump Finley had learned how to use both an ironing board and a razor.

Who says there aren't any modern-day miracles? Addy thought as she grinned at her neighbor.

Bump rubbed his chin as if it were still covered with stubble and shook his head. Then he cleared his throat. "Well, Miz Addy, I reckon you could say I got my hands full, all right."

"Who's your little friend? I can't say that I remember her."

"Well, Jake here says she's Gabrielle. I can't rightly say for sure, though."

Addy frowned, then looked down at the little girl, who still smiled as if she'd just been given the keys to a doll store. Sure enough, her name was embroidered on her collar. Gabrielle.

"Who does she belong to, Mr. Finley?"

"We-e-e-ll, now that you mention it, Miz Addy..." Bump kept his eyes carefully trained on Jake's antics with Barney. "We don't rightly know."

Addy felt a familiar lurch. The one that was part dismay and part apprehension and a whole bushel basket of mother instinct. She looked down at the little girl, who looked up at her cheerfully.

"Well, where'd you get her, Mr. Finley, if you don't know where she belongs?"

"Found 'er."

"*Found* her?"

"Smack dab in the middle of the park."

"Alone?"

He nodded solemnly. "You got that exactly right, Miz Addy. Just sittin' there all by her lonesome."

Addy felt a renegade excitement swelling in her chest and tried to beat it into submission. The house was full. Past full. Danny had made that abundantly clear. They would take in no more children.

Until the addition was completed. At least, that was Addy's addendum to Danny's edict. She hadn't actually spoken it out loud, of course. But when the time came, she was certain she could make Danny see things her way. Didn't he always come around?

She looked down once again at the little girl. "Where's your mommy, sweetheart?"

The little girl was silent.

"Yep. That's precisely what she said to me."

"Mr. Finley, she didn't say anything."

Again, he nodded. "Yep. That's the way it happened, all right."

"But did you look around? Or—"

"Wasn't a soul in sight, Miz Addy. We waited almost two hours. Missed my favorite show, too. The one where families get up and yell at each other and act like dang fools. Figured somebody'd show up, but..." He shrugged.

"Oh."

"That's when I figured I'd better bring her over here."

"I see. But—"

"Figured you'd know what to do."

Addy sighed. Well, Danny would understand. In fact, this would no doubt be settled by the time Danny got home tonight. They would call the sheriff and he'd be here in no time flat, and probably they already had a report from someone whose little girl had wandered off.

By the time Danny came home at suppertime, this little angel would already be home safe and sound.

Addy took the little girl's hand from Bump and they started toward the house. "Come on, sweetheart, let's go find your mommy."

The little girl's hand was cool and soft in hers, a perfect fit.

DANNY COULDN'T WAIT to get inside his office and close the door. Then he could throw something. Swear a blue streak. Vent all this frustration some blasted way or another.

All day he'd been fighting to get his people back to work. But with the shredder down and the only employee who knew how to repair it vacationing in Biloxi, Danny's hands had been tied. He'd been at the mercy of a repair crew from Tuscumbia, which hadn't arrived until after lunch. And to be efficient, manufacturing recycled paper had to be a twenty-four-hour-a-day process.

So Danny had watched his production schedule get shot to hell and back. He'd concentrated on things like unloading the boxcar full of airline tickets, all of them cut wrong and therefore unusable for anything except recycling. The paper could be put in the hopper and ground up, but without the shredder, the process broke down right there.

Today Danny was responsible for letting the process grind to a halt. Ben understood, of course. But the frustration of it had Danny at the end of his tether. And as soon as he was alone, where the men and women who worked for him couldn't see it, he was going to—

When he closed the door behind him, Danny saw at once he wasn't alone. His frustration rose up another notch.

Heather Yates sat in his desk chair, hunched over and peeling bright orange polish off her nails. Danny noticed right away that she must've been looking at his favorite picture of Addy, because the brass frame now faced the wall. Heather grew instantly still when she became aware of Danny's presence.

"Well, hey, Mr. Mayfield."

Her voice was soft and shy, the same as it always was inside the glassed control room where a handful of people pushed the buttons that kept the plant running. But she looked different today. He couldn't put his finger on it, but something about timid Heather Yates had changed.

"What can I do for you, Heather?"

She smiled and stood slowly. A tall redhead, Heather seemed to fill up the tiny room. She was wearing jeans today. Tight ones. They looked about the size of Addy's jeans, but Heather filled them out a whole lot different. That was one of the things that was different. For the first time, Danny realized that Heather wasn't just tall, she was also built. Today she was dressed to make sure somebody noticed.

When she spoke, however, her voice was still so soft he barely heard her. "I've been waitin' to talk to you."

He walked around to the far side of his desk. Heather sidled around to the far side, too. Close enough for a cloud of her perfume to engulf him.

His irritation growing, he repeated, "What can I do for you, Heather?"

"Guess it's been a rough day for you, huh?"

"Yes, it has." He tried his damnedest not to snap at her. He'd learned firsthand from Ben McKenzie how to treat the people who reported to you. Snapping at them wasn't part of the treatment.

"Bet you could use a little relaxation after work, huh?"

After work. The houseful of kids came immediately to mind. Bickering and squealing and splashing water all over the bathroom. Another mountain of dirty jeans and T-shirts to replace the mountain that Addy would have somehow found the time to turn into neatly folded stacks of sweet-smelling clothes during the day. The frayed edges of Danny's temper unraveled just a little more.

"You want to get to your point, Heather?"

She smiled with something bolder shining in her baby blues. "I heard some of the gang goes over to the new tavern after work. Have a few beers. I never wanted to go alone. But maybe...well, if you were there, I wouldn't feel so funny, I guess."

Something about the invitation gave him a queasy feeling in his gut. "Thanks, Heather. But I have a wife and family. I like to get home to them after work."

Something inside his traitorous head, some gruff old voice gave a big harrumph at that one.

"That doesn't mean you have to quit having fun, does it?"

Now he was beginning to get it. That funny look in her eyes, these clothes that didn't quite suit her personality. Heather Yates was trying to... well, she was acting downright...well, what she had in mind was...

Nah. That was the craziest thing he'd ever come up with. Wait till he told Addy that one.

"What I'm saying is, I like you, Mr. Mayfield. I trust you, you know, the way I don't trust most of the guys. I'm not one of those party girls, Mr. Mayfield, but I think you and me could have a lot of fun." Then she put her fingers on the top button of his shirt as if she might just unbutton it if he was thick-headed enough to mistake what it was she had on her mind. "Don't you think so, too?"

He almost reached for her wrist to remove her hand. Then he thought about all this talk about sexual harassment and how careful you had to be around women workers these days, and wasn't sure exactly whether he ought to touch her or not.

"I think we ought to forget we had this conversation."

But she didn't stop touching him. In fact, he had the strangest feeling that her next move was going to be to lean and push her breasts right against his chest. He knew it, yet he didn't have the foggiest notion what to do to stop her.

Then his office door opened. Heather didn't move right away, but sighed first and sent him a shy glance from beneath her lowered lashes. A calculated gesture if he'd ever seen one, designed to give whoever was at the door an eyeful.

Swallowing the uncomfortable lump in his throat, Danny turned to see Ben standing in the door, taking in the scene with a frown on his square-jawed face.

"I think you'd better get home, Danny. Somebody just called and said the sheriff was over there. Something about one of the kids, I guess."

The bottom dropped out of Danny's stomach. And the last frazzled thread of his nerves snapped right in two.

CHAPTER THREE

DANNY THOUGHT HE'D HAD his share of living slap in the middle of chaos and crisis after fourteen years of being married to Addy. But nothing had prepared him for what was going on at 619 Mimosa Lane.

For starters, he couldn't even get into his own driveway. Three sheriff's cars sat in front of his house—he hadn't known the county *had* that many sheriff's cars. Then there was one of those TV news trucks from one of the stations in Muscle Shoals. And most every neighbor, from nosy old Betsy Foster to his boss's wife, Rose, were standing around on the sidewalk. All of them were looking at his house, and only Rose raised her hand in greeting.

All the way home, Danny's heart had clattered like the old hopper at the mill when it was spitting out ground-up paper at full throttle. Now his heart wanted to jump right out of his chest.

He barely got his pickup stopped before he jumped out and ran up to the knot of people standing in the yard. One of them was Addy.

Thank God! Nothing wrong with Addy.

"Addy, what the holy hell is going on?"

She turned at the sound of his voice and smiled that sweet, serene smile she used when she wanted him to calm down. The adrenaline pumping him up immediately changed from worried adrenaline to potentially ticked-off adrenaline.

"Oh, Danny, hi! You're early. Aren't you early?"

"Hell, yes, I'm early! The damned militia's in my front yard! Damn right I'm early!"

The little fine lines around her eyes tightened; her way of warning him that she didn't want to have to get angry, but she was perfectly willing to if he saw fit to push her.

"Danny, you know Sheriff Baylow, don't you? And Deputy Fenton?"

She knew damned well he'd gone to school with Mikah Baylow and Orvis Fenton, same as she had. Still, he smiled at the two men. He knew it was a tight smile and he knew they would know it, too. But the South was ever polite, even in the midst of crisis.

At least, he supposed this must be a crisis even though Addy clearly had it in mind to keep him in the dark about the exact nature of this further upheaval in their already-heaving lives.

"How you fellas doing today?" he asked. Mikah and Orvis replied with equal civility. "Maybe one of y'all would like to tell me what's going on here."

"Listen, Danny, we're real sorry about these TV folks," Mikah said. "But as soon as we put the word out on the wire, I guess they got wind of it, and we can't get 'em to move along."

"Got wind of what, exactly?"

His wife spoke up just as Mikah opened his mouth. "Now, Danny, it's really nothing. We're almost finished and—"

"Addy."

She smiled again, in response to the threat implied in his tone. "Sheriff Baylow and Deputy Fenton are just trying to find out all they can about the little girl Bump Finley found in the park," she said soothingly. She even patted his arm. He really didn't like the fact that she felt the need to pat his arm. This must be really big.

Well, of course it was big. Hadn't she said something about a little girl somebody found in the park? And what did she have to do with it, unless... "What little girl?"

Addy was beginning to look exasperated. "The one Bump Finley found—"

"I know, I know. In the park. What's she got to do with *us* if Bump found her?"

Her expression changed abruptly. Now she looked as if she'd been caught with her hand in the cookie jar. "Well, he didn't know what else to do."

Yep, he was definitely operating on ticked-off adrenaline now. "So he brought her here."

She smiled again, daring him to make a scene. "That's right. Now, sweetie, if you could run around back and make sure David hasn't torn down the tarp you put up where you're working on the addition, that would really be a help. I saw him heading toward the creek with some blue tarp about half an hour ago and I hollered after him but he didn't stop. I think he got it out of the garage, but I'm not sure and—"

"Who is she?" he interrupted.

"Who is who?" Addy asked, disguising her stalling as patience.

"The little girl."

"Well, we don't know, Danny," she said. "If we knew that, do you think we'd all be standing here like this, just talking about it?"

Danny turned to Mikah. "Sheriff, would you mind if I had a moment alone with my wife?"

"Um, sure, Danny. Listen, I think we have everything we need now. Why don't we just move along? If anything else comes up, we'll be in touch." He was backing up as he spoke, grabbing hold of his deputy's shirtsleeve as he did so.

In seconds, the two officers were at their cars, signaling the other deputy, who proceeded to talk to the woman with the minicam who was hanging around the TV truck. In another couple of minutes, all four vehicles were pulling away.

Danny turned to look at Addy. She was glaring at him. "Danny Mayfield, what in the world is wrong with you?"

"Me? What's wrong with *me?*" He could see it clear as day. This was going to be the occasion everybody in Sweetbranch would come to think of as The Day Danny Mayfield Finally Snapped. And even seeing it coming, he couldn't stop it. "I come home to a front yard full of sheriff's deputies and TV reporters, my wife won't do me the courtesy of explaining what's going on, and you wonder what's wrong with *me!*"

"Danny," she said, yanking her glasses down from atop her head, "I hope it makes you happy that the neighbors are listening to you raise your voice like that."

"Hell, the neighbors know more about what's going on around here than I do! If it weren't for the neighbors calling the mill, I'd still be in the dark!"

Addy's big eyes were now the muddy color of Willow Creek after a week of thunderstorms. "I have to start supper," she snapped, then whirled and started for the house.

Danny began to follow her, then remembered that his pickup was still in the middle of the street with the door standing open. He turned back toward his truck, at which point all his neighbors politely turned their backs and pretended intense interest in their rosebushes or the crabgrass growing up between the cracks in their sidewalks.

With a roar of the engine designed to let everyone who hadn't already figured it out know how royally peeved he was, Danny pulled his truck into his usual spot at the back of the driveway. Then he headed for the kitchen, where he planned to get the rest of the story out of his once-loving wife who now seemed hell-bent on driving him crazy.

Addy was grating cheese for macaroni and cheese for all the world as if nothing had happened.

Casey and Elisabeth lay belly-down on the floor, under the picnic table, coloring, Casey's short dark curls bobbing up and down next to Elisabeth's honey-colored ponytail. Reno was meticulously placing dots of butter atop the brown-and-serve rolls she'd lined up evenly on a cookie sheet. No dot of butter varied a milligram in size from any of the others. Reno was like that. Danny could hear Brook and Terrell in the other room, arguing over the remote control. David, he knew, was at the creek, doing God knows what with a sheet of blue tarp.

And sitting quietly on a picnic bench, watching Reno, chubby legs swinging back and forth, sat the little girl he knew must have caused all the commotion.

"Who is that?" he said as quietly as he could manage.

The little girl turned to look at him. Her smile was enough to stop his anger dead in his tracks. He turned his eyes to Addy, because he wasn't about to be sidetracked by another one of Addy's angelic-looking charity cases. Even David had looked angelic for about twenty minutes.

"Why, that's Gabby," Addy replied without looking up from her grating.

"Addy, what is she doing here?"

"Now, Danny, what do you *think* she's doing here?" she said so softly he knew she didn't want the little girl to overhear this conversation.

Danny drew a long, deep breath and walked over to the picnic table. He sat down on the bench across from the little girl and was once again drawn into her smile. He smiled back and said, "How are you doing, darling? I'm Danny."

She didn't say a word. Just kept smiling.

"Daddy," Reno said as she snapped the lid back on the tub of butter, "she doesn't talk."

Danny looked down at Reno, whose dimples twitched in a sympathetic smile. He looked at Addy, whose back was to him, and noted that she had paused to await his response. Fine, a little girl who couldn't talk. Why not? They had orphans and abused children and even one whose mother had been HIV positive when the baby was born. What was wrong with a little more variety?

He blew out a loud breath and said, "Reno honey, why don't you take everybody into the bathroom and have them wash up for supper?"

Reno gathered up the butter and her knife and frowned at him. "Daddy, it's not time to wash up yet. It isn't even time for the rolls to go in the oven."

"You're right. But I want to talk to Addy, and I'd sure be grateful if you'd take everybody and go play somewhere else."

Reno nodded, then leaned over and gave him a kiss on his cheek. "I understand. Grown-up talk."

Her little face was warm and sweet so near to his, and he experienced a flash of gratitude for having such special kids in his life. "Thank you, sweetie."

Then sanity returned and he acknowledged that two or three special kids would have been plenty. Seven was over the edge. *Anybody* could see that.

Anybody but Addy.

After stashing the butter in the refrigerator and dropping the knife into the sink, Reno clapped her plump hands together and said, "Okay, kids, let's go watch TV with Brook and Terrell." Then she took Gabby's hand and said, more softly, "You come, too, okay?"

And they were gone. Even the wails of protest from Terrell and Brook didn't last long. Someday, Reno was going to make somebody a great little drill sergeant.

"Addy, you want to tell me why that little girl is still here?"

Addy set the grater and the block of cheese on the counter and turned to face him while she wiped her hands on her homemade blue-checked apron. She was barefoot, only her ankles showing beneath her long, full skirt. He loved the way she looked, like something sweet and unspoiled, straight off the prairie. "You know good and well what she's doing here, Danny Mayfield. Where else is she supposed to go?"

"Anywhere else but here." He saw the color rise in her cheeks and knew her anger was rising with it. "Give me some good news here, Addy. Is somebody coming to pick her up in a few minutes? Is that it?"

She yanked at her apron strings and flung the cover-up onto the table. "Nobody knows who she is, Danny. Who do you suppose would be coming after her?"

"I don't know! Some of the other crackpots who collect stray kids, maybe! Surely you aren't the only one, Addy! Or are you? We had six this morning. Now we have seven. What'll it be next month, Addy? Ten? Twenty?"

"It's David, isn't it," she said. "You think David is a handful and—"

"All six of them are a handful!" He rose to his feet. "Addy, the house is too small. My paycheck is too small. I—"

"Don't you act like you're the only one earning money around here. I do my share."

"I know you do." How could he be so angry and still want to take her in his arms when he heard that little catch in her voice? "And you're knocking yourself out trying to keep up, too. Did you even eat today?"

"I don't see what that's got to—"

"You didn't, did you. Dammit, Addy, how many times do I—"

"Too many times, I'd say."

He summoned as much patience as he could muster and tried to start over, slowly, calmly. "Addy, everything has its limits. There's only so much floor space for spreading out sleeping bags. There's only so much money for flu vaccinations and jars of peanut butter. There's—"

Addy wasn't swayed by his patience. "There's no limit on my love, Danny Mayfield. So you can just quit trying to put one on it!"

That stopped him cold. He knew it was true. Addy had a heart as big as that hundred-foot magnolia at the south end of Main. But it was a heart with a fracture in it—a heart that remained empty of the one thing Addy was convinced she needed in order to be empty no more.

"Addy," he said softly, moving around the table so he could take her shoulders gently in his hands, "all the abandoned kids in the world aren't going to make things any different."

The stony glare in her eyes didn't soften at the sound of his voice or his touch. "Leave it alone, Danny."

"If it's supposed to happen, it will," he said. "The doctor said—"

She jerked away from him. "We are not talking about that, Danny! Quit trying to change the subject on me. We're talking about a little girl who's lost and alone, and there's no good reason on earth why she shouldn't stay here. So quit trying to turn this into something it's not!''

''I wish you'd quit being so damned stubborn for a change. Just because you haven't been able to—''

''I said stop it! Are you going to calm down so I can get supper on the table or are you going to try to psychoanalyze me to death?''

''Addy, this is wearing me out. We've got to set some limits here, can't you see that?'' He felt the anger welling up again and knew there was no stopping it, just as there was no stopping Addy once she got like this.

''I'm warning you, Danny—''

That did it. Everything behind his eyes turned red. ''*You're* warning *me*? How about *I'm* warning *you!* That little girl and about four others go. Right now! This week. And that's that.''

''Are you giving me an ultimatum, Danny Mayfield? Are you trying to order me around? Just because you've got a big-shot job at the paper mill doesn't mean you can come home and act like cock of the walk, you know.''

''Dammit, Addy, it's not like that and you know it.'' *Anything but,* he thought. He felt defeated and exhausted. More than that, he felt hurt that she couldn't seem to understand him the way she once had. ''But this is my life, too, and I can't take it anymore. I've been telling you that for months. And now I come home after a rough day and find out you haven't been listening to a word I've said. You have to—''

"I don't *have* to do anything. And if you think I do, I'll...I'll...I'll go stay with my mother until you come to your senses."

He and Addy had both stormed out too many times for him to take that kind of threat very seriously. "Oh, no, you don't. Don't you think for one minute you can go running home to mother and leave me here with six...*seven*...kids to deal with."

"Fine. *You* go." She gave him a little shove in the chest toward the back door.

"Now, Addy..."

She continued backing him toward the door one stumbling step at a time. "I mean it! Get out of here! Now!"

"Now, Addy..."

"You get, Danny Mayfield. And don't come back until you've remembered we're supposed to be partners."

His back was against the screen door now and he felt it give. He was outside.

"Now, Addy..."

She slammed the big door in his face. Hard. Then he heard the dead bolt slam into place.

Danny sighed.

The only thing bigger than Addy's heart was her temper. Shaking his head, he turned away from the house and headed for his pickup. Looked like another night on the sofa bed in the den at his mother-in-law's house for Danny Mayfield.

SOME FOLKS IN SWEETBRANCH said gossip officially became gospel once it was talked up in The Picture Perfect beauty salon on Main Street.

If that was so, the latest gossip made its miraculous transformation into the gospel truth at 7:29 the following morning. Heather Yates made it her personal business to be sure of it.

"Guess y'all heard about the big breakup," she said, studying herself in the mirror as Rose Finley McKenzie snipped away at her hair. She liked her eyes this way, with a little extra liner in the corners. Made her look sultry, she thought. Never mind what her loony mother said. She thought all women who wore makeup looked like tramps. But Heather knew that was because Pop had run off with that painted woman who made change at the all-night convenience store.

Heather, however, could understand why her pop had wanted a little something more out of life than a passel of brats and a wife who couldn't be bothered to keep herself up.

Heather could understand it because she'd grown tired of it herself. Look where it had gotten her, trying to do things her mother's way. No friends. No fun. If she didn't expect to end up like her mother, it was time for a change.

Noticing that everybody in The Picture Perfect was looking her way, Heather paused for a moment to savor the attention.

"Danny Mayfield and that wife of his have split up," she said. "Heard there was an awful row."

At that moment, the rat-tail comb in Rose's hand gave a particularly sharp tug on Heather's hair.

"Ow! Rose, take it easy. You know I'm tender-headed."

"Why, honey, it slipped my mind."

"Anyway, I heard it all had to do with that little girl Addy brought home with her yesterday," Heather continued. She wasn't sure she'd ever had so many people paying attention to her all at once in her whole life. Besides Rose, there was Rose's partner, Alma, the wife of the new elementary school principal, whose name escaped Heather, and Mrs. Rennie May Jemsen, who was waiting for her permanent wave.

Heather's excitement built with the attention, and she thought it wouldn't hurt to embellish the story just a tiny bit. "She just thought she could slip this little girl in with all the rest—you know she's practically got her own softball team over there now—and thought nobody would notice this little girl looked exactly like her. How she thought she could get that one past Danny I'll never—"

Rose dropped the lock of Heather's hair she was holding and stepped back, hands on her hips.

"Heather Yates, that's a big, ugly fib and you know it."

Heather felt color rise to her cheeks. "Now, Rose, all I'm telling you is what I've—"

"I know. All you're telling me is what you've been told by some other nosy old gossip."

Rennie May leaned forward and caught Heather's eye in the mirror over Rose's station. "You mean that little girl is Addy's? But I thought she and Danny had been married forever. How could she manage to hide something like that?"

Rose turned to Rennie May. "Some spiteful old soul made that up, Miz Jemsen." Then she turned back to Heather. "I don't suppose you saw this little girl who's supposedly the spitting image of Addy?"

"Not me, exactly, but—"

"Well, I did. My Uncle Bump is the one who found her in the park. And she definitely does not look like Addy Mayfield." She leaned over Heather's shoulder and studied her customer closely in the mirror. "Fact is, she might look a little like you, except her curls are genuine. You haven't been hiding a love child in your basement, have you, Heather?"

Alma laughed and Heather gave Rose a shriveling look in the mirror. Anybody in this town who knew anything knew that Heather Yates had never had one single opportunity for a love child, thanks to her holier-than-thou mother.

"I know Addy is your friend, Rose, but that doesn't change the facts," she said, enough injury in her voice to take care of not only Rose's slight, but every slight she'd ever felt from being a nobody in this town. "Danny Mayfield did not sleep at home last night."

"That's true enough," Alma said tartly. "He slept at his mother-in-law's. Reckon there's something kinky going on there, Heather?"

"Okay. Make fun of me. But you won't be making fun of me when I become the next Mrs. Danny Mayfield."

A heavy silence settled over the shop. Nobody moved a muscle. Alma's hand, and the can of spray she wielded, paused. Rennie May had leaned over about as far as she could without going face-first onto the yellow-and-white linoleum, just to get a better look at Heather.

Rose paused, too, for a moment. Then, laying her scissors on her workstation, she hit the lever on the back of Heather's chair and snapped the seat up as high as it would go. When they were nearly eye level, Rose twirled the chair around to face her.

Then, with deadly slowness, Rose said, "Danny Mayfield already has a wife."

Heather stared at her with genuine concern in her blue-shadowed eyes. "But he needs a woman like me. Somebody who'll put him first. You'll see. You'll all see."

CHAPTER FOUR

ADDY REFUSED TO CRY, even though watching her mother wash up Danny's breakfast plate made her sad and mad and embarrassed all at the same time.

"Looks like you cried all night." Eulainie Cook turned the clean plate bottom-side-up on the blue-checked kitchen towel she had spread on the counter and dried her hands on her faded yellow apron.

"Did not," Addy said.

"Stubborn girl."

Eulainie warmed their coffee and sat down across the kitchen table from her daughter. Addy stared into her coffee. She didn't have to look up to know what she would see in her mother's face. She also knew Eulainie wouldn't be handing out a lot of unasked-for advice. Addy almost wished she would. She hated having to admit she didn't know which way to turn.

"He's a stubborn man," Addy replied at last.

"He's a good man," Eulainie countered. "The best."

Addy happened to agree, but she wasn't about to admit it. "It's not like he's perfect."

"Close to it."

"And I'm far from it. Is that what you mean?"

"You don't want to know what I think," Eulainie said, stirring a little extra cream into her coffee.

Times like this, Addy tried to figure out how she'd ended up in this family. Eulainie, with her soft white hair, unlined alabaster skin and placid disposition, seemed to be no relation. Even Jed, her father, who had died six years ago, had been easygoing to the point of making Addy feel like screaming sometimes. Addy's brother was just like Jed.

It would explain everything if Addy had been dropped off on the doorstep at the farm as a baby. Her obsession with mothering all the unwanted babies in the world and her hair-trigger temper would be explained in one fell swoop.

Addy sighed and pinched a nibble from a cold biscuit on the plate in the middle of the table. "You think I ought to patch things up."

"That's part of it."

Impatient, Addy said, "Okay, what's the rest of it?"

Eulainie smiled, but it wasn't even one of those smug, know-it-all mother smiles that would have made it hard for Addy to sit still for whatever was coming. It was all tenderness and understanding; Addy wished she had inherited about one-eighth of her mother's sweet nature.

"Addy, I think Danny is more frustrated than you realize. You've forced a lot onto him, you know."

"But Danny loves the children. I know he does."

Eulainie nodded. Everybody knew how Danny was with the kids. He played ball with them and took them fishing and entertained them with air guitar whenever an oldie came on MTV. He made them laugh, and he tucked them in, and he stayed up nights when they had a stomach virus.

"Of course he does," Eulainie said. "But he's not a saint. And you can expect him to take only so much."

She looked as if she wanted to say more.

"But he understands," Addy continued to protest, determined to convince someone she was right. "You remember what it was like for Danny. He hasn't forgotten that."

"He might like to," Eulainie said.

That took Addy by surprise, and she didn't have an immediate comeback. What could her mother mean by that? she wondered. It wasn't as if Danny had anything to be ashamed of. Why, he had a lot to be proud of, pulling himself up by his bootstraps the way he had.

Addy hadn't noticed Danny until they were sixteen, although they'd gone all through school together. Oh, she could remember giving him half the sandwich out of her own lunch box plenty of times, just the way she had for other kids who didn't always come to school with lunches of their own. She could remember thinking it awfully smart the way he always got his jeans a size too big and several inches too long, so he had plenty of room to grow into them over the course of the school year, unlike Petey Whitlaw, whose jeans always got too short and showed too much white sock by the time spring rolled around.

But she hadn't really thought of him in *that* way until he made the football team their junior year. She noticed the way he ran with the ball, so fast and slick the other team couldn't lay a hand on him. She noticed the way he didn't swagger or dance when he made a touchdown, just set the ball down in the end zone and walked back to the sidelines.

She also noticed that no matter how much yardage he piled up or how many footballs he carried into the end zone, Danny Mayfield never got the adulation other hometown football heroes got.

The local paper didn't go on about his successes the way it did some of the other kids. The cheerleaders didn't make up chants using his name. Danny Mayfield was poor white trash and everybody looked down on him, no matter how much he seemed to accomplish.

Estes and Alvice Mayfield scratched out a living on a dusty piece of ground outside of town, the way Mayfields had for generations. They had lots of kids and not much education and even less money. What they did have, some folks said, was moonshine. So when Addy saw the way the town kids treated Danny, she took him under her wing the same way she'd adopted the squirrel with the broken leg the summer she was twelve and swapped her fluffy, sweet-faced kitten for the one in the litter that was blind. She told him how smart he was and how talented he was and told him to listen to his coach and not his father, who insisted Danny ought to stay home from school to help on the farm. She helped him fill out the applications for football scholarships, even when he was skeptical of the whole idea of college.

Somewhere along the way, she fell in love with him and convinced him no one was going to protest if he fell in love with her in return.

And when he got the scholarship and was added to the team roster at Auburn University, Addy married him and clerked at the grocery store for extra money, even though it meant she had to work most Saturday afternoons when he was on the football field.

But she listened on the radio, because the Piggly-Wiggly turned off the Muzak on Saturday afternoons and piped in the game instead, which all the customers appreciated.

Danny, of all people, should understand and support her in what she was doing now. Why couldn't anybody seem to see that?

Eulainie poured one final cup of coffee into her cup and unplugged the pot. "Do you *want* Danny sleeping on the sofa bed in my den?"

"Well, of course not." Addy stood and rinsed her cup at the sink, setting it upside-down beside the one Danny had used for his breakfast. Longing washed over her. "He'll be home tonight."

Eulainie was silent.

"Well, he will."

"Don't count on it." Then her mother walked out of the kitchen and down the hall toward Addy's old room. It was a playroom now, for all her grandchildren, including Addy's ever-changing brood. Addy stomped after her. She found her mother kneeling beside the child-sized table where Gabrielle was coloring.

"What's that supposed to mean?" Addy demanded.

Eulainie gave her a frown, then turned her attention back to the little girl. Gabrielle wore one of Elisabeth's T-shirts, bearing a long-faded purple dinosaur, tucked into a pair of Brook's rolled-up jeans. Her pink sneakers peeked brightly from beneath the table, their newness a startling contrast to the worn hand-me-downs. Reno had brushed her ringlets into a mass of downy frizz. She looked up from the drawing of the Three Little Pigs she was coloring and smiled at Addy.

The anger and frustration around Addy's heart melted at the sight of the sunny smile.

"Gabby, would you like to stay with Grandma for a while?" she asked.

Gabby turned questioning eyes on Eulainie, who nodded her enthusiastic agreement. Gabby dimpled and nodded until her fuzzy curls shook.

Addy brushed her fingertips along the little girl's plump cheeks, then looked at her mother. "Maybe I'll hang out the truce sign this time."

"That's my girl." Eulainie's hazel eyes crinkled, and her voice went soft and motherly.

Gabby dropped her carnation pink crayon onto the page and clapped, although Addy was certain the little girl couldn't possibly have any idea what was going on. Still, she dropped one kiss on her mother's cheek and another on top of Gabby's head.

When her lips touched Gabby, she could have sworn the little girl's delight fluttered right up through her and straight into Addy like a living thing.

Rose McKenzie stood at the cash register at the Around the Clock Diner haggling with Mellie over the two biscuits she wanted with her take-out lunch in place of one biscuit and one square of corn bread, which the menu specified.

"Now, Rose, you know if I start breaking the rules for you, soon I won't have a biscuit left in the house and poor old Mr. Pedersen won't have any when he drags in here at one-thirty, and I'll have to tell him Rose McKenzie started the whole thing."

"Mellie, what's got you in such a snit this morning?" Rose said, aware that the eyes of everyone at the counter were on the two of them.

"Me? *I'm* not in a snit." The stocky waitress pointed her pencil at Chester Melton. "Am I in a snit?"

Chester looked from one woman to the other, shrugged and reached for the hot pepper vinegar. "Whole town's in a snit, y'ask me." He doused his collard greens with vinegar. "Betsy Foster ain't speakin' to half her kinfolk, and young Malorie Roberts has scandalized half the town with that news about her son, and now Danny Mayfield's cussed out the county's entire law enforcement staff."

"Now, Chester, that's just not so," Rose said, her irritation mounting. It was then she realized *she* was probably the one in a snit, not Mellie. She'd been in a rotten mood all morning, ever since that misguided Heather Yates was in the shop boasting about making a play for Danny Mayfield.

That wasn't all, either. There was the business of Krissy's mother. Rose's six-year-old stepdaughter had cried herself to sleep again last night, shuddering and sobbing in Rose's arms, because her mother hadn't called her in months. No one knew where Cybil Richert had disappeared to, but Rose was ready to snip her head off with her sharpest pair of scissors the minute they heard from her. Cybil had a history of problem drinking and had been married to a second husband, who abused Krissy. In a dark part of her heart, Rose feared Krissy was better off not knowing where her mother was, or what was going on in her life. Chances were good it wasn't pretty.

But Rose couldn't stand to hear Krissy cry, and for that reason she hoped they heard from Cybil soon.

"Well, I don't know how you heard it," Chester said, "but the boys down at the barber shop had it that way."

"The boys down at the barber shop don't know spit," Rose said. "If you want the straight story, you'll have to come to The Picture Perfect."

Chester and two of the other men on stools at the lunch counter shook their heads. "Ain't likely," one of them said.

"Nope," agreed the other.

"If that's not what happened, s'pose you fill us in," Mellie challenged.

Before Rose could work up a retort, the bell over the door jingled, and she knew from the way conversation in the diner stalled that one of the gossipees must have just walked through the door. The guilty look on Mellie's face as she glanced over Rose's shoulder confirmed Rose's suspicion.

"Well, hey there, Addy." Mellie's greeting was too bright; as bright as her electric blue eye shadow, which Rose figured someone had once told her looked good with red hair.

"Hi, Mellie." Addy walked up and stood by Rose at the counter, her voice as determinedly cheerful as Mellie's. "Rose. Boys."

"How's that little girl Uncle Bump found down at the park?" Rose asked, further miffed that everyone was so breathless over a little domestic tiff that they'd all forgotten a little lost girl was involved.

"She's doing good," Addy said, looking over the menu. "Staying with Mama right now. I'm...uh... going on a picnic. Over to the paper plant."

Rose shot Chester a told-you-so look over Addy's head. "That's a nice idea, Addy. Mellie, you give her some extra cobbler, you hear? She's got blackberry today. Danny's partial to blackberry, isn't he?"

Addy looked up and smiled gratefully. Rose gave up her argument over biscuit versus corn bread and put her money on the counter while Addy ordered fried chicken and potato salad. Mellie fit the order into the shiny metal clips for Marty in the kitchen, then slid Rose's change across the counter.

"Heard that little girl Bump found is deaf," Chester said, finishing off his iced tea and gesturing toward the pitcher behind the counter.

"No." Addy's forehead furrowed in a frown. "She can hear just fine."

Rose knew the truth of the matter—that for some reason the little girl didn't speak. But she didn't see that the gossips at the Clock needed any more fodder at this particular moment.

"Here," she said as Addy's boxed order came up. "Let me help you take this out to your... You're not on your bike, are you?"

"Borrowed Mother's car," Addy said. "It's right out front."

Rose followed Addy out to the station wagon, carrying the bag with the foam glasses of tea and containers of blackberry cobbler.

"You all right?" she asked as Addy slid into the driver's seat.

Addy smiled sheepishly. "You know Danny and me. We just get a bit carried away. It'll be all right."

Rose hoped that was the case and decided there was no point in warning her young friend about Heather. Addy did tend to fly off the handle with very little provocation. A picnic lunch was a good sign. No reason to give Addy something else to get riled about.

She waved as Addy drove off, went back in to pick up her own boxes, then started down Main Street toward The Picture Perfect.

On her way down the street, she saw a woman who clearly wasn't a local standing uncertainly in front of Agnes Sauter's Sweet Boutique. The woman didn't look as if she'd ever bought a stitch of clothing at the Sweet Boutique and wouldn't even if it was end-of-season markdown. As Rose approached, wondering about the sleekly dressed blonde in the designer suit, the woman looked in Rose's direction. To Rose's surprise, the woman seemed startled, turned abruptly and hurried into the store.

Rose told herself there was nothing to feel uneasy about, although strangers in town often gave her moments of unease, ever since Krissy had been snatched out of her hands by her abusive stepfather a few years earlier. She tried to shrug it off, but as she passed the Sweet Boutique, she glanced in the window.

Staring out at her was Cybil Richert.

Pretending she hadn't recognized Krissy's mother, Rose quickly averted her eyes and hurried toward The Picture Perfect. Her hands trembled so badly she almost dropped their lunches. And her stomach twisted, so she couldn't eat hers, anyway.

When the shop hit a lull in the middle of the afternoon, she picked up the phone and dialed the paper plant. When her husband answered, she whispered, "Ben, she's here. Cybil. I saw her on Main Street."

"Oh, my God."

"Ben, you don't think she'll… Should one of us go to the school after Krissy this afternoon?"

"I'll go."

Rose felt better, knowing Ben would take care of it. She would never have met Ben if he hadn't been so determined to protect his daughter—he came to Sweetbranch to hide out with Krissy when the courts did nothing to protect her. But if Cybil was drinking again, who knew what she was capable of?

Rose wanted nothing more than to be home, to protect Krissy and her own little Jake herself.

What was Cybil up to now?

THE TAP ON DANNY'S OFFICE door beat out a timid little rhythm. With both hands on the back of his neck, he kneaded the sore muscles that didn't like the mattress on his mother-in-law's sofa bed. "Come in."

The door opened slowly. A face framed by soft red curls peeked in at him.

"Hey there, Mr. Mayfield."

"Heather." He looked at the clock on the wall over the blueprint of the equipment that was giving him such a headache. Half past noon. "I thought you were on second shift."

"That's right." She slid through the door, closing it quickly behind her. She stood there, hands behind her back, eyes downcast. She looked for all the world as if she was afraid someone would strike her at any minute. Danny didn't like thinking about the implications of that. "I thought you might want company for lunch."

She took a few steps in his direction and he stood, seized by the uncomfortable sensation that he would be trapped behind his desk if he didn't act immediately. When she reached the edge of his desk, she pulled her hands out from behind her. She had a wicker basket in her hands; she set it on the edge of his desk and smiled shyly.

"I knew you didn't have anybody to fix you lunch today and I didn't want you getting hungry, Mr. Mayfield."

Danny started to perspire. He had to remember to talk to Ben McKenzie about this. Ben would know what to do. "I made my own lunch this morning, Heather."

"Oh, shoot, Mr. Mayfield, a man can't be fixing his own lunch." She took another step in his direction, but

Danny was frozen with indecision. Her cheeks were flushed, and she couldn't quite meet his eyes. "I brought fried chicken."

Danny thought of Addy's fried chicken. Second-best in town, he always said, right after his mother-in-law's. That didn't get him into trouble with anybody; besides, it was true.

"Heather, why don't you take the basket out to the break room and share it with some of the rest on first shift."

How, he wondered, did a gentleman tell a lady her cooking didn't make his mouth water? Especially a lady who looked like nothing so much as a young pup who'd already been kicked too many times in its young life.

Even so, he thought Heather ought to know better than to try sharing her fried chicken with married men.

Heather walked over to him and stood inches from his chest. She smiled in a timid way that reminded him she might not have had anybody to tell her the right and wrong of things. But as he studied her brightly colored lips, he wondered. That was pretty much an industrial-strength coating of hot pink she was sporting there. It struck him it'd take more than a shy little kiss to rub that stuff off.

He thought again of Addy and the way her wide, soft mouth was always the color of a barely ripe peach. Her own color. She wore lipstick on Sundays, but it seemed like she always talked it off before they even made it to the opening hymn. That was another of the many things he loved about Addy. Soft, kiss-able lips.

Heather leaned right against him now, bearing down with those lips. "Mr. Mayfield, I know you must be lonely," she whispered, and her voice was as trembly as her lips. "I wouldn't ever let a man of mine get lonely."

He put his hands on her shoulders then, although the idea of touching her scared the bejesus out of him. She had to be too naive to have any idea what she was starting here. But before he could push her gently away, the door to his office opened once again. He looked over his shoulder, expecting to see Ben, knowing he was going to have to explain this for sure now.

Standing in the doorway, boxes from the Clock stacked in her arms, was Addy.

Danny knew right then that things were about to go from bad to worse.

"Now, Addy," he said, but he got no further.

Addy dropped her boxes to the floor. Danny flinched. Heather's eyes widened and she turned slowly to face Addy.

"I'm so sorry, Mr. Mayfield. I thought you said we'd be alone."

Danny flinched again. What had he been thinking, seeing her as shy and innocent? Here she was, acting as if she had it in mind to provoke Addy. And sure enough, Addy was provoked. She marched right up to Heather, close enough to personally wipe the hot-pink smile off the girl's face. Danny expected it to happen, any minute.

"Who the devil are you?" Addy glared at Heather. "And before you answer, I suggest you take your hands off my husband."

"Now, Addy..."

Heather looked at him, all wide-eyed innocence, and wrapped her hand around Danny's arm, as if to gather him close for protection. "It's all right, Mr. Mayfield. She don't mean to be rude."

"The heck I don't." Addy snatched Heather's hand off Danny's arm and flung it aside. "I'll be as rude as I please."

Heather emitted a tiny bleat of surprise, mustered a wounded look and backed off. Again the trembly lips. "No wonder you moved out," she said in her little girl voice.

"I didn't move out."

"What exactly have you been telling this girl, Danny Mayfield?"

"Nothing, Addy. I... She..."

"He's lonely," Heather contributed, giving him a little wink behind Addy's back as Addy turned her hellfire-and-brimstone gaze on him.

"Heather works here, Addy. That's all. And... uh..."

"How convenient."

"We like it. Don't we, Mr. Mayfield?"

Addy quivered with rage clear down to the ends of her long cinnamon-and-nutmeg curls. "Danny Mayfield, is this what happens whenever we have a little spat?"

"Addy, it's not what you think." *Weak, Mayfield, very weak.*

Heather didn't help a whit by laughing.

"It better not be what I think."

"Heather thought I might be hungry."

"For lunch," Heather said, picking up her basket and waving it shyly in his direction.

"If my husband is hungry, I'll feed him."

Heather shrugged and looked down at the boxes Addy had cast onto the floor. Potato salad oozed out of one of the crushed containers. Heather set her basket back on Danny's desk, patted it and said, "I'll just leave this, Mr. Mayfield. I think you're going to need it."

She sashayed toward the door, turning only to say, with a disapproving look, "Does she always boss you around like that? Why, I'd never boss a man of mine."

Then she was gone.

His stomach churning, Danny reached out for Addy. She flung his hand aside.

"I never in a million years would have believed you would treat me this way," she said, her voice soft and ominous.

"Addy, it's not like that. Let me explain."

"I'll pack your clothes. Pick them up sometime when I'm not there."

"Now, Addy—"

But she was gone as quickly as Heather had disappeared. He was alone in his office with the smell of fried chicken and the heated words of the past ten minutes milling around in his head.

The words that roared the loudest and the most persistently were Heather's. *Does she always boss you around like that?*

CHAPTER FIVE

DANNY WASN'T PREPARED for what he found when he got home that afternoon.

He'd been calling the house every half hour since Addy stormed out of his office, but he never got an answer. Even after the kids should have been home from school, the phone continued to go unattended.

Nevertheless, he figured Addy would have cooled down by the time he got home. Then he'd be able to talk some sense into her. He damn sure didn't plan to spend another night on Eulainie's sofa bed. He'd had a crick in his neck all day. Enough of Addy's temper. *She* could listen to reason for a change.

Full of the self-righteousness of the falsely accused, Danny pulled his truck into the driveway on Mimosa Lane late that afternoon. But for the second afternoon in a row, he didn't make it all the way to his parking space in the back.

What stopped him this time was the wheelbarrow in the front yard, piled high with suspiciously familiar clothes.

Danny slammed on the brakes, jumped down from the cab and stalked across the lawn. He nearly stumbled over Barney, who lumbered into his path with a friendly woof and demanded a head rub.

"Not now, Barney."

He reached the wheelbarrow, Barney still at his side, wagging his big shaggy tail and slobbering doggy kisses all over Danny's wrist and hand. Danny stared into the wheelbarrow. Yep, he knew these clothes, all right. His flannel shirts. His jeans. His Auburn University sweatshirt with paint stains color-coordinated to every room in the house. Underwear. Socks. The toes of his dress shoes poked out of the pile.

"What the... Addy!" He started toward the house. "Addy, you come out here right this minute!"

He stopped when nine-year-old David rose from the top step of the front porch. He stood there, straddle-legged and tough-eyed, a miniature John Wayne with carrot red hair, freckles to match and a gap between his front teeth.

"You can't come in," David said, his tone belligerent. Danny thought the boy looked as if he were enjoying his macho role as protector of the home front a tad too much.

"The heck I can't." At least he remembered to keep his language in line. Which, under the circumstances, he felt showed remarkable restraint.

He took another step toward the porch. As he did, David dashed past him in the direction of the wheelbarrow, pulling something out of his jeans pocket as he went. Danny watched, interest changing to horror as David waved a book of matches over the wheelbarrow full of clothes.

"I'll do it," David said, his tone as menacing as his high-pitched voice allowed.

"David, hand 'em over." Danny's heart pounded uncomfortably as he held his hand out for the matches. The boy tore a match off the book and Danny wondered what your next move was supposed to be when confronted with a four-foot delinquent with arson in his heart.

The squeak of the screen door broke the tension. David glanced toward the sound, and Danny turned to look, as well. Addy stood beside the door, arms folded, glasses atop her head, one bare foot wrapped around a slender ankle. Even from across the yard, Danny could see the stubborn set of her chin and the anger blazing in her eyes.

"Addy, what's going on here?"

"I told you I'd pack for you."

"Addy, you're being ridiculous. Let me—"

David interrupted. "Want me to do it, Mom? Can I?"

Danny's determination that they wouldn't have another fight began to dissipate. "You see what one of your precious angels is doing?"

"You'd better go now" was her only answer.

"Now, Mom?"

Danny heard the scrape of the match, heard the tiny spit as fire struck. Addy remained unmoved. Clenching his lips tightly to keep from saying exactly what he thought, Danny turned, grabbed an armload of clothes from the wheelbarrow, threw them into the bed of his truck and roared down Mimosa Lane. Through the rearview mirror, he watched his Auburn sweatshirt fly out the back of the truck. He didn't even slow down.

AS A SECOND DAY PASSED, then a third, without a word from Danny, Addy felt as if she'd stepped into a nightmare. All she wanted to do was wake up, but the nightmare wouldn't let go of her.

The first two nights, she let the children stay up an hour later than usual. But bedtime still came around, and she was still alone in a bed she was accustomed to sharing. In fact, she hadn't slept alone two nights in a row since she and Danny married fourteen years earlier.

But she wouldn't think of that, she told herself as she kissed the boys good-night and clicked off the light in their room. Thinking only served to remind her that their anniversary loomed, little more than a month away.

Thirty-eight days, to be exact.

She told herself this silly mess would be resolved long before that. Danny would come around. Danny always came around.

Hoping that thought would cajole her heart into a lightness it didn't feel, she walked down the hall to the girls' bedroom. She stood in the door, watching with a full heart as Reno oversaw bedtime prayers.

"You have to close your eyes," the eleven-year-old whispered.

"No," five-year-old Elisabeth whined. "Then it'll be dark."

Reno sighed, exasperated. "Okay, just pray, then. But God might not listen if your eyes are open."

Addy smiled, despite the catch in her throat.

"My knee hurts," Brook whispered, pointing out the adhesive bandage that covered most of her bony kneecap.

"Then hurry so you can get up," Reno said.

Only Gabrielle prayed without prodding or correction or guidance. Head down, hands clasped, she moved her lips in silent prayer. Once again, something about the tiny girl crept close to Addy's heart and gave a tug.

Reno stepped back when all three little girls were caught up in their Now-I-lay-me's, surveying them with satisfaction.

"What about you?" Addy whispered, putting her arm around the girl.

Reno shook her head. "I never pray. Not anymore."

"Why not?"

Reno looked up at Addy, her dark eyes solemn, too solemn for one so young. "Because He never listens to me."

The sweet comfort Addy had felt moments earlier abandoned her. Aching with the memory of all the abandonment Reno had experienced in her short life, Addy pulled the girl closer. "Of course He does, sweetheart."

Reno shook her head against Addy's chest. "I asked and I asked and He never brought anybody back to me."

How do you answer that? Addy wondered. "You keep praying, sweetheart," she said.

"But I'm afraid. What if...what if I ask Him to bring Danny home? Maybe, if I ask Him, He won't listen to that one, either."

Reno's tremulously spoken fears kept Addy awake most of the third night that Danny was gone.

The next day, tired and unable to concentrate, Addy packed up her most pressing projects, took Gabby by the hand, and walked down the street to knock on the Foster front door.

She waited patiently, listening either for the squeak of Susan's wheelchair or the thump of the walker she'd used periodically these past months. She looked down, about to explain things to Gabby, but Gabby looked up at her with such a serene smile that Addy almost felt the little girl understood without an explanation.

"Mrs. Hovis was hurt last year," she said, feeling foolish at the idea. "For a long time, she rode in a wheelchair. Then she started using a walker."

But now she's okay.

"Yes, she is," Addy said, then realized she must have been answering her own thoughts. For Gabby, of course, had done nothing but nod and smile. "Okay, I mean."

The front door opened and Susan broke into a big smile. "Well, what a wonderful surprise! And this must be our newest little neighbor."

Addy noticed that the walker had now been replaced by a beautifully carved cane. "No, *this* is a surprise! A cane! And a pretty glamorous-looking one at that."

Susan's freckled face pinkened in delight. "Isn't it exciting? One of the men at the church carved it just for me."

"It's wonderful. I can't believe how well you're doing!"

"Sam says I'm a miracle-in-progress."

Sam was Susan's physical therapist and her new son-in-law. He was probably right, Addy decided. Not only was Susan now walking with a cane, her voice was hardly slurred at all, despite the severe brain injuries she'd suffered less than a year ago.

As Susan ushered them in, Addy couldn't help but notice that the Foster house grew a little more dreary with each week that passed. Addy had been coming on a regular basis since Susan returned to Sweetbranch for her recovery, first at Sam's suggestion, then simply because she enjoyed the company.

But coming to the Foster house sometimes brought her down. Betsy Foster had a way of doing that to people.

Addy followed Susan out to the side porch, where they would sit and work and talk.

"Have you set a date yet?" she asked as they settled down in the wicker furniture.

Propping her cherry-wood cane against her chair, Susan shook her head. "Not yet."

Addy knew she should bite her tongue, but she couldn't. "Why not?"

"You know why not."

Addy knew. All of Sweetbranch knew. Betsy Foster had suffered a stroke the day before the original wedding date a few months back. The stroke was minor, but it had served its purpose. Susan had postponed the wedding until her mother came home from the hospital. Betsy had recovered completely, but the postponement had become lengthier as Susan became more afraid that her engagement to Tag had caused the stroke.

Betsy Foster's long-standing opposition to Tag Hutchins went back twenty-five years to when he and Susan were high school sweethearts. She had managed to stand in their way once. More and more, it looked as if she would do so again.

"Susan, you can't change your mother."

"But I keep thinking if I give her a little time, she'll surely come around."

"Has she come around for Mal?"

Susan looked down at her hands and shook her head.

The whole thing was more complicated than any soap opera, Addy knew that much. First there was Susan's dreadful accident. Then her daughter, Malorie, had married Susan's therapist, Sam Roberts, on Christmas Day. Sam happened to be Tag's nephew, which didn't please Betsy Foster, either. But the real icing on the cake had been when Malorie dropped her bombshell about two-year-old Cody, to whom she had given birth when she was barely out of high school.

Betsy had shamed her daughter and granddaughter into hiding the truth about Cody. She was displeased when Malorie revealed the family secret, although Addy couldn't help thinking it was for the best. Now Betsy's stroke had postponed Susan's happiness yet again.

"But you should see her," Susan said, frowning. "She isn't well. It's as if she's grown old overnight. I...I just can't bring myself to deal her one more blow."

Addy doubted anything much was wrong with Betsy Foster, but for once she kept her mouth shut.

"Set the date, Susan. You deserve to be happy."

Susan nodded, then looked at Gabrielle and said, "My little grandson is in the other room. His name is Cody, and he's building a fortress out of plastic blocks. I'll bet he'd love some help."

Gabby looked at Addy for permission and was off like a shot when Addy nodded.

"How is that working out?" Addy asked. "Is he adjusting to the change?"

"Beautifully," Susan said. "He's too young to do much questioning. And I expect by the time he's Gabby's age he'll have forgotten what a mess we all made of things."

Addy smiled wryly. "We can do that, can't we?"

Susan studied her. "Want to talk?"

Addy stared at the bag of work in her lap. She remembered all the times she'd sat on this side porch, listening to Susan sort through her slowly recurring memories in the months after her auto accident. She remembered Susan's painstaking first efforts at sewing, which Addy had helped her with in hopes Susan's fine motor skills would improve. Helping someone else was one thing; asking for help was something else entirely.

Could she be that brave?

"I just don't know what to believe, Susan." But even as she said it, Addy knew exactly what she believed. "That's not true. I don't believe for one minute that Danny is...is...fooling around with someone else."

Susan looked dumbfounded, and Addy hoped that meant the gossips in Sweetbranch hadn't latched on to any juicy news about the sweet-faced redhead she'd caught making cow eyes at her husband.

"Well, for heaven's sake, Addy, I don't, either! What on earth are you talking about?"

Addy shook her head miserably. "I didn't come over to unload on you. I thought maybe you could give me a hand with some of these projects. Bunny called yesterday and said her inventory is down and she needs some stuff and I...I just can't seem to concentrate."

She paused for a breath, afraid of the wobble she'd heard in her voice.

Susan leaned over and took the sewing bag out of Addy's lap and set it aside. "If you'll get what's bothering you off your chest, you'll probably find it a lot easier to get your concentration back, young lady."

Addy laughed, although it was a weak sound. "I'm not sure you're old enough to be calling me young lady."

"I may be young, but I'm a grandmother, and that qualifies me for dispensing wisdom. So let's have it."

Addy felt bare without her sewing in her lap and wished for something to fidget with. "Well, I thought he was... At first, it just seemed to be about the kids.

Our fight, I mean. I guess we've been fighting about the kids nearly as long as I've known you, haven't we?"

"It does seem to me we've talked about this before," Susan said softly.

"Maybe I should've listened before." Addy pulled a throw pillow into her lap and hugged it against her chest. "Anyway, when he came home and found Gabby there, that was the last straw, I guess. Maybe...maybe if we can find out where she belongs, who her parents are, maybe then everything will be all right."

Addy glanced up only long enough to catch the doubt in her friend's face.

"Any word about who she is, where she came from?"

Addy shook her head. "I talked to the sheriff again this morning. Nothing. He said it's gone out over some kind of national computer network and there's nothing. Can you believe that?"

"It is hard to believe nobody's missing a little girl that precious."

"She *is* precious, isn't she?" Addy found that even in her bleakest moments, simply being with Gabrielle gave her a measure of serenity she found nowhere else these days. "I mean, who wouldn't want her, even if she can't talk, right? Why, if Danny would just get to know her—"

"She can't talk?"

"Doc Newman ran all kinds of tests the day before yesterday. Maybe we'll find out what's wrong." She looked up sheepishly. "I think that bothered Danny, too. Just one more thing he didn't think he could handle. Oh, Susan, you don't think Danny's found somebody else, do you?''

"What makes *you* think that?"

Addy huddled into the corner of the wicker love seat, squeezing the life out of the throw pillow, uncertain she could bring herself to talk about what she'd seen that day in Danny's office. What if saying the words out loud made her ugly suspicions true? What if... What if?

Then she looked at Susan again, remembered all the hard times her friend had faced over the past few months, and decided the only thing to do was plunge ahead.

"I went to his office and this woman was there, a girl, really. She couldn't have been much older than Malorie, and she was all snuggled up to Danny and—" Her voice cracked, and Addy knew she couldn't say another word without breaking down. And she was afraid if she broke down she'd never stop crying.

Now, why in the world should she feel that way when she knew darn good and well there was nothing really seriously, irreparably, wrong with her marriage? If there was, she would have seen it coming long before now. Wouldn't she?

After a few moments, Susan asked, "What did Danny say?"

"He said—" Addy stopped. She really couldn't remember what Danny had said. She wondered, suddenly, if she'd given him much chance to say anything. She wondered if she'd gotten so worked up and angry over her own hurt pride that she hadn't let Danny get a word in edgewise.

How many times had he accused her of that?

Addy loosened her hold on the throw pillow, swallowed hard and experimented with a weak smile. "Maybe we ought to work for a while. I've got some place mats that are just dying to be finished. Would that be okay?"

They spent the rest of the morning working with their hands—Addy's stitches were a little shakier than usual—and looking in on the children and talking about anything but Danny and angel-faced Gabby. They talked about the way business had taken off at Hutchins' Lawn & Garden since Malorie took over running the store. They talked about the newfangled aerator Tag had bought with the money from the sale of his motorcycle and how he could barely keep up with calls from people who wanted their lawns aerated. They talked about the way Bump Finley had stuck like glue to Betsy Foster after her stroke, despite the way they argued. They'd been engaged once, a lifetime ago, and Susan still had hopes that relationship would motivate Betsy to change.

By the time Addy left at lunchtime, she had a much calmer head and an ample supply of place mats and toaster cozies for Bunny's Country Bumpkin Boutique.

Nevertheless, when another check with the sheriff at the end of the week turned up no leads on Gabrielle's identity, Addy started feeling frantic again. Every day she'd hoped for some word so she could call Danny and tell him things were back to normal. And every day that passed without a resolution was a day when she imagined Danny growing impatient with waiting.

Of course, she had to admit that Danny wasn't the one who had the problem with patience. Danny would have been content to wait until after college to marry, for example, but Addy had insisted otherwise.

"Addy, we've got the rest of our lives ahead of us," he'd said, holding her in the crook of his arm on her mother's couch.

"But why should we wait, Danny? We know what we want. Let's do it. Now."

He'd looked at her with that slow-spreading smile of his and taken her glasses off. "What do you want?"

Even without her glasses, she could see him well enough to know exactly what she wanted. She had nuzzled just a little closer, pressing herself to the length of him, and whispered, "I want you, Danny Mayfield. And I don't have the patience for waiting four years."

They hadn't waited.

And Danny had been the patient one when the babies didn't come along as quickly as Addy thought they should. He hadn't seen the point in all the tests, all the visits to the doctor.

"It'll happen when the time is right, sweetheart," he'd whispered against her ear when she was disappointed to realize she wasn't pregnant after all.

"The time *is* right," she had insisted. "I'm going to be too old before too much longer."

He hadn't laughed. "You're twenty-five. I don't think the clock's going to run down anytime soon."

"Maybe you just don't want to be a father," she'd said, determinedly gloomy.

"I love being a husband. And I'm going to love being a father. When the time is right."

And he'd gone on telling her so, but right now, Addy wasn't so sure Danny liked being a husband *or* a father. What if he decided he liked being a bachelor, instead?

Stop being a ninny, she told herself. *He's not a bachelor. He's living at mother's. How much trouble can he get into living at my mother's?*

But she couldn't help remembering that he didn't spend nearly as much time on her mother's sofa bed as he did at the paper plant. And she'd already seen firsthand how much trouble he could get into there.

CHAPTER SIX

EXHAUSTED BY A WEEK of managing seven children on her own—while covering up her own emotional distress—Addy slept long and deeply Friday night.

Faintly aware of the first soft rays of sunshine and the good-morning chirp of the birds, Addy didn't even open her eyes at her usual wake-up time, merely drifted back into sleep.

The next thing she heard was the familiar rumble of Danny's old pickup. Still half asleep, she smiled at the sound, burrowed deeper into the warm sheets and drifted once again, this time on a silken thread of anticipation.

Then she remembered.

Her eyes flew open. Her body went stiff beneath the sheets. Danny was here. Omigosh, and here she lay, still in her nightgown, her hair a mess. She'd wanted to look her absolute best the next time he saw her, although she told herself she shouldn't give two hoots what he thought. After all, he'd seen her in every kind of disarray imaginable and always seemed to find her plenty desirable before. Including—no, *especially*—first thing in the morning.

She smiled. Danny always said he liked her best when her body felt soft and warm with sleep.

She closed her eyes and listened to his progress from the truck to his toolshed. She listened for the children, too, and heard not a peep. She snuggled against her pillow, suddenly aware of the brush of the sheets against her legs, the whisper of her nightgown over her bare breasts. She heard him now, at the back of the house, where the blue tarp once again covered his work. He could walk right in through the back wall of the master bath. Right into the bedroom. She stretched and yawned and smiled again.

She heard the rattle of the tarp. Heard his voice, softly calling her name. She pretended to sleep. She heard his footstep on the bathroom tile and gave the sheet a gentle kick. Just enough to bare one leg.

She heard him at the bedroom door, felt his presence with heart-thumping certainty. Still feigning sleep, she felt his gaze on her, and with it the insistent pulse of her body that said she'd been without his touch too long. She held her breath.

"You'd better get your shower," he announced brusquely. "I'm going to be hammering soon, right outside the bathroom. I don't want to disturb your privacy."

She shot up in bed, instantly furious. But by the time she swept the tangle of hair out of her eyes, he was gone. She flailed around in her sleepy brain for a biting retort and came up empty.

"Disturb my privacy, my fat Aunt Fanny," she muttered all the way to the shower.

Then she dropped her gown right in the middle of the floor and dared him to step back through the tarp while she waited for the water to reach the perfect temperature for her shower.

He didn't.

By the time she dried off—a process that was much too slow without him to dry her back—she was spitting mad.

DANNY HEARD THE FAMILIAR sounds of Addy's temper tantrum through the tarp. The slamming of the medicine chest. The muttering. The shower curtain being yanked into place. Addy wasn't singing in the shower this morning. Ordinarily he would've smiled. But five nights on his mother-in-law's sofa bed had robbed him of every ounce of humor. Addy's temper had ceased to be funny.

He felt like doing a little slamming and muttering of his own as he rummaged through his toolbox, but he refused to give her the satisfaction. Just the way he'd refused to give in to his impulses when he'd walked into her bedroom.

Expecting to find her up and about, as she normally would be at this time of day, he'd been stunned to see her lying there, tangled in the sheets, her hair fanned out over the pillow, a tangle of curls kissed by the early-morning sun. Stunned wasn't the half of it. He'd wanted her, immediately and desperately.

Dammit, there he went again! He slammed the lid of his toolbox shut. Damn her for not understanding. For not even being willing to listen. And double damn her for not trusting him.

He heard the snap of the tarp, followed by the snap of her voice. "It's your own fault if you wake up the kids with all that banging around."

"*Me* banging around? What about you?"

He didn't want to look at her, but he couldn't help himself. And sure enough, there she stood in that green-print dress he liked so much, hair still damp and a little wild, cheeks still pink from the hot shower. He liked to shower with her, on weekends, and watch the water sluice down her breasts, pausing on the small, high tips that were precisely the ripe-peach color of her lips.

Dammit!

"I figured I better get this finished," he said, turning his back on her. "Don't want you sitting out here alone with the back of the house wide open like this."

She was silent. She didn't protest his implication that she'd be here alone for a while. Until *she* came around, he'd vowed to himself. *She* was the one who had kicked him out. *She* was the one who'd piled up his clothes in a wheelbarrow in his own front yard. *She* was the one who was so all-fired determined to have every little thing exactly the way she wanted it.

"I'm not alone," she said at last. "I've got seven kids to keep me company."

"Don't I know it."

Another long silence.

"I'm fixing biscuits."

He knew she hadn't been into the kitchen yet, but he could smell her biscuits already. He wondered if she would have country ham, scrambled eggs, maybe a little red-eye gravy. His mouth watered. He'd left the house before Eulainie was up. That was how eager he'd been to get here.

To see Addy.

"So?" he said, hoping to coax some kind of gracious invitation out of her.

"So, are you hungry?"

Just for spite, he said, "I've already eaten."

"Fine."

Then, for extra spite, he added as she turned and walked away, "Waffles."

It was a fib, of course. But he knew that she knew Eulainie Cook had never made waffles a day in her life. Wouldn't hurt her a bit to worry about who might have fixed him breakfast while she mixed up her damn biscuits.

ADDY HAD A PLAN. She worked it out while she banged around in the kitchen, making a mess out of everything, mixing up biscuits and frying country ham. *He might be able to resist me,* she thought, *but this'll get his mouth watering. Waffles, my foot!*

Her plan was to give her hardheaded husband a dose of the idyllic family life he was missing. Starting with home cooking.

Before the day was out, Danny got a good dose of Mayfield family life, all right. But it was far from idyllic.

What happened first was that the fire alarm went off when the biscuits burned because Addy got distracted when Terrell broke his glasses and cut his nose.

"Want me to go down to the Clock and bring back some breakfast for the kids?" Danny asked as he fanned smoke out through the back door with one of her gingham-checked kitchen towels.

"No." She snatched the towel out of his hands, thinking it might be just as well if he couldn't see her for the smoke. Her cheeks were red, that much was certain. "I can do that."

Danny backed out the door to join the smoke. "Fine."

He looked way too calm to suit her. And he'd handled the crisis way too calmly, too. There she'd stood in the middle of the kitchen, terrified to open the oven door, wondering where the smoke alarm was located and how to turn it off, a screaming Elisabeth clinging to her skirt. If Reno hadn't had the presence of mind to herd the other kids out the front door and Danny hadn't come in to turn off the stove, disconnect the alarm and open windows and doors to shoo out the smoke, Addy supposed she would have stood there till doomsday.

Maybe she had no business having kids around in the first place, she thought, scratching burned biscuits into the garbage and wondering if she'd ever manage to round up the kids for a bowl of Cheerios now that they were scattered all over the yard and beyond.

That was the first time her plan went awry.

Then David fell off the roof of the house after sneaking up Danny's ladder.

Addy heard the crash from Danny's work site and went flying, fear choking her heart. The first thing she saw was Danny, standing there with a screwdriver stuck in his back jeans pocket, his T-shirt clinging damply to his back and a saw in one hand.

Thank God, Danny was okay.

The next thing she saw was David, lying in the middle of the window Danny had been framing up. The carefully measured and cut boards were splintered and broken and one of Danny's sawhorses had been crippled beyond repair. David's big blue eyes looked stunned; his freckles stood out on a pale face. Addy waded into the wreckage.

"Addy, get out of there with those bare feet," Danny said. "You'll pick up a nail and—"

She ignored her husband and knelt beside David, hoping that wasn't a nail poking into her knee. She put tentative hands on David's arms and legs, feeling for anything broken or bleeding. "Are you okay?"

His mischievous smile was beginning to emerge and he squirmed away from her touch. "Yeah. I'm fine. Leggo, okay?"

She helped him up, still searching for gaping wounds. He scrambled out of the pile of broken wood that had almost been a bedroom window and prepared to scoot away. Danny had him by the collar of his striped polo shirt before he'd taken two steps.

"Not so fast, sport."

"Now, Danny—"

"You've got some cleaning up to see to," Danny said, gesturing to the mess and ignoring Addy. "I suggest you get busy."

David looked up at Danny with the same impish grin that was his answer to everything. "You said I couldn't help."

"And you ignored me, didn't you."

David shrugged.

"Now, get busy."

David stared uncertainly at the mess he'd landed in the middle of. Danny pointed out the giant garbage can he was using for scraps. "Clear away everything that's broken. Then we'll see to repairing this sawhorse."

"No foolin'?" David looked delighted with his fate.

Danny looked as if he didn't know what to make of a boy who relished his punishment. "Yeah. No foolin'."

"He'll get splinters," Addy protested as the boy grabbed the corner of the broken window frame and started hauling it toward the garbage can.

"They won't kill him."

"What if he steps on a nail?"

"As I recall, he had a very expensive tetanus shot right after he got here," Danny retorted. "And those sneakers cost so much they ought to keep out most of the nails around here."

"Fine. But if he gets hurt—"

"He just fell off the roof, for heaven's sake. That's an injury-repellent menace you're looking at there, Addy."

"He's just a little boy."

Danny grunted and gave his broken sawhorse a tug. Addy watched the play of muscles beneath his T-shirt and ached to be held against his chest. "He's a little boy who's just cost me a morning's work."

"He's not a bad boy, Danny."

"I know he's not, Addy. But he's a handful. He needs more attention than we can give him."

"That's not true," she said, although the tiny voice of doubt in her heart wondered again if she might be the wrong person to take care of all these kids, to make sure they were safe and warm and well fed.

Faced with Danny's determination to focus on his project and not on another futile conversation with her, Addy went back into the house and her own Saturday-morning chores, only to be distracted when the usually meek Terrell punched Casey in the nose and Casey bled all over Brook's favorite doll. That, in turn, prompted a fit of tears and anger that echoed through the house for a good half hour.

The only children who didn't contribute to the ruckus were Reno, who as usual helped dry tears and clean up messes, Elisabeth and Gabby, who played so quietly Addy didn't notice right away that they had disappeared.

"THE CREEK IS FUN," Elisabeth said, taking Gabby by the hand and leading her to the edge of the woods. "But Mommy says not to go by myself. So you can come with me. Okay?"

Gabby nodded, which made her curls bob up and down like the jack-in-the-box at Gramma Eulainie's. Elisabeth laughed.

"You've got funny hair," she said, touching one of the younger girl's curls. "I like it."

Gabby squeezed her hand, and Elisabeth decided that must be her new little sister's way of saying thanks. Funny, but they had been playing together all morning and Elisabeth had almost forgotten Gabby didn't talk. So far, Elisabeth wasn't having a bit of trouble understanding her.

"Want to catch frogs?" Elisabeth asked, hoping Gabby would say no but knowing she needed to at least make the offer. After all, frog-catching was the best entertainment the creek had to offer. David said so, although Reno seemed to think otherwise. But then, Reno was more like a grown-up than even Addy sometimes.

Gabby gave the question serious consideration, then shook her head.

"Okay. Then we'll...look for shiny rocks."

She started to tell Gabby about the shiny rocks she'd found the last time she came to the creek and how they all turned out to be ugly and dull once she got them up to her room. But when she looked at Gabby, it was almost as if Gabby knew already.

This time, Gabby seemed to be telling her, they'll be shiny for sure.

So they reached the creek and took off their shoes and waded into the ice-cold water, giggling as it tickled their toes and swirled around their ankles. Elisabeth guided Gabby to a nice, flat rock in the middle of the creek, then found one for herself and squinted into the burbling water.

They talked while they searched. At least, Elisabeth talked, and imagined she could hear everything Gabby would say to her if she could speak. They talked about learning to read, which Elisabeth hated, and learning numbers, which Elisabeth liked. They talked about having straight hair instead of curls and white sneakers instead of pink ones.

"I hope you can stay and be my sister a long time," Elisabeth said. "Sometimes we have brothers and sisters who only stay a little while. I've getted to stay two whole years now."

Gabby seemed to think she would be Elisabeth's sister for just the right amount of time, and that sounded good to Elisabeth.

Soon Elisabeth decided it was time to tell Gabby about her real mommy and her real daddy, who hated each other and hated her, too.

"They hate me so much they ran away from home," she said, jingling the six rocks she had collected in her pocket.

Gabby didn't seem to think they hated her.

"'Cause if they didn't hate me, they'd come back for me, wouldn't they?"

Gabby seemed to think Elisabeth shouldn't be afraid. And the funny thing was, by the time they each had a wet pocket heavy with rocks, Elisabeth wasn't quite so afraid. Maybe her mommy and daddy did love her. And maybe soon they would come back for her.

But right this minute, it just felt good to be looking for shiny rocks with her new little sister.

ADDY TOLD HERSELF there was no reason to panic.

"Yet."

She looked in the girls' bedroom again, although she had looked in there first.

"Elisabeth! Gabby!"

They still weren't there. And they weren't in the boys' room or in Addy's room playing with her lipstick or in the garage or the front yard. They weren't at Susan Hovis's playing with Cody, because she'd already called there to check.

Addy's heart began to pump painfully. It wasn't like any of the children—with the possible exception of David—to go off without letting someone know where they were. Unable to draw a lungful of breath, Addy wanted nothing more than to run to Danny, to fling herself into his arms. Danny would know what to do. Danny would make everything all right.

But that was the last thing in the world she *could* do right now, darn his stubborn hide.

She went back out to the front porch, where Reno was teaching Casey how to play the keyboard they'd picked up at a yard sale in Muscle Shoals a month earlier. Once again, she looked worriedly up and down Mimosa Lane. Her heart was ready to burst right through her rib cage.

"What's wrong, Mommy?"

"Nothing, sweetheart. I just haven't seen Elisabeth and Gabby for a while." She looked into Reno's dark, solemn eyes. "You haven't seen them, have you?"

Reno shook her head.

"I seen 'em," Casey said.

"*Saw* them," Reno corrected her.

"Yeah. Saw 'em. Goin' down to the creek."

Addy's hand flew to her mouth. *Now* it was time to panic. "Oh, God."

She did the only thing she knew to do. She ran straight to Danny.

"Oh, God, Danny, they're gone! They went to the creek!"

Danny grabbed her by the shoulders. His big, strong hands gave her an instant shot of courage. "Who? Calm down, now. What's wrong?"

"Elisabeth and Gabby. They went to the creek. Alone."

"Addy, it's okay. It's a shallow creek. I'm sure they're fine. Now—"

"Are you going with me or not?"

She knew she sounded desperate and she didn't even care. She felt a lump in the back of her throat. She hated hearing him sound so calm when he knew darn well what could happen to two little children— And yet wasn't that why she'd sought him out?

"Why don't I go?" he said. "You stay here and—"

"No! I'm going, too. I have to go."

"Not until you calm down, Addy. You're scaring the others. Okay?"

She tried to draw a long, slow breath to show him how calm she was, but it didn't work. She was almost panting. She turned to Reno and said, "You take everybody into the house until we get back. Okay?"

Big-eyed, Reno nodded and started rounding up the rest of the big-eyed children. All except David, who had a hammer in his fist and said, "I've got work to do. I don't have to go in the house like a little kid."

Danny put his hand on David's shoulder. "That's fine, Dave. You stay here and see if you think we've got enough nails to finish up the rest of the windows before supper. Addy and I'll be back shortly."

David nodded solemnly.

Impatient, Addy headed toward the woods. Danny caught up with her halfway there.

"Addy, you're—"

"I know," she snapped. "I'm overreacting."

He sighed. "If this damned creek scares you this much, why don't we just move? I've told you a dozen times—"

"Not now, Danny. Please?"

So they tramped toward the creek in silence, except for Addy's periodic calling of the girls' names. She tried not to think why her calls weren't answered. Tried not to think about how she would feel if anything had happened to either of the girls. Because Danny was right. He'd told her a dozen times they could leave, move away from the creek. But something held her here. Something that was as irrational as her fear.

At least, Danny thought the fear was irrational. But Danny hadn't been the one whose little sister had been found facedown in this very place. Danny didn't know. She'd told him, but he *couldn't* know because he hadn't been through it.

"Elisabeth!"

The closer they got to the clearing at the creek bank, the calmer Addy grew. Cold and calm. Then she realized it wasn't calm at all. It was numbness. So she wouldn't be hurt, no matter what they found.

When they burst into the clearing, the first thing she saw was Elisabeth bent over Gabby's feet, tying her left pink sneaker onto the younger girl's right foot. Both were wet and smiling serenely.

Elisabeth looked up and said, "We didn't go in the creek, Mommy. I promise."

Addy couldn't figure out how to scold them and hug them all at the same time. So she settled for hugging them.

CHAPTER SEVEN

TOO MUCH ADVICE gave Addy a headache. Right now, she felt a migraine coming on. She'd heard enough well-meaning advice in the past week to fill a number-ten washtub.

"No time for a migraine," she said, giving the knot in Gabby's sneakers another tug to test it.

Gabby frowned, her lips curled up in a skeptical pout. Whether for the shoestrings or Addy's timetable for headaches, Addy couldn't have said.

"Well, it's true," she replied to the frown, as she often did to Gabby's expressive face. "Right now, we've got an appointment with Bunny at the boutique, which means you and I have to walk over to Grandma Eulainie's to borrow the station wagon, drive back here and load up the back seat with tea towels and angel dolls and baby comforters."

She gestured to the colorful, cushy pile on the sofa. Gabby climbed down from the rocker and walked over to the pile of quilting, laying her cheek on one of the comforters.

"So, let's make it march," Addy said, taking Gabby by the hand. "We've got to do all that and get back here before the other kids start trickling in from school."

Her hand was on the front doorknob when the telephone started ringing.

Addy glared at the jangling contraption, opened the door and said, "Let it ring."

Gabby didn't budge.

"If it's important, they'll call back," Addy explained, giving Gabby another gentle tug. Gabby frowned. "It's probably some sales associate offering me a free trip around the world if I'm one of the first happy couples to tour their new resort."

Actually, Addy expected it was probably another well-meaning friend or neighbor with good advice on how to win Danny back from the other woman, how to get even with him but good or how to get back into the swing of being single. But that would probably be even harder for a five-year-old to understand than the irritation of telemarketing. Gabby frowned again. So did Addy.

"For heaven's sake, Gabby, I'm not even a happy couple right now. No sales associate in her right mind would even want to talk to me."

Gabby's chubby face looked suspiciously close to tears.

"Yeah. I know. Me, too."

Addy closed the door, dropped the little girl's hand and snatched up the telephone. She was immediately glad she had. Doc Newman was on the other end. Addy glanced at Gabby, who had plopped down on the couch and proceeded to examine each of the items Addy had carefully stacked for delivery to the boutique.

"Don't know if this is good news or bad," Doc Newman began.

Addy's frustration shifted into uneasiness.

Doc Newman cleared his throat. "The tests don't show a blessed thing wrong with that child, Addy."

"Oh. Well, that's good, isn't it?"

"Well, yes. And no. What it means is, there's nothing *medically* wrong. And that leaves something psychological."

Addy's heart wrenched in her chest. She glanced over her shoulder again at Gabby, who now held one of the angel dolls in her lap. She was staring at it intently, her little heart-shaped mouth barely open, tracing the doll's gilt-trimmed halo with one tiny fingertip.

"Then, what do we do?"

"Well, I suppose we have to assume Gabrielle has experienced something traumatic. Something she needs help getting over."

"But how do we do that if—"

"I don't know, Addy. But I can recommend someone who's very good with children."

Addy stood with the phone to her ear for several seconds after Doc Newman hung up, trying to compose herself before she turned back to Gabby. She didn't even want to think about what kind of awful things might make a child unable to speak. She didn't want to think about how difficult it could be to help a child recover from whatever that trauma might be.

And she didn't want to think about the look Danny would give her when he heard this little bit of extra news.

"Let's shake a leg, Gabby," she said at last, facing the little girl with a big smile. "When you've got angels to deliver, you have to get them there on time."

Forty minutes later, they were walking through the back door of Bunny's Country Bumpkin Boutique. Addy carried the big box, Gabby carried the doll with the gold rickrack halo.

Bunny welcomed them warmly, but Addy saw the speculative look she gave them as she set the box on a worktable in the storeroom. The look generally preceded a surefire tip for getting her life in order again.

"I don't need any more advice," she said as she and Bunny unpacked the box.

Bunny glanced at Gabby, who had marched straight to a child-sized rocker and sat down to hug her angel. "Who said I'm in the advice business?"

"If you aren't, you're the only one in town," Addy said. "I've got so many tips already, I'm thinking of writing my own self-help book. That way, anybody out there who wants a headache from listening to so much advice can just pick up a copy of my book. Save a little trouble for everybody."

With a muffled snicker, Bunny drew out her consignment book and began to log in Addy's items. Bunny, with her platinum highlights and gravity-defying bangs, still looked as if she worked at The Picture Perfect in town. Without looking up from her book, Bunny muttered, "Then I'll just save my breath and let you screw up all by yourself."

"Thank you."

"So, you going to the wedding?"

Addy's spirits dipped a little lower. She'd all but groaned when she heard the news that Susan and Tag had finally set the date, even though she'd been hoping for this very thing. A wedding was the last thing she wanted to attend right now. But how could she not go? Susan Hovis was too good a friend.

"Sure. Looking forward to it," she lied.

Bunny grunted. "Yeah. I think half the town's going just to be sure Betsy Foster doesn't throw a monkey wrench into things again. Wouldn't put it past her to have a heart attack right in the middle it."

Addy murmured something noncommittal and wandered off, browsing through the store while Bunny finished her paperwork. She remembered the extra angel doll, which was now sleeping peacefully in Gabby's pudgy arms. She knelt beside the rocker. "Sweetheart, it's time to give this doll to Miss Bunny now. Okay?"

Gabby looked distinctly doubtful. She kissed the doll on the forehead and hugged it closer to her chest.

"We've got lots of dolls at home, Gabby." At least three angel dolls, early versions that didn't quite hit the mark, sat on a shelf in the girls' room. "But Miss Bunny needs this one so that someone who doesn't have an angel can take one home. Don't you think that's a good idea?"

Gabby's dark blue eyes grew misty, but she gave the doll one more kiss, then held it out for Addy.

Everyone needs an angel.

Addy almost gasped, she was so certain Gabby had spoken the words. "What?"

"I didn't say anything," Bunny called out.

"No, I—" Addy caught herself, stared at the little face that so soothed her aching heart these days, and sighed. "You didn't, either, did you, sweetheart?"

Gabby shook her head solemnly. The movement shook one little tear off her eyelash. It trickled down her plump cheek.

"That's okay, Gabby," she whispered, placing her own kiss on the little girl's forehead in exactly the spot where Gabby had kissed the doll. "Maybe you do need your own special angel."

Then she placed the doll back in Gabby's arms. Gabby lowered her cheek to the doll's cloth cheek and smiled. The sight was well worth the small loss. Addy's heart lost some of its ache.

She walked around some more, Bunny's earlier words haunting her. She went back over and signed the papers. "What makes you think I'll mess up? You like being pessimistic? Or do I look that befuddled?"

Bunny tucked her paperwork back in a drawer and stared at Addy. "You really want to know?"

"Why not? I've had everybody else's two-cents' worth."

"I'm figuring you haven't heard what Heather Yates is saying all over town."

A tiny shock wave of alarm shot through Addy. She shoved her copy of the consignment contract into her skirt pocket. "No, and I don't want to, either." She grabbed up her empty box. But she didn't move. "What did she say?"

"She's practically got Las Vegas giving odds on how long it's going to take her to become the next Mrs. Danny Mayfield." Bunny picked up an angel doll with a pink lace collar and waved it in Addy's face. "The way I figure it, Addy, you ought to be whipping up a guardian angel of your very own."

IF ADDY HAD A GUARDIAN angel, she would have asked it to transport her home. She wanted to hide there. She wanted to curl up in her favorite chair, the ugly orange one they'd bought at a yard sale for their very first apartment in Auburn, and nurse her wounds. She wanted to shut off her brain and pretend she'd never heard the nasty gossip that another woman was actually spreading to people all over town about stealing away Addy Mayfield's husband.

But she had no guardian angel, and all she could do was drive her mother's station wagon back to her mother's house, get out and walk home with Gabby. First, however, she had to listen to her mother.

"Are you getting enough rest?" Eulainie asked.

Which Addy took to mean she looked haggard, that she had circles under her eyes, that she couldn't possibly hope to hold on to a man looking as downright pitiful as she did.

"Well, of course I am," she said. "I've got handling seven kids down to a science. Practically all my time these days is spent napping or soaking in a scented bath."

"Cranky, too," Eulainie added as she slipped the extra set of car keys on the hook by the back door. "You want me to come stay with you until one of you hardheaded young 'uns comes to your senses?"

"No!" Addy looked away. She wanted her mother right where she was to make sure Danny had no op-

portunity to stray! No. He wouldn't. He wouldn't!
God, how she missed him.

"I could take care of the kids. Feed you," Eulainie
added, giving her daughter a pointed once-over.

Fine. So she was scrawny, too. She recalled Heather
Yates's round, young shape and prayed that at least
some of it was thanks to one of those new Wonder-
Bras.

Somehow she escaped and made it back to Mimosa
Lane. She was almost home—and safe from more
prying, more spying—when Bump Finley and Betsy
Foster came around the side of the Foster house. They
were exchanging words, as polite Southerners said
when an argument was in progress. Addy couldn't
avoid overhearing.

"Goldang it, Betsy, it's none of your business! Like
every other goldang thing you stick your nose in."

Betsy primly peeled off her gardening gloves. "Well,
I suppose I have as much right as anyone else in
Sweetbranch to express my opinion. After all, they are
my neighbors."

Addy flinched, told herself she was being para-
noid. After all, surely there was something else in
Sweetbranch for the gossips to talk about besides the
Mayfield mess. She walked faster, far from eager to
hear any more of Betsy Foster's pontificating. Gabby
gave her hand a squeeze.

"Besides, Jacob, all I said was that young woman
ought to get herself to an attorney before another day
passes. A scoundrel like that could leave her high and
dry. And her with all those children on her hands."

"Now, Betsy, I ain't heard a soul say a thing about Danny Mayfield being a scoundrel. 'Cept you, of course. And you can't even recognize a good son-in-law when you're about to get one."

"Hush up, Jacob."

Addy sucked in her breath and almost ran the rest of the way home, Gabby toddling along beside her. She had to get home, behind closed doors.

But even home turned out to be no haven that afternoon. When the children poured in after school, David and Terrell were already arguing. When she followed them into their room to urge them to quiet down, she found out why.

"It's *his* fault," Terrell said, pointing at David.

"Is not. He had it coming to him."

Addy refrained from rubbing her temple, but the throbbing was definitely insistent. "Now, boys, I don't want to hear it. Whatever it is. I've had a long day and I'd appreciate it if you just drop it."

They grew quiet, still glaring at each other. But as Addy turned to leave, she heard David whisper, "I'd break his other nose if he had one."

Addy whirled, turning the throbbing behind her eyes into a full-fledged pounding. "Whose nose are you talking about?"

Absolute silence descended. Addy folded her arms across her chest. This was where Danny usually came in and saved the day. Getting tough with the kids wasn't her strong suit.

"I'm waiting."

Terrell grabbed his favorite diversion, a catalogue of computer software, and flopped down on his bunk.

His blond hair flopped, too, and the glasses he had taped together slid down the end of his short, eight-year-old nose. "He punched Jimmy Linton in the nose. It bled all over. I bet he broke it."

Addy tried not to allow her exasperation to show. "David, you know better than to fight."

"But he…he said it was my fault." David pulled his gangly legs up against his chest, propping his pointy chin on his knees. For once, his devilish smile had vanished. "About you and Dad."

"Then David cussed him out," Terrell said from behind his catalogue.

"Did not!"

"Did, too!"

Sighing, Addy dropped to the floor beside David. She, too, was out of smiles. "It's not your fault, David. Sometimes grown-ups just get mad at each other."

He shrugged, and Addy doubted if he believed her. She wanted to give him more reassurance, but right at this moment, she probably needed even more than David.

"How long are you gonna be mad at each other?" he muttered.

Addy's throat felt thick. She swallowed hard. "Not much longer. We just need a little time to simmer down."

"Like time-out."

She nodded. "Exactly."

David picked at the worn spot on the knee of his jeans. It would be a hole soon. Thank goodness it was almost summer and she wouldn't have to spring for new jeans right away. He squeezed the tip of his pinky into the frayed spot. "Maybe one of you'll just go away for good."

"Nobody's going away for good, David." Oh, how she hoped that was true. But she had to say it because she knew where David's mind had wandered. His own father had gone away for good. Then his mother had gone to Chicago, leaving him with friends while she looked for work. She never came home. Addy knew by now how children interpreted the abandonments and tragedies in their lives. It was always their fault.

How well she knew that feeling.

"Promise?"

The hope and dread in the barely whispered word constricted Addy's heart. Could she promise this little boy who had already been betrayed so many times something she couldn't be sure of delivering? On the other hand, could she deny him his hope that this time things would turn out differently?

Perhaps a compromise. She put her hand on his spiky red hair, gave it a ruffle and pulled him over for a brief hug—all that he would allow, she knew. "That's not something you have to worry about."

As she was closing the door behind her, she heard David whisper to Terrell, "You notice she didn't promise."

Addy's heart sank. How had she ever thought she had what it took to be a good mother? Worse, how had she managed to forget what being a good wife was all about?

ADDY HAD NEVER INTENDED to show up for Susan's wedding alone. Despite the tiff between them, she'd figured she and Danny would be side by side for the wedding.

That was before she knew that everyone in town knew about Heather Yates.

The worst of it was, there was no one she could talk to. These days her closest friend was Susan, who didn't deserve to be burdened with broken dreams and betrayed promises in the days right before she said her own vows. And aside from Susan, Addy had to admit, her best friend in the world was Danny. Always had been.

That made the hurt even sharper.

She tried not to think about being alone as she sat in the pew at the Sweetbranch First Freewill Baptist Church. She wore her most festive floral-print dress and her mother's strand of pearls and her one-and-only pair of high-heeled shoes, unearthed from the back of her closet. She'd seen Danny's good navy suit while digging for them and almost broke down into tears.

"Darn you, Danny Mayfield," she had muttered, slamming the closet door, "I can get through this alone. And I won't make a fool of myself crying, either. I won't give this town the satisfaction."

She figured she could keep her pledge by thinking about something else—*anything* else—besides the wedding ceremony and all that it meant.

So she sat on a pew near the back. She didn't look through the ivory-colored program with the gold bells embossed on the front.

"Oh, Danny, look!" They'd showed up early for rehearsal and found the box of wedding programs that

would be handed out the next day. Her heart pounded as she looked at the printed words, as the meaning sank in. She looked up at him, her first moment of prewedding jitters taking hold. She was only eighteen. Was she ready for such a grown-up step? "Is it really going to happen, Danny? Really?"

"You're not scared, are you?"

She hesitated, nodded. "Maybe. Looking at it in print like this, it's so . . . final."

He lifted her chin and looked into her eyes. Her jitters didn't stand a chance, not in the light of the self-assurance in Danny's face. "We can do anything together, Addy. You're the one who showed me that, don't you know?"

Addy swallowed hard and shut out the organ music echoing majestically, triumphantly, through the sanctuary. She looked but did not see when the bridal couple met at the altar, the same altar where she had taken Danny's hand years before.

Her heart felt like a wild bird in her chest, wings clamoring frantically against her ribs. Clutching her father's arm, she heard the first strains of the wedding march and knew with a certainty that her feet were rooted in place.

"Come on, baby," Jed Cook whispered, his usually stoic face full of emotion—pride and joy and wonder. "It's time."

"Oh, Daddy, I can't. I just . . . can't."

"You love him, don't you?"

"More than anything. But—"

He gave her a little smile, his chin wobbling a tad, and nodded toward the altar. "There's a fine young fellow up there counting on you."

She looked toward the altar and, through the shimmering softness of her veil, saw Danny turned their way. He looked awkward and uncomfortable in his tux. And this morning his face looked as young and uncertain as she knew hers had looked before rehearsal the night before.

Somehow, that gave her courage. It meant he wasn't going into this lightly. It meant he knew this was forever and he wanted it, anyway.

Whatever fear had held her in its grip released her, and she walked down the aisle, her arm through her father's, her eyes on Danny's.

Dragging herself back to the present only to discover herself on the brink of tears she'd sworn not to shed, Addy heard the Reverend Weston Siske begin speaking the words of love and loyalty and commitment.

When someone slid onto the pew beside her, Addy knew before she even looked that it was Danny. She felt his presence like a summer storm vibrating through the air. The tears almost fell then, and that made her angry enough to get past the moment.

"What are you doing here?" she whispered.

He touched a finger to his lips.

She glared at him. He'd been to the house after she left because he was wearing his navy suit. She told herself it was only seeing him dressed up like this that made her heart race. The white collar of his shirt made such a breathtaking contrast to his sun-browned skin.

His hair was so neat, a little damp even, the way it was for a while after he got out of the shower. She could smell his shaving cream and instantly remembered the smooth feel of his chin and jaw right after he shaved.

No wonder Heather Yates wanted him. Who wouldn't?

She jerked her head around and pointed it once again toward the front of the church.

Tall, dark Tag Hutchins made a devilishly good-looking groom, with his strong arm around the waist of his bride. But Addy barely noticed. Now she had plenty to be aware of besides the wedding ceremony. Now all her senses were consumed by the presence of the man at her side.

And when the Reverend Siske asked Susan Hovis if she would love and honor Tag Hutchins until death do them part, Addy once again felt the tears gathering in the backs of her eyes.

What had gone wrong? When things had been so very nearly perfect, what had happened?

She could come up with only one answer. A shy redhead with plenty of curves.

Danny chose that moment to take her hand in his. Addy froze. As much as she wanted to sit there and hold hands like lovers, how could she humiliate herself by letting all the gossips in Sweetbranch see how easily she caved in?

CHAPTER EIGHT

DANNY HAD WAITED until the ceremony started before he took his seat beside Addy. That way she wouldn't be able to start up with him. But something about her was different today. He knew that the minute her eyes locked with his, before she even spoke.

This was more than her usual mule-headed temper. Behind the anger in her eyes, he saw a deep well of hurt and disappointment. Much like what he'd seen each and every time she'd found out she wasn't expecting.

Is that what's bugging her now? he wondered.

That's when he reached out and took her hand in his. The moment he did, he knew something else—something worse—was afoot. Before, when she'd been so disappointed, she had always turned to him. He had done his best to comfort her, to reassure her, to coax her back to an awareness of all the blessings they did have in their life together. He'd liked to think he was her rock at those times, the way she'd been there for him so often.

This time, she snatched her hand away and whispered sharply, "Cut it out!"

Wounded, he let his hand fall to the pew between them. How had things gotten this bad? he wondered.

They couldn't talk. They couldn't touch. She didn't seem to want him within a mile of her.

At that moment, a twinge of guilt nipped at him.

He told himself he had nothing to feel guilty about. He'd tried to tell Addy the same thing, but she wouldn't listen, any more than poor, misguided Heather would listen when he tried to explain that he had a wife he loved and wasn't interested in her attentions.

Still, some part of him couldn't help but feel flattered when Heather said, in that sweet, breathy voice of hers, "You would always be first with me, Danny. You'd never have to worry about me neglecting you."

There was that guilty twinge again.

He looked up as a collective sigh quivered through the church. Tag and Susan had just turned to face their friends and family. Mr. and Mrs. Eugene Hutchins, Junior.

Danny never had been big on weddings. He'd only shown up today for Addy's sake. Because he wanted to see her and because he worried she might feel bad facing this alone. But as he looked into the faces of Tag and Susan, Danny felt the power of a commitment between a man and a woman as he'd never felt it before.

Tag's rugged, time-worn face looked ten years younger today, softened by a hope for the future that only love could create. And Susan, who had been through so much since her accident, smiled and wept at the same time. Tears trickled slowly down her cheeks, glistened in her eyes. She had the radiant look of a young woman embarking on a lifetime of limitless possibilities.

Danny felt a thickness in the back of his throat as he contemplated a love that could so transform two people, one who had lived a bitter, solitary life for decades and another who had almost lost her past and her future to injuries.

He swallowed hard as the couple came down the aisle slowly, Susan leaning on Tag for support and taking each step with careful deliberation. He studied Addy's back as the new Mr. and Mrs. Hutchins passed, captivated by the strength in his wife's squared shoulders and the vulnerability in the back of her neck, revealed now by her upswept hairstyle. He ached to touch it, to inhale the scent of her that was like the breath of life to him.

The first thing he thought when she walked down the aisle was that he'd never seen her hair up before and she looked so grown-up, so mature.

He wasn't sure how guys were supposed to feel during their wedding. It wasn't something guys talked about. Was it normal to feel scared and excited and so full of hope all at once? Danny had never felt normal in his whole life. But now, looking at Addy in her pretty white dress and her veil, those flowers cradled in her arm, he thought maybe his life was about to change.

In Addy's arms maybe he could learn all the things the rest of the world must already know about love and happiness and family and home.

He sniffed. Damn! *He might not know much about how other guys felt, but he did know they didn't cry at anybody's wedding!*

Before Danny realized it, Addy had stepped into the aisle, into the midst of the departing guests.

"Addy," he called after her softly.

She didn't pause, didn't turn, did nothing to acknowledge him. He followed as quickly as he could work his way into the stream of guests and headed for the Fellowship Hall in her wake. He caught up with her at the door and put his hand on her shoulder. He noticed for the first time how loosely her best dress hung on her and felt a wave of guilt. She might not know it, but she needed him there to take care of her.

"Addy, don't be like this."

"You've got some nerve showing up here like this to embarrass me," she said under her breath.

"What?" Danny felt his temper begin to rise, but he coached himself to calmness.

"I wish you'd just leave."

"I came for you, for Pete's sake." He knew his voice rose a notch and he tried to hang on to his temper. "I'm still your husband, for crying out loud."

She leveled a devastatingly cold look on him. "I'm surprised you remember."

Then she shook his hand off and entered the Fellowship Hall. Danny could see no good reason to turn the wedding reception into a battleground. Or maybe it was that little bit of guilt tweaking his nose that persuaded him to leave.

BEN MCKENZIE WASN'T one to stop at a bar on the way home from the plant, even when the place was as friendly and cozy as Tony de Fuente's Holy Spirits Tavern. But tonight he had a mission.

Tonight, he hoped to save Danny Mayfield from his own pigheadedness.

Rose had told him the gossip before they fell asleep the night of the Hutchins wedding. If he had noticed how Addy brushed off Danny's presence at the wedding, Ben was certain everyone else in town had noticed, as well. But Rose had said talk was that Danny was dropping by Tony's after work most days and staying later every night. In itself, that wouldn't have been enough to prompt a little crusading, because Danny still did his job as production manager and did it well. But the rest of Rose's information could affect Danny's performance. Could even land Ben's company in court. And he had no intention of losing all he'd worked for because of some scheming little girl.

He looked around for Danny. The tavern, housed in a one-time Episcopal church at the west end of Main Street, was quiet by neighborhood bar standards. A country ballad wailed on the jukebox; the cue ball hit a rack of balls at the pool table along one side. People talked and laughed, but nobody sounded raucous or out of control. Very little smoke hung in the air, and the strongest aroma was fresh popcorn, not stale beer. Pewlike booths lined one wall. Tony de Fuente, a dark-haired newcomer to Sweetbranch whom Ben recalled having an interesting story of his own, pumped beer behind the bar, which snaked across the far end of the old sanctuary, where the pulpit used to be. A neon clock touting a low-alcohol beer hung over the baptismal, and the stained-glass windows gave the place a mystical air. Smiling, Ben wondered if the setting weren't at least partly responsible for the subdued mood at the Holy Spirits.

About two dozen young people filled the booths and stools, hung around the pool table and the electronic bowling machine. Most of them Ben recognized. Young, unattached plant workers. People who would have left the town as soon as they had their high school diplomas in the days before the plant opened. None of them was Danny.

Ben walked toward the bar, thinking Danny might show in the next few minutes. Or he might ask Tony a few gentle questions. But before he got halfway across the room, a voice beckoned to him from one of the booths.

"The upstanding Ben McKenzie hanging out at the local bar?" The voice was low and sultry and uncomfortably familiar. "I'm shocked."

The uneasiness Ben had felt the moment Rose told him about seeing his ex-wife threatened to escalate into full-scale anxiety. He'd been tempted to snoop around, try to find her. But he'd decided to let it rest and maybe she would turn around and go back to Winston-Salem. For much the same reason, he now clamped down on his reaction and turned toward the voice.

"And here I thought you were in town to see Krissy." He glanced around him pointedly. "I guess you had something else in mind."

Cybil gazed at him, her hand draped loosely around a tall glass filled with ice and pale liquid. She looked as regal as always, her cool blond hair swept up in a Grace Kelly knot, her expensive clothes fluid over her slender body. Her gray eyes didn't look hazy, and Ben had a moment of hope that her drinking wasn't out of hand again.

"Can I buy you a drink?" she said.

"No, thanks." She hadn't invited him to, but Ben slid into the booth and stared at her across the table. He hoped the fear didn't show in his eyes; he wondered what it was he feared most. "What are you doing here, Cybil?"

She smiled, that mystery smile that had so intrigued him when he was younger and subject to being intrigued by women who had a hard edge to them. He'd had a hard edge then himself. The birth of his daughter had smoothed his rough spots; Cybil just kept sharpening hers.

"Thought I'd see what kind of little burg it took to lure you away, Ben."

He wanted to ask how long she planned to stay. Whether she wanted to see her daughter, who had cried for her mother these past few months when no one knew where Cybil was. He wanted to know how much she was drinking and exactly what kind of plans were clicking and whirring in that methodical little mind of hers. But he knew better than to ask. Cybil had always enjoyed the game of withholding whatever it was Ben had wanted most.

"Quaint, isn't it?" he replied instead, knowing his comment about Sweetbranch would feed into her cynical outlook.

She laughed softly and raised her glass to her lips. "You would think so."

She drank, a long swallow that seemed to replenish her spirits the way ice water on a summer day revived a jogger. Except that it was early spring and Cybil looked as if the most exertion she'd experienced recently was hanging semiprecious stones from her ears.

"Nice seeing you again, Cybil." He made a move to leave. He had better things to do than let his ex-wife jerk him on the end of her string.

She put her hand on his wrist. He thought he saw a touch of loneliness, of vulnerability, in her eyes, but the look vanished quickly. The old, hard Cybil returned. "Don't be in such a rush."

She sounded as if it didn't matter to her one way or another, but Ben suspected her casual unconcern lay pretty much on the surface. He stood and tried to remember that the distaste he felt would hurt no one but himself. And maybe Krissy, if she were ever to detect it. "Call Krissy. She misses you."

Cybil looked down, but not before Ben saw the surface toughness crumple again. She recovered quickly. "Oh, don't worry, Ben. I have no intention of writing off my daughter."

The bitterness in her eyes when she looked up chilled him. He had run once before to protect Krissy, had broken the law. But now he had a son, a wife, a business. What could he do now if push came to shove?

DANNY SAT IN HIS PICKUP, hands gripping the steering wheel, staring at the muted light filtering through the stained-glass windows of Tony's tavern. He didn't want a beer. He didn't want to listen to another country song about love gone wrong. He didn't want to laugh or shoot pool or be sociable.

But he also didn't want to sit in his mother-in-law's kitchen eating meat loaf that tasted just like Addy's. He didn't want to wonder what Addy was doing and what had happened to the kids at school that day. He didn't want to ache himself to sleep from wanting to hold Addy so bad.

What he wanted was to go home.

He jerked the keys out of the ignition and jumped down from the truck. After what happened at the wedding Saturday, it was clear he was the only one who wanted that. And damn if he'd go home as long as he wasn't wanted there.

Ben McKenzie was walking out the door of the Holy Spirits as Danny was walking in. Danny's surprise must've shown on his face. Ben said, "I've been looking for you."

All kinds of anxieties rushed into Danny's head, the biggest and most frightening being that something had happened to Addy. "What's wrong?"

Ben put a hand on his arm and maneuvered him back out the door into the parking lot.

"Ben, what's happened?"

Leaning against the hood of his car, one foot on the ground and the other on the bumper, Ben gave Danny a long, hard look. Danny began to understand that nothing had happened to Addy. But something might be about to happen to him.

"I want you to tell me what's going on with Heather Yates."

Knowing he had nothing to feel guilty about didn't do Danny one lick of good. He felt the perspiration, hot and prickly, on his neck and back. Whatever he said, it wouldn't sound good. If Addy thought the worst of him, how could he expect anyone else to believe him? "Nothing."

"That's not what she's saying."

Danny's gut did a plunge into the dirt. "What do you mean?"

"Danny, I know you're having trouble at home. But I can't have that spilling over into my plant. This kind of thing—"

"What's she saying?"

"All she's saying is she's going to be the next Mrs. Mayfield." Danny groaned at Ben's words. "What she's hinting at... Well, you can pretty much guess. What I want to know is whether there's anything to it or not."

Danny looked Ben straight in the eyes. "Only in her overactive imagination."

Ben held his gaze for a long time, trying to gauge the truth of his words. "What are you going to do about it?" he asked at last.

Danny's shoulders sagged. "What *can* I do? I can't fire her, can I?"

"No. You can't fire her."

"We could transfer her somewhere else in the plant."

"Make her somebody else's problem?"

Danny sighed. "Yeah. Something like that."

"If word gets around I moved her out of your reach, it might not look good."

"And it looks good now?"

"It can always get worse."

"I don't see how." Then it dawned on him. "Has Addy heard this?"

"What do you think?"

What Danny thought was that it would be a cold day in hell before Addy asked him to come home.

"Stay away from Heather," Ben said. "I don't want you within ten feet of her, anywhere, anytime. If she comes into your office, get out of there."

Danny nodded. Ben clapped him on the shoulder and reached into his pocket for his car keys. "And go home. The best way to fight a rumor like this is by getting rid of any reason for the rumor."

"But—"

"How long have the two of you been together?"

"Thirteen years." Then it came to him. Their anniversary was just weeks away. His lungs squeezed shut on him.

"Thirteen years is a lot to throw away. Work it out, Danny."

Danny shook his head miserably, walking toward the tavern door without conscious thought as Ben pulled out of the parking lot. Addy was his whole life. Had been since he was just a kid.

How had things gotten so screwed up? And how did you reason with somebody who could get so mad she'd sic a delinquent with a matchbook on your clothes?

Maybe he should have done things differently that Saturday morning when she was lying there in bed, so soft and warm with that lazy smile on her lips. If she couldn't be reasoned with, maybe he could find another way to get her attention.

He shoved the door of the tavern open. Something about the idea of having to seduce his own wife made him hot under the collar. And why should she have things all her own way?

The stool at the crook in the bar suddenly looked inviting. Tony had a cold beer sitting in front of him almost before he was settled down.

"You look like the unhappy man tonight, *mi amigo*," Tony said, pausing in front of Danny's stool to rerack wineglasses.

"'Course he is. He's married, ain't he?" said a man down the bar.

"Not exactly," said someone else at the other end of the bar. Everyone within earshot laughed. Everyone except Danny. And Tony. Tony just looked at him.

When the other conversations resumed, Tony leaned his elbows on the bar and said softly, "Sometimes the relationships are difficult to work."

Danny found a small smile for Tony's awkward English. Tony was all contradiction. Tall and good-looking in the way of a Latin movie heartthrob, Tony never seemed to have a woman on the string. And despite owning a business that seemed tailor-made for an extrovert, Tony often struck Danny as shy, reluctant to share himself.

"Yeah," Danny said. "And once they get off track, getting 'em back on track can be darned tough."

"But it is this that you want? To get back to the tracks?"

"Yeah. Sure." Of course he did.

"Then you tell her the way of it and that is that," Tony said with all the confidence of a man raised in the kind of culture that obviously didn't produce stubborn women like Addy. "She is waiting for you to do this thing."

"You don't know her," Danny said, shaking his head.

"She has face to save," Tony insisted.

As Danny contemplated that, the woman sitting next to him suddenly pointed her finger at Tony. "What about Danny's face? Don't he get to save his face?"

"His face is saved when he is once again sleeping in his own bed," Tony announced as he pulled the tap and filled another mug.

The man on the other side of the woman who had spoken up turned to them and said, "But she's the one who threw him out. Threw all his clothes right out in the front yard. That's what I heard."

Danny cringed.

The woman nudged Danny's shoulder with hers and raised her glass in his direction. "You've got your rights. Don't let her shove you around."

"Aw, Ginny, that's a bunch of baloney and you know it," said another woman, two stools down.

"The way you talk, there's only one side to this. You know what men are like." She leaned around the man between them and glared at Danny. "What do you expect when you have a little honey on the side, May field?"

The other woman slammed her mug on the counter. "Oh, shoot. That's just talk. Heather's hoping for somebody to save her from that rotten family of hers. Everyone knows that. The truth of the matter is—"

The man gave her a sign and she grew quiet. All eyes turned toward the door. Danny was afraid to look.

"Speak of the devil," said the second woman.

And they all sat back to see what would happen next.

Danny could feel Heather's eyes on him as she walked toward him. All activity seemed to have stopped—the pool table was silent, the talking ceased, the clink of glass on tabletops came to a halt. All he could hear was the slow throb of a country love song and the deliberate click of high-heeled boots on the hardwood floor.

Ben's warning came back to him. All the other advice he'd heard was a jumble, but not that. Without taking another swallow of his beer, Danny stood, threw a couple of bills on the bar and turned toward the door. Heather stood there smiling at him. He walked right past her without a word.

Heather's soft voice was unnaturally loud in the silence. "You know it just breaks my heart when you treat me mean, Danny."

The buzz resumed instantly, lower and more intense than it had been seconds before. Danny felt his face grow hot. As he reached the door, he heard someone in a nearby booth say, "I told you. She's got him on a leash just like one of those kids of theirs. Always has."

No words could have had a more disastrous effect on him. They reminded him of what Heather had said before. About what he'd finally said to himself less than an hour ago.

What had happened to him? And how had he been the last one to see it?

CHAPTER NINE

WHEN YOU HAVE KIDS, Danny told himself, you end up in hospital emergency rooms. No biggie, as Brook would say.

Didn't help. As he dashed through the double doors into the county hospital, his heart raced painfully and he couldn't calm the apprehension prickling beneath the surface of his skin.

He'd barely spotted Addy when she threw herself into his arms and clung to him. She was little more than a wraith. But he closed his eyes and wrapped his arms around her slight figure, feeling a rush of relief that she had once again turned to him in her distress.

"Oh, Danny, I'm so glad you're here," she whispered, her voice frantic.

"It's all right now," he said, knowing she was far more distraught than a little boy's broken arm warranted. "I'm here and everything is fine."

He also knew the source of her out-of-proportion fear. She had always blamed herself for her little sister's tragic death, and he supposed she always would.

He held her until she stopped trembling, murmuring to her the way he had many times. The times she'd thought she was pregnant, then discovered she wasn't. When her father died. When Brook's influenza escalated into pneumonia and they'd both feared that she had been infected by her HIV-positive mother, after all. He hardly knew what he said; he doubted if Addy did, either.

She went still in his arms, finally, and he led her to a bank of dingy blue chairs along one wall, out of the flow of ER traffic. She hadn't been crying, but her eyes still looked frightened.

"Tell me what happened," he said, holding her icy hand.

She nodded, took a second to find her voice. "It's David. He was in the tree house at the McKenzies' and he and Krissy had fixed up this rope so they could play Tarzan. He had to go first, of course, and when the rope didn't hold, he broke his arm."

Danny had to smile just a little. David would be rambunctious, no matter what. And he'd probably smiled that devil-made-me-do-it smile all the way to the hospital. "How bad is it?"

She shook her head. "Not bad. They—"

"Mr. and Mrs. Mayfield?"

They looked up into the friendly face of a clerical worker. She wanted insurance information, and they spent ten minutes on that.

"Just a simple fracture, they said," Addy continued when the admissions clerk left them alone again. "But he wouldn't let me stay in the examining room with him. He said he was fine and I should wait out here for you."

Danny wanted to take her hand in his again, but the intrusion of the woman in uniform had taken the intensity out of their closeness. Once again, Danny felt like the husband brought in from the doghouse only temporarily.

"Boys break their arms," Danny said. "He'll be fine."

"But I should have—" Danny watched as she floundered, trying to find a way to blame herself "—been there. I could have done something."

"Addy, he's nine years old. Old enough to use his head a little bit. And you can't watch his every move."

"But he doesn't even want me around. If I hadn't—"

"Mr. and Mrs. Mayfield?"

Danny sighed, exasperated. This time, it was a nurse wanting to know if David had ever had any allergic reactions. Once again, Danny saw his wife's feelings of inadequacy all over her face when she had to admit she didn't know the answer.

When the nurse walked off, Danny simply said, "It's not your fault."

"It feels like my fault," she said miserably.

Danny knew without being told that it wasn't just the broken arm that Addy blamed herself for. It was all the bad colds and the poison ivy rashes and the strep throats over the years. It was the abandonments and the abuses and the deaths that had left little ones alone. All of it Addy's fault. All of it Addy's responsibility to cure, to fix, to heal.

And all of it because of the one child she hadn't been able to save.

"Addy, you can't blame yourself for everything," he said softly, putting his arm around her narrow shoulders.

She gave him a look that said she could most certainly try—and succeed more often than not.

"It wasn't your fault then and it isn't your fault now," he said.

Addy tensed. "I don't want to talk about it."

"You were eight years old, Addy. You couldn't have—"

"Mr. and Mrs. Mayfield?"

Danny thought he might just slug the person with that cheerful voice, but when he looked up, he realized she probably packed more of a wallop than he did. The fullback in the nurse's uniform also had her arm around a beaming David, who practically swaggered with pride over his pristine cast.

"Your young man is ready to go home," the nurse said. "Now, David, you have your instructions on caring for your cast?"

David pulled a rumpled sheet of paper from his hip pocket and passed it to Addy. "This was so cool," he said as the threesome headed to the exit. "You won't believe what all they did."

Danny didn't mention that things probably hadn't changed dramatically since he'd broken arms at ages eight and fourteen. And he barely registered David's enthusiastic telling of his war story. As he ushered David and Addy to his pickup—Eulainie had dropped Addy and David off, then rushed home to feed supper to the others and get them off to bed—Addy was all he could concentrate on. The look in her eyes, the quaver in her voice, the fragile feel of her shoulders in his embrace. He resented the interruption. And he was grateful for the chance to take her home, to be with her this night.

Maybe tonight, after shooing David off to bed, they could patch things up. The signs were there that it was what she wanted, too. Hadn't she rushed into his arms? Hadn't she grown calmer when he held her? Wasn't that the way things were supposed to be between them?

David had fallen asleep by the time they reached Mimosa Lane, and Danny carried him in, held him while Addy pulled back the sheets. They tucked him in together, shoulders brushing.

It felt so right.

Eulainie had already tucked the girls in. That only left Casey and Terrell. After seeing his mother-in-law safely to her car, Danny came back inside and stood in the doorway to the bathroom, where Addy was supervising toothbrushing.

"Need some help?" He held his breath, hoped he sounded casual.

She looked at him, a look that was at once as familiar as his favorite sneakers and at the same time excitingly, strangely new. She nodded. And Danny knew she was agreeing to more than sharing child-care duties.

The two boys had a million questions about David's broken arm, which they agreed to wait to ask him until he woke up the next morning. They settled instead for a silent and reverent inspection of the cast that lay atop the sheet. Clearly jealous, they crawled into bed, accepted Addy's kiss and Danny's tug on their toes. The lights went out, the house grew quiet.

Danny took Addy's hand and led her into the living room. He wanted to take her straight to the bedroom—*their* bedroom—but he didn't want her thinking he was taking their relationship for granted. If she had heard those stupid stories, she probably figured she deserved to be wooed. So he would woo. In fact, he wouldn't mind wooing one little bit.

He pulled her onto the couch with him, drew her into the crook of his arm. She snuggled against him, not the least bit reluctantly.

"Where were you when I called Mom?"

Danny frowned. He wasn't in the habit of fibbing to his wife, but he figured she wouldn't be crazy about hearing he'd stopped at Tony's for a beer, either. "I hadn't come in from work yet."

Not exactly a fib, he told himself.

She turned her face up to his. "You're not working too hard, are you?"

Danny discovered he didn't like the feeling of guilt that came with even such a tiny shading of the truth. He leaned his head into hers, just close enough to feel her hair brush against his cheek. "No. But you are."

"I don't mind."

Her husky whisper felt as soft against his senses as her hair, her curves, her skin. A deep, hard longing gripped him, reminded him how empty he'd been without her. He brushed his lips against her forehead, inhaled the fresh, clean scent of her, a scent that made him think of nuzzling the soft valley between her breasts.

"I hope you're not waiting for me to make the first move, Danny Mayfield," she whispered, her sharp tongue as endearingly familiar as her fragrance.

Danny smiled. "Lord, I've missed you."

"You couldn't prove it by me."

She glanced up at him and he caught her sly grin. He would've liked to tease her, play the game with her a little longer. But it had been too long already, and he needed her too much. Without preamble, he pulled her into his lap, settled her slim, firm bottom over the swell of his erection. She smiled.

"Why, I guess you have missed me."

He took her face in his hands, pulled her lips to his. He buried his fingers in her hair, his tongue in the warmth of her mouth. She responded hungrily, made those little sounds in her throat that always made him grow hard. He lowered a hand to her breast, small and high and perfect. He tugged at her buttons. She tugged at his zipper.

His zipper slid down, her buttons popped open, and the doorbell rang all at the same time.

"Ignore it," he whispered, seeking the taut crest of her nipple with his fingers.

"Can't," she gasped, nevertheless touching the tip of her tongue to his lips. The chime reverberated throughout the house once again. "The kids'll wake up, anyway."

She was already wiggling off his lap, straightening her clothes, smoothing her hair. Danny's excitement crashed, the mention of the kids as effective as a deep freeze in killing the heat of his desire.

"Addy," he called out, protesting, knowing it was futile.

She was already at the door, standing on tiptoe to peek out. She turned an apprehensive look on him, then opened the door. Maxine Hammond and her attorney husband stood on the porch.

"I'm sorry, Addy," Ragan began. "I told her this could wait till morning."

"It most certainly could not," his wife said. She was smiling broadly.

Danny thought perhaps it was the male perspective, but he, too, felt certain whatever it was could have waited until morning. Waiting until morning might have made all the difference in the world.

Addy ushered their visitors in. A regal woman the color of rich coffee, with beaded braids and clothes that reflected her Bermudian ancestry, Maxine had a hand in most of the charitable work that went on in Sweetbranch. Ragan, with his red hair and freckles, looked like anything but an attorney. As they made their way into the living room—Maxine sat on the other end of the couch and Danny grew another degree or two grouchier—Ragan began to explain his efforts at locating a relative for an estate that was still in probate.

"Oh, for goodness' sake, Ragan," Maxine interrupted. "They are not interested in that."

At least she had that right.

Maxine turned to Danny, then to Addy, who was now sitting all the way across the room in the old orange rocker. Addy was curled up in a characteristic pose, skirt pulled down over her knees, bare toes peeking out. Her skirt was snug against the curve of her hip and thigh, and Danny's body filed a protest that he could no longer touch her.

If the Hammonds could manage to get their news out and then get on their way back home, Danny told himself, maybe it still wouldn't be too late.

Then he heard a soft rustling from the hallway. His jaw automatically clenching, he looked toward the sound. Brook stood in the doorway, rubbing her half-closed eyes, standing with one bare foot on top of the other.

"I heard a noise," she said so sleepily no one else heard her.

Damn! The path to reconciliation was growing bumpier by the minute. Danny's optimism grew dimmer.

"Ragan has located Elisabeth's father," Maxine announced at last.

Addy almost fell out of the rocker. "What?"

Brook gasped. Danny heard her bare feet headed toward the bedroom. He almost groaned aloud.

"Omigosh!" Addy was sitting on the edge of the rocker now, her hands clasped together tightly, her face aglow with an excitement Danny had certainly hoped to see tonight, though not quite for the same reason. "Oh, Danny, isn't that wonderful? What happened? What happens now?"

Little squeals came from the back of the house, followed by the muted thunder of other sets of feet. Danny knew what happened now. And it wasn't what he had planned. Not even close.

By the time seven children stormed into the room, adding their shrill voices to the din and demanding their own sets of answers, Danny barely heard Ragan Hammond's explanation. What it boiled down to, though, was that Elisabeth's father was now living in another state, running his own small business and happily remarried to a woman with a young daughter of her own. Elisabeth's mother had moved around so much that her father lost track of them. So he'd been unaware that his daughter had been motherless for the better part of a year.

Elisabeth's father was coming for her within the week.

Joy reigned. And with it came plenty of hugs and shouts and excited chatter.

The enthusiastic celebration infected Danny, too. He had to blink to keep the tears back when Elisabeth first absorbed the news. The shy little blonde with the timid smile and the dimple just below her right eye covered her face and hid her eyes. Then, unable to contain herself, she began to dance around the room in her Sleeping Beauty nightshirt.

"My real daddy's coming! My very own real daddy's coming!"

Above the heads of all the little ones crowded into the living room, Danny locked eyes with Addy. She, too, was crying. He understood too well the mixed emotions flitting across her face: the happiness she shared with this little girl for whom something was finally going right; the satisfaction in knowing she had made a safe and happy home when that little girl had nowhere else to go; and the poignant sadness of knowing she would soon be losing a little girl she loved like a daughter.

Danny smiled at Addy, hoped he had a chance to tell her, before the night was over, what a triumph this moment was for her. Here he stood, in the midst of a half-dozen parentless children, and none of them was standing on the sidelines indulging in self-pity. Each felt secure enough, loved enough, to rejoice with Elisabeth. Addy deserved the credit for that and his heart swelled with love for her.

The only child remaining still and quiet in the middle of the happy turmoil was Gabrielle, the newest of Addy's little angels.

Gabby sat on her knees in an armchair, one of Addy's angel dolls clutched to her chest, her face aglow with happiness. Danny felt drawn to her. Telling himself she might not feel comfortable with his presence the way the others did, he nevertheless walked over to kneel beside her.

He realized, when he did, that he didn't know what to say to her. Addy had told him Gabby and Elisabeth had become inseparable, but Gabby didn't look the least bit concerned about losing her new friend. Addy had also told him Doc Newman had found no physical reason for the girl's speechlessness. But as he looked into her big, blue eyes, Danny found himself thinking he didn't need to say a thing.

He just squeezed her hand. Or had she squeezed his? He wasn't sure. He only knew he felt reassured.

Danny tried, for the next half hour, to get to Addy. He wanted to put his arm around her shoulders, to share a joyful kiss. To stake his claim, he supposed, and maybe even to whisper some encouragement for the idea of herding the children back into bed. But whenever he got close, someone else seemed to get to Addy first. One of the children or Maxine. When he finally reached her side, it seemed clear no one would sleep for some time to come and the popping of the celebratory popcorn had begun.

Danny gritted his teeth. *Tonight? This had to happen tonight?*

"Addy, don't you think—" he whispered.

"What?" She looked down at Casey, who was tugging on her sleeve.

Danny gritted his teeth some more while she took care of Casey's problem—his favorite Power Rangers glass wasn't clean and he didn't want to drink his soft drink out of anything else.

"Addy, maybe it's a little late for them to be drinking soft drinks, anyway." Danny walked into the kitchen to protest.

"Hmm? Oh, Danny, could you see if there's a bag of ice in the freezer?"

There was. Soft drinks it would be.

Danny looked at the clock. Now it was past *his* bedtime. He turned down a soft drink.

"Addy, if these kids don't get to bed soon, you'll never get them up in the morning," he said once the popcorn littered the living room rug.

Maxine looked around and chuckled. "I fear there is little chance they would sleep even if you could get them back into bed."

She was right, of course. Danny looked at the roomful of giggly, sleep-silly kids. He looked at Addy, who appeared to be the only one in the house ready to doze off. And he looked at the Hammonds, who were finally shifting on the couch, preparing to leave.

An hour too late, Danny thought, disgruntled.

Addy barely kept her eyes open until the Hammonds were out the door. The children were now arguing over whether to watch a late-night movie or a comedy sketch, both of which apparently had R ratings.

"I'll be back in two minutes," Danny said to the children as he swept Addy into his arms. "Do all your whining between now and then because when I get back, it'll be bedtime."

The whining started and he turned his back on it. He carried Addy into the bedroom, stuffed down the pangs of disappointment as he contemplated the reconciliation that had seemed so close just an hour earlier, and tucked Addy gently between the sheets. She roused a little as he pulled the sheets up around her shoulders.

"Come to bed, Danny," she whispered, her voice heavy with sleep.

He wanted to. Ached to. But what he didn't want, he realized now, was to wake up in the morning with everything unchanged. Earlier, he'd let himself get caught up in desire for his wife, ignoring the fact that passion was not going to solve their differences.

Now he knew better. He'd seen proof of it first-hand. The kids still came first. Nothing had changed.

But right now, he couldn't even explain that to her. She was too sleepy to take in his explanations. Too sleepy to understand that tonight had turned into another example of the way their plans always took a back seat to the children.

"I have to take care of the kids first," he said.

As always.

She nodded, her eyes already closed again.

CHAPTER TEN

THERE WERE FEW THINGS Addy hated more than shopping for a baby shower. Unwilling to face the task alone, she asked Rose McKenzie to go with her to shop for one of their neighbors, who was expecting her second child.

Wistfully, Addy fingered the ruffled edge of a bib, smiled at the tininess of a knit sleeper striped like a baseball uniform.

One day. She used to think that whenever she passed the children's store on Main Street. She'd given up even letting the thought cross her mind. Especially now.

"I was thinking something practical," Rose said, tugging a bulky box off a nearby shelf. "How about a diaper-disposal system? Now, that's something to get any new mother's heart going pitty-pat."

Addy grinned and wrinkled her nose. Rose's wry sense of humor was exactly why she'd invited her neighbor along. It was hard to be gloomy for long with Rose around.

"I was leaning toward something a little sweeter than that," she admitted, waving the sleeper.

Rose nodded and studied the outfit. "That's gonna

be sweet for about ten minutes. Until he spits up on it.''

Addy laughed, which was a first for quite a while. Probably her first since the night they'd learned about Elisabeth's father. Although the children had been giddily happy ever since, Addy still hadn't forgiven Danny for the way he'd left that night. She continued to be humiliated by the memory of asking him to come to bed and waking up the next morning alone.

Oh, he'd tried to talk about it since. Some nonsense about all the things that had come between them in the first place still being unresolved. Addy knew rationalization when she heard it. He had walked out to spite her because their lovemaking had been interrupted, and she knew it.

''Oh, look,'' Rose said, drawing Addy out of her reverie. ''You want to talk sweet, now this is sweeter than sucking on sugarcane.''

She held up a musical mobile featuring nursery rhyme characters. It was sweet. So sweet Addy felt the familiar ache. Oh, to be fixing up a nursery.

Before she could decide between the mobile and the sleeper, a crash at the corner of the aisle caught her attention. She turned in time to catch David cutting the corner of the aisle too close and knocking over a display of formula.

He looked up and caught her eye, grinning from ear to ear. ''Oops.''

As he haphazardly began replacing the cans, he said, ''Guess what I saw? A ball glove. You know, I never had a ball glove, and Danny said we'd start practicing softball as soon as it got warm enough, and

I was thinking it was probably warm enough because all the kids are wearing shorts to school now, so I probably need a ball glove. Dontcha think?"

Terrell and Casey had showed up by then, and all three of them stared up at her expectantly while Addy's heart turned to a hard lump in her chest.

Softball practice. It was one of Danny's traditions. Every year, starting in May, he got the kids together a couple of evenings a week and drilled them on pitching and catching and batting. To get them ready for summer Little League, he said.

Because the boy in him couldn't wait to hear the soft thud of a softball against a bat, Addy always thought. She loved watching him with the kids, his face as flushed and excited as theirs as they ran the bases and dropped high flies and tossed wild pitches. Danny loved softball practice.

But how could she stand to watch it this year? Worse, how could she stand it if he didn't show for "spring training"?

"I don't know, David," she said, putting the sleeper back on the rack, her enthusiasm for the little outfit vanished. "I'm not sure we'll have practice this year."

David's grin wavered slightly. "But we have to have it. I wasn't here for it last year. So we have to have it."

Terrell took off his glasses and wiped a smudge on his grass-stained T-shirt. "You mean 'cause Danny's not here this year?"

David thumped the younger boy on the shoulder with his cast. "That's a doofus thing to say."

Addy put her arm around Casey, who had snuggled up to her when Terrell mentioned Danny's absence. "Yes, David, because Danny's not here. I'm…I don't know how to pitch or catch myself. I wouldn't be much help to you guys."

That much was true. But the greater truth was that she simply couldn't face the idea of doing it without Danny.

"Then we'll teach you." David grabbed her by the hand and started tugging her toward the toys. "Come on, I'll show you. This glove fits just right. You'll see."

Two minutes later, she was standing in the midst of the toys while David demonstrated why the glove had been practically custom-made for his hand.

"David, I said—"

"Aw, come on. Please?"

"Yeah, we really need practice," Terrell added.

"We'll help with supper every night," said David, who somehow managed to avoid helping with meals even when he was asked.

"And brush our teeth wif only one remembering," Casey said.

Their bright, hopeful faces tugged at her even more powerfully than her complicated misgivings. She looked over at Rose, who had followed them with a buggy filled with the diaper disposal and the musical mobile. Her friend gave her a sympathetic look.

"The smart general knows when to wave the white flag," Rose said.

"But—"

"I've got an idea," Rose said. "Uncle Bump could help."

"Well—"

"Krissy would love to join you."

Addy sighed. Outnumbered and outmaneuvered. "Okay. I give up."

A whoop of triumph went up from the three boys. The girls heard the ruckus and joined them. Negotiations for new ball gloves ensued, and once again Addy found herself unequal to the task of resisting.

Addy left them rummaging through the display of gloves and followed Rose back to the infants department.

"You're sure Bump won't mind?"

"He'll love it. Nothing he likes better these days than being around young 'uns. Besides, he needs something to get his mind off Betsy Foster."

Before Addy could respond, they rounded the aisle and almost rammed their cart into Heather Yates. Addy almost cried out in surprise and dismay.

Heather held the same little sleeper that had captured Addy's fancy. As she recognized Addy, her dreamy expression became more calculated.

"Well, hello there," she said, all sweetness.

Addy nodded, unable to coax a word out of her mouth.

"I was just daydreaming," Heather said, returning the outfit to the rack. "After all, it may not be that long before I have a little one of my very own. You know?"

She smiled again, turned and walked away, the sway of her hips exaggeratedly provocative.

Rage and disappointment and shame all came roaring to the surface in Addy, leaving her red-faced and speechless. She was fine until she felt Rose's hand on her shoulder. Then the tears filled her eyes.

"Don't pay any attention to her," Rose said. "She's nothing but a sad little girl making up fairy tales because she can't stand real life."

Addy drew a long, deep breath and tried to calm herself. "Maybe."

But the truth was, that sad little girl saw Addy's husband every day. And Addy couldn't see him for ten minutes at a time without causing another spat. She shook her head miserably and said, "Oh, Rose, I don't know what to do anymore. And whatever I do, it seems like it always turns out to be the wrong thing."

Rose pulled a tissue from her skirt pocket and passed it to Addy. "I know. When I first met Ben, I seemed to do one darn fool thing after another."

Addy managed a faint smile. "Not you."

Rose chuckled. "Men do that to us. Make even the best and wisest of us leave our brains in the bureau drawer."

"I love him," Addy said, although she wasn't sure why it seemed important to say so right at that moment. Maybe because she missed saying it so. "But I don't know how to fix things."

"Did you tell him that?"

Addy shook her head. "Every time we try to talk, we end up in a fight. Or the kids get in the way." She dabbed at the tear drying in the corner of her eye. "I just...I'm so scared. I guess everybody knows about her. Rose, do you think there's anything going on?"

"Have you talked to Danny about it?"

Addy darted a panicked look at her friend. She'd hoped Rose would offer heated denial in the face of the rumors.

"I've been too chicken. Do you believe he's . . . up to something?"

Once again, Addy prayed for a confident denial. Rose only replied, "Do you?"

Deep in her heart, Addy simply couldn't believe that Danny would betray her. And she wanted to think that no one else in Sweetbranch would believe it, either. She searched Rose's face and found a challenge.

"What I think doesn't matter much," Rose said. "What do *you* think?"

Addy drew a long breath and after she let it out, she knew there was only one answer. "I believe in Danny."

Rose smiled. "Good. You want to know what Ben says?"

"What?"

"He says Heather has a terrible crush on Danny, but Danny's doing his best to stay away from her. He even asked Ben to transfer the girl."

Hope fluttered in Addy's chest. "Will he? Transfer her?"

"I don't think he can."

"Oh." Heather's face floated in Addy's memory. She remembered the worshipful look Heather had given Danny, as well as the heart-shaped lips and the young body she flaunted so heedlessly. "Still . . ."

"What?"

"How long could any man resist a twenty-year-old in tight jeans?"

Rose shook her head. "Good question. Maybe not as long as he would if he had a good woman waiting for him every night."

Addy flushed. But wounded pride festered in her chest because of the rumors and the way Danny had walked out the other night. No, Danny had to be the one to come to her.

"Ask yourself this, Addy," Rose said as they pushed their cart toward the checkout. "Would you rather be right or would you rather be happy?"

Addy contemplated the question. But as she trudged home with her seven little ones in tow, she wondered stubbornly why she couldn't be both.

DANNY HAD ALWAYS BEEN the one to come around before. This time, he figured Addy could darn well make up her mind to do the coming around.

He'd heard that Bump Finley was going to be taking his place at weekly softball practice. That stung. Not that he planned to let Addy find out. He'd also heard that the latest rumor making the rounds was that he'd given Heather Yates a ride home from work one day when her car was in the shop.

This particular rumor was true. But maybe it hadn't been smart. Danny had just heard about Bump Finley, and he'd been just ticked off enough to do something colossally stupid.

He and Addy brought that out in each other sometimes.

Besides, he was ready to explain things anytime she got ready to listen. The next move was up to Addy.

"If this is the way she wants to play," he told Tony at the tavern, "I can play it right back at her."

Tony pretended to give Danny's reaction plenty of consideration, then shrugged. "If these are the games that make you happy..."

Danny didn't know how to explain to a man who wasn't even married that it had nothing to do with being happy. It had to do with making a stand. At least, that's what he told himself.

By the time Saturday rolled around and he showed up to work on the addition to the house, Addy had heard the latest story. And she was steamed. He knew that because all morning the children streamed in with messages from her.

Brook came first, pointing at her front tooth. "It's loose. Mommy said to ask you if it's time to pull it."

Danny squatted and peered into the little girl's mouth, then gave her front tooth a gentle wiggle. "Nah, I think that one needs about two more days of wiggling first. Think you can handle that?"

She grinned, nodded and ran back into the house calling out a report to Addy.

Next, Terrell dragged a catalogue outside and plopped down in a puddle of sawdust, pushing his glasses back up on his nose. "Mommy said I should show you the computer I picked out for us all to get for Christmas this year."

Danny balanced his level between the sawhorses and dropped to the ground beside the eight-year-old. "Okay, let's see 'er."

Terrell pointed. "Right there. And we could all play on it and do homework on it, so it wouldn't really be that expensive, since Santa could bring it to all of us, not just me.''

Danny hid his grin by taking a swipe at the perspiration on his brow with the sleeve of his work shirt. "Is this what the others want for Christmas, too?"

Terrell thought before he answered that one. Danny studied the boy and thought how much like Addy he seemed with his big glasses. He used to wonder if their own son would wear glasses—before he gave up wishing for one of their own.

Terrell pushed his glasses back on his nose again and said, "Well, I'm not sure they're smart enough to know this is what they ought to want. Sometimes they act like babies, you know?"

Danny smiled. "I know. Tell you what, Terrell. Christmas is still a long way off, and we'll have to have a lot of consultations with Santa between now and then. But we'll keep this in mind."

Terrell closed the catalogue, holding his place with his thumb. Instead of taking off right away, he looked solemnly at Danny. "If you don't come home, will Santa come at all? The year my real dad left, we didn't get to have Santa."

Danny felt a pang of guilt for what he and Addy were putting the children through. Most of them already knew way too much about abandonment. He didn't want them learning more on his account. He put his arm lightly around the boy's narrow shoulders. "Addy and I will make sure Santa comes no matter what."

Later, Casey came with news of the leaky bathroom faucet, and Reno gave a medical update on

David's broken arm. Gabby simply stood with an angel doll tucked under her arm and smiled at him in a way that made it impossible for him to do anything but stop and give her a hug. And Elisabeth brought a breathless report on the telephone call she'd had from her real daddy, who would arrive soon to take her to her new home with her new baby half brother. She'd already started packing because Addy said she could have all her clothes and one of the angel dolls.

"So will you come say goodbye, Daddy?"

Danny looked down at the little girl with the soft blond hair and the excitement glowing in her eyes. He remembered the day she scraped her leg on the sidewalk while learning to ride a bike and lay on the pavement crying until he carried her into the house, where she insisted Danny be the one to patch her up. He remembered lots of days. A lump rose in his throat and he swept her up in his arms. He had to admit, he hated seeing them go more than he dreaded seeing them arrive. "I sure will, sweetheart. I wouldn't miss it."

The last to come out was David. "I have to go with the little kids to a dumb birthday party, so I can't help out today, even if I didn't have a broken arm. Okay?"

Danny gave him the okay and examined all the autographs and personalized artwork on his cast.

Then the kids headed out for the birthday party and the house grew quiet. Danny grew restless. He kept pausing to listen for signs that Addy was still in the house. When he was too antsy to pay attention to the siding he was hanging, he decided to go in search of a drink of water. After all, the soft drink he'd brought had gone flat. Well, pretty flat.

He found her in the living room, curled up in the orange rocker, dozing. A quilt square hung over the arm of the chair, abandoned. She had pulled the afghan around her shoulders; one set of bare toes peeked out the bottom. The other leg was stretched out, her foot resting on Barney's back. Her thick waves tumbled around her shoulders and clung to one cheek. Her glasses had dropped to the carpet beside her chair. Danny wanted to wake her, yet at the same time he wanted to savor her just the way she was, serene and unflustered. He stood in the doorway undecided.

She shifted, and the quilt square slid off the chair arm. Danny told himself he would quietly rescue it, stack it on top of her bag and back away again. But when he got that close, he found he couldn't move away. He got caught up in the familiar pattern of freckles on the wrist that now poked out from beneath the afghan. He remembered how silky her skin felt on the inside of that wrist. He knew his thoughts were getting into dangerous territory, but hadn't yet figured out how to reroute them when Barney yawned and rolled over.

The loss of her furry footrest roused Addy. Her eyes had that unfocused look that always stirred his fantasies. She yawned and stretched. The afghan fell away from her shoulder, as did her knit top, revealing a bare shoulder. She was all delicate skin and sparse flesh, the very thing about her that brought out Danny's protective urges. His head told him the last thing Addy needed was someone to protect her. Ah, but when she looked this way, so soft and fragile, his heart wanted to believe it.

He dropped to his knees, hands folded on the chair arm. She was close enough to touch. He leaned forward and brushed his lips across her naked shoulder. He felt her shiver.

"I like watching you wake up," he whispered.

She turned those blurry eyes on him and spoke in a voice muzzy with sleep. "Oh, really? I guess that's why you were so eager to stay the other night. I hated having to run you off like that."

"Let's not fight." He blew on her cinnamon brown hair, watching it drift up and down on her shoulder.

"Don't," she said, but her voice was weak in a way he recognized.

He kissed her shoulder again. Her jaw. Little sounds of desire started in her throat and brought his own need to full alert. He tugged her knit top lower; the top button popped open. He reached up and released the next button, then the next. A peach-colored camisole was all she wore beneath her top, and through it, he could see the dusky, erect tip of one breast.

"Don't," she said again, but all he heard was the breathlessness that made her plea sound like anything but a protest.

He touched the outline of her nipple with his tongue, wetting her camisole, drawing more little sounds from deep in her throat. He tugged gently with his teeth, opened one more button and covered her other breast with his hand.

Suddenly, he felt her hand on his wrist. "Danny, wait."

He stopped, eyes closed, and took a moment to regain his composure.

"You're not going to back off at the last minute again, are you?"

He pulled his hand away, let her knit top fall back into place. "I didn't back off the last time."

"You most certainly did."

He knew better than to argue, but that stubborn edge in her voice always set him off. "The doorbell rang, then the kids woke up and boom! We were in the middle of a party."

"See." She shrugged her top back up to cover her shoulder. "It's easier if we just give in and fight."

"I wouldn't mind, except we never get to the making-up part anymore."

"Whose fault is that? Seems to me I asked you to stay." She looked away, played at having a consuming interest in refolding the afghan. "If you hadn't been in such an all-fired hurry to go sleep on my mother's couch, we might've made up the next morning."

He put a hand on hers to still her busy work and force her to look him in the eye. "I didn't want us to wake up the next morning and be right back where we started, Addy. If we don't reach an agreement about the kids, it's just going to keep coming up over and over."

"Not if you wouldn't keep making such a fuss about a few kids in the house," she retorted.

"Do you just want to fight or are you willing to talk about this? *Really* talk about it?"

She draped the neatly folded afghan over the chair

arm, squarely between them. "Okay. I'm calm. Let's talk."

For Addy, she *was* calm, he decided. "Okay. If we could agree to limit the number of children staying with us at any given time, that would be a start."

She drew her lips into a thin, hard line. "Fine. And what do we do, just tell the others to come back later when we're under quota?"

"Addy, every needy child in this county isn't your responsibility."

"I know. I know."

"Then what do you suggest? Where do you think it stops?"

She stared at her hands in her lap for a long time, then said softly, "When God stops sending them to us, I guess."

Danny groaned softly. How was he supposed to reason with a woman like this? "Let's think about, say, four. Four children at a time."

She stared at him as if he were speaking a foreign language. "We have seven right now. What do we do with them? Have a lottery? Pack lunches for the three losers, pat them on the head and wish them good luck?"

"Elisabeth goes with her father next week. Gabby's only been here a few weeks. Maybe—"

"No!"

"Addy—"

"Not Gabby. She's... I can't explain it. But she's... I just feel so connected to her, Danny."

"All I know is, six kids is about three too many. But I'm willing to compromise."

"What you mean is, you're willing to come home as long as I do it your way. Isn't that what you mean?"

He stood, his frustration beginning to get the better of him. "Yeah. Maybe I do think it's time we played Danny Makes a Decision for a change."

"Oh, so now I'm bossy."

"You said it, not me."

"Maybe you just aren't that interested in coming home."

"Yeah, I love sleeping in your mother's living room."

"Is that the only place you've been sleeping?"

Danny felt the color rush to his face and cursed himself for reacting like a guilty two-timer. "Addy, have I ever given you reason not to trust me?"

"You've never stayed away for weeks at a time."

"If you'd just be a little, tiny bit reasonable—"

"I've never caught you with some woman hanging off you before, either."

"If you'd try listening to me, I've already explained a dozen times that Heather has a...a...sort of a...crush. Like girls get on teachers. That's all."

"She's not built like a schoolgirl."

"If you think this is about Heather, you're just looking for excuses, Addy Mayfield. This is about restoring some sanity to our house. This is about taking some of the load off so we have some time for each other again."

"I'll bet Heather doesn't make you feel short-changed, does she?"

Now Danny was really steamed. Apparently more than a decade of loyalty didn't count for much with this woman. "Well, I don't know. But you could be right. You could just damn sure be right."

CHAPTER ELEVEN

DANNY HEFTED GABBY above his head so she could see over the others and wave goodbye as Elisabeth rode off in a dusty yellow sedan with her father, a young electrician with an adoring look in his eyes and a dimple to match his daughter's. Her new family had hugged her enthusiastically, and Elisabeth already looked at home.

Although the occasion had started out buoyantly enough, with all the children nearly giddy with excitement, by the time Elisabeth's father placed her small suitcase in the trunk of the car, the mood had begun to shift. Danny could see it on the faces of the six children left behind as the car door closed, leaving them on the outside again.

Terrell scuffed at the driveway with the worn toe of his sneaker. Casey wrinkled up his nose and screwed up his face the way he did sometimes when he was determined not to give in to the temptation to cry. Reno's eyes grew red. Even David's always-beaming face lost a bit of its glow.

Happy as they were here, all of them wanted their own families.

Lifting Gabby off his shoulders and allowing her to snuggle into the crook of his arm, Danny watched

Addy turn her attention to the children. They huddled around her. She comforted them with a touch, a smile, a kiss from her fingertips to their cheeks. And he realized all over again what a gift Addy gave to these kids, and all the others who had come before. Without her giving heart, where would they be? What would they be learning about life?

She's their angel.

The words in his head came to him in a sweet, tiny voice he didn't recognize, and for a moment, he thought Gabby had spoken. Startled, he glanced at the little girl, whose cheek rested against his shoulder. She smiled as if they shared a secret. Danny opened his mouth to ask an absurd question, then clamped it shut. Of course she hadn't spoken.

Still, wherever the thought had come from, it stuck. The truth of it couldn't be denied.

Holding Gabby snuggly, he walked over to his wife, who was still surrounded by the children. Kissing the tips of his fingers, in imitation of her actions, he then pressed his fingertips lightly to her cheek.

"There goes one more you saved," he whispered.

Addy's cheeks grew rosy. "I didn't do anything," she protested.

Danny shook his head. "Hey, kids, who's the best mom in Sweetbranch?"

A chorus of young voices shouted, "Addy is!"

"In the world!" Terrell added.

Not to be bested, David said, "In the universe!"

"Oh, pooh!" Addy pulled her glasses down from atop her head and hid behind them once again.

"You're all just trying to butter me up, thinking I'll bake brownies."

That, too, was met with a chorus of agreement. Addy laughed, darting a quick, uncertain glance in Danny's direction as they started toward the house. Danny hung back, setting Gabby down so she could follow. He wondered if he should join the family and risk another scene with Addy, no matter how he ached to be with them.

Gabby took two steps before turning back and holding out her hand to him.

Danny stared into her face, felt himself enveloped in her sunny, accepting smile. Guilt gnawed at him. Hadn't it been his protest against bringing Gabby into the house that had caused this rift in the first place?

As if impatient with waiting for him to make up his mind, Gabby walked back, took his hand in hers and led him toward the house. His uncertainties about whether he still had a place in the family disappeared with each step he took behind the little girl with the mop of strawberry blond curls.

The other children were running helter-skelter around the kitchen by the time Danny and Gabby arrived. Dragging out mixing bowls, egg beaters, cocoa and eggs, they formed a small but frenetic hurricane, with Addy at its eye. Fallout from the storm would be brownies.

Danny sat on the bench at the picnic table, marveling as Addy called out instructions that seemed to spin some form of order out of the chaos. Soon, chocolaty batter was swirling in the mixing bowl, the oven was preheating, and the fine dusting of flour that covered the countertop also covered the bottom of a baking pan.

And children were everywhere.

"You have to clean up the smashed egg," Reno was telling Terrell.

"How come I have to?" the put-upon boy protested.

"Because you're the one who smashed it."

Brook, a veteran of many brownie-making episodes, was the first to remember to call out, "First dibs on licking the bowl!"

Followed by the howls of protest.

Watching his wife as she guided Casey's unsteady hands in pouring the batter into the pan, Danny marveled that none of it flustered her. He looked with new eyes at this woman who had lost her cool every time the two of them exchanged two words for the past month, but who could maintain her serenity while six children trashed her kitchen. Well, five children, he amended. David had disappeared. Which figured. Hardly the domestic type, David would no doubt reappear as soon as the brownies came out of the oven.

"You're a miracle worker," Danny said, sidling up beside Addy while Reno gripped the pan tightly in both fists, held her breath and slipped it carefully onto the oven rack.

Addy's smile looked less than convinced. "I wish."

Cleanup commenced as soon as the pan disappeared into the oven, a process Danny discovered was even louder than the measuring-and-mixing stage. But not loud enough to cover the horrendous crash that came from the backyard two minutes later.

David was nowhere in sight when they reached the backyard, which was probably just as well. Danny might have been sorely tempted to break the boy's other arm.

The doorframe Danny had spent the better part of a morning cutting and squaring up now jutted through the middle of one of the Sheetrock inside walls Danny had completed just days earlier. The doorframe was ruined and so was the wall.

The children stared in wide-eyed silence. Addy, too, stood by in silence, not even daring to look in Danny's direction.

"David!"

Danny walked in the direction of the woods, calling the boy's name, trying to keep the anger out of his voice and knowing he couldn't be succeeding very well. Behind him, he heard Reno rounding up the other children, shooing them back into the house. He stared at the woods, quivering inside with an anger he knew was far too big to be solely about this one incident. He also knew it reflected his anxiety about how this would serve to widen the gulf between Addy and himself.

"I'll help fix it," she said softly, just over his shoulder.

"No," Danny said. "*He'll* fix it."

"He's just a little boy, Danny."

He whirled on her, was momentarily sidetracked by how tired she looked. All her radiance from a few moments before had disappeared. "He's a destructive little boy, Addy."

"He didn't do it on purpose."

"How do you know that? He's always doing things like this. He's into something all the time."

She looked at her wit's end, the same way he felt, and he wanted nothing more than to take her into his arms and comfort her, offer her rest and respite.

"I know he's a problem sometimes, Danny. But he's been abandoned. He—"

"I know, Addy. I know. But he's also disruptive. He needs more discipline."

"He needs more love," Addy said, defiance now blazing in her eyes.

"Addy, you give him as much love as anybody could."

"Maybe he needs more than a mother."

That stopped him. He stared at her, anger and frustration and uncertainty mixing explosively in his heart. "Fine. Now this is my fault."

"Maybe if you didn't have such a soft spot for wayward young women, you'd have something left over for little boys who need fathers."

She stomped off then and left him standing by the edge of the woods, feeling very, very alone.

THE BROWNIES BURNED.

The children played quietly, the way children will when they sense something is wrong. The spirit of closeness had fizzled.

David came home just before dark, smiling sheepishly and vowing he could fix everything himself. Beneath his devilish smile, Addy saw a forlornness she wasn't used to seeing. Elisabeth's reunion with her real father had touched off something in him, she was certain. She hugged him, and for once he didn't wiggle away.

Addy felt forlorn herself. Her weariness went bone-deep as well as spirit-deep. She fixed soup for the children's supper but could barely swallow a bite herself. Chicken noodle wouldn't fix what ailed her.

She sat in a lawn chair in the backyard, barely aware of the mild spring air enveloping her. She stared at the blue tarp Danny had yanked haphazardly back into place before he roared off in his pickup. The gigantic tarp barely covered the mess, the pile of scattered tools and splintered wood. Addy couldn't see how the mess could ever be cleared away, how this assortment of debris could ever be restored to some semblance of home.

"Oh, Danny," she whispered. "How'd things ever get in such a mess?"

Her heart hurt so badly she wanted to cry. She wanted to go home to her mother and sob in her arms. But she had children of her own who looked to her to make sure their world was still on its axis. She couldn't let them down.

She stood and wandered through the house to see that the children were okay. Reno sat in the orange rocker reading *Little Women* while David and Terrell watched a video on TV. Brook colored at the coffee table. Addy moved down the hall, looking for Casey and Gabby.

She heard them before she saw them. They'd made a tent by draping a blanket between the desk and the bunk bed in the boys' room. Casey's voice floated through the blanket, into the hall.

"I'm not here 'cause my mama and daddy don't love me," he was saying. "I'm here 'cause my mama had to go to the hospital for a while."

Addy folded her arms across her chest and leaned against the doorframe to listen. Casey's father, she knew, was married to someone besides Casey's mother. That was sad enough. But Casey's mother was in Birmingham, undergoing intensive treatments for cancer. The last time Addy had spoken with her, the outlook remained bleak.

"But she's almost well now," Casey continued. "And soon I'll get to ride off with my mama, the way 'Lisabeth did today. Real soon."

Addy remembered his mother's exact words the last time they spoke. "I tell myself I ought to get you to bring the boy to Birmingham so I can see him one last time, but I hate for him to see me this way. And...the truth is, I just don't know if I can face that yet, myself."

Then what? Addy wondered. Then what became of Casey? They couldn't even think about adopting him permanently with their own family in shambles.

The rest of the weekend, everyone at the Mayfield house seemed subdued. Now that her favorite playmate was gone, Gabby latched on to Casey and they spent their time in quiet play. Reno and Terrell studied. Brook tried to help Addy catch up on her projects for the boutique, her assistance slowing things down more than anything else. David rummaged around under the blue tarp and Addy decided it would serve Danny right if she left the boy alone to get into whatever mischief he wanted.

By Monday, Addy was having trouble pulling herself out of the morass she'd let herself sink into over the weekend. She tried to work but couldn't concentrate. She offered to take Gabby to Susan Hutchins's, where she could play with Susan's grandson, Cody, and little Jake McKenzie. But Gabby shook her head and dragged a pillow off the couch to sit on the floor as close beside Addy's rocker as she could get.

Addy smiled at the little girl, but Gabby wasn't fooled. She put her cheek on Addy's knee. Addy realized she felt comforted just by Gabby's nearness. That didn't surprise her as much as the realization that she was on the verge of talking to the child about her worries—about Danny and David and even Casey— the way she would to another adult.

That would never do.

She tried telling Gabby stories while she sewed, thinking that would keep them both occupied with something pleasant. But for some reason, the story that kept filling her head was not a story she could share with Gabby.

Wynona kept popping into her head.

She shook away the intrusive memory, tried to pick up the threads of the story of Jack and the Beanstalk. The story of Addy's little sister was no fairy tale, had no happy ending.

Addy focused her thinking, but before she got Jack out of trouble with the giant, Wynona was back. With a clarity Addy hadn't experienced in more than a decade, she saw her little sister flounce out of their bedroom, tossing her curly blond hair, her rosebud lips pursed defiantly. Her last image of Nona.

The quilt square in her hand was crumpled. Addy tried to spread it on her lap, smooth out the wrinkles. Her hand trembled.

It's okay.

The voice in her head was her own, Addy supposed, but it sounded like Gabby's. Which she realized immediately was foolish, for she'd never heard Gabby's voice. She looked down at the little girl, whose cheek still rested on Addy's knee. Her angel doll lay in her lap, grasped loosely in one little fist.

Addy closed her eyes, even though she knew that would merely invite all the memories to roam freely in her head. She'd stuffed them down for so long, had kept them under control so well, she wondered why they were surfacing so insistently.

Addy could still smell the damp, loamy scent the banks of Willow Creek had given off that afternoon. Her eighth summer had been a wet one. Big, ugly toadstools protruded from the base of every tree trunk, and moss was thick and slippery on the bare earth. Water swelled and gushed over rocks and tree limbs in the creekbed.

They had played on the banks of Willow Creek all afternoon. Nona was four. Addy's bare feet were muddy, and Nona's hair clung to her cheeks and neck in damp ringlets. As late afternoon crept into the woods, bringing a chill with it, Addy decided it was time to go home for hot chocolate and dry clothes.

They were barely clean and dry when Nona remembered her doll.

"Come on, Addy," Nona said, tugging on Addy's hand. "I forgot S'mantha. Wanna go get her, okay?"

Addy looked down at the dry socks she was just pulling on. She weighed that against the goofy-looking doll with her yellow yarn hair and painted-on freckles. "I'm not going back out there and get all yucky again. You can get your stupid doll tomorrow."

Nona crawled onto her bed and looked out the window. "But it's gonna be dark. S'mantha'll get scared in the dark."

"She's just a stupid doll. She won't get scared."

Nona turned to glare at Addy, her chubby face puckered in a frown. "Yes her will. You got to help, okay?"

Addy shoved her feet into her shoes. "I don't 'got to help.' We'll get Samantha tomorrow. So don't bug me anymore."

"You're a mean sister!"

Then Nona was out the bedroom door and Addy lay back on her bed, glad to be alone. She might read a book or she might write a letter to her pen pal in Arizona or she might just close her eyes and take a nap until suppertime. But at least she didn't have to listen to her pesky little sister.

Addy had woken with a start from her dream about meeting her pen pal at Disney World. No light came in through the bedroom window. Her heart pounded. Something felt scary and she couldn't think what.

Then she had heard the sound that had startled her awake. Her mother, crying. Addy shot upright. She'd never heard her mother cry before. Something was bad wrong.

The sound of someone sobbing brought Addy back to the present. Now, too, her heart pounded. Something still felt scary, but this time she knew what it was. This time, the tears were hers.

Gabby had climbed into Addy's lap and put her arms around Addy's neck. Addy held Gabby close, taking comfort in her warm little body. She waited for the rest of the memories to subside, the bleak memories of learning that Wynona had gone back for her doll, after all. But the woods had been dark by then, the ground slippery and the water swift. Wynona had drowned.

Eight-year-old Addy had known immediately that her little sister's death was her fault. She was the big sister. The responsible one. And she'd refused to help Wynona, had let her go off to the creek alone.

Thirty-two-year-old Addy still believed that her little sister's death was her fault. And nothing she had done in the years since could repay that debt. None of the children she saved made up for the one she'd lost. The one who was her own flesh and blood. The guilt still weighed on her mind.

How many times in all the years she and Danny had been trying to have a child of their own had the voice of Addy's guilt told her that she and she alone was the reason there would be no other child of her own flesh? That, she knew, was her punishment.

Danny, cried a tiny voice in her heart. *Oh, Danny, I wish you were here. Just to hold me.*

Gabby wiped at the tears on Addy's cheeks with her fingertips, looked at Addy with sadness in her own big, blue eyes. The sensation that the little girl understood her sorrow—and her guilt—overwhelmed Addy.

And that must prove you're losing it, she told herself, trying to find a reassuring smile for the little girl. The smile felt wobbly and she couldn't hold on to it for long. When it faded, Gabby snuggled more closely against Addy's chest, putting her warm cheek against Addy's. They sat like that for a long time. The little girl's closeness was a soft, warm comfort, filling her, easing the hurt. She even felt, after a bit, as if some of the guilt had been siphoned off and drained away into the quiet morning.

After a while Addy lost track of time. Gabby finally scrambled down from her lap, took Addy by the hand and led her out the kitchen door into the backyard. As if in a trance, Addy followed the little girl without question, even when their path led to the edge of the woods and beyond, toward Willow Creek.

They walked along Willow Creek holding hands. Addy felt as if she were being shown the creek for the first time in more than twenty years. She heard the clear, soft sounds of the burbling water—sounds she had heard in her head many times and transformed into the dangerous hiss of rushing water. She saw the sunlight sifting through the tall pines and the new spring buds on the oaks, finally spilling into the rippling water of the creek. She heard the trill of a spring robin and the fierce chatter of a squirrel who didn't welcome their intrusion.

She looked down at Gabby, who looked back at her expectantly. Addy nodded, as silent as the child. But the air around them sang with the understanding that flowed between them.

Addy knew that Gabby felt how much she was loved. And Addy felt forgiven, although she couldn't have said why walking this creek bank with a little girl who didn't even know the story of her crime could bring her forgiveness. How many times had Danny held her hand or cradled her in his arms and tried to tell her that no one blamed her for Nona's death? How many times had he reminded her that she had been nothing but a child herself, and not responsible for the actions of another little child?

One of the first times Addy had thought herself in love with Danny Mayfield had been on the anniversary of Nona's birthday, the year Addy was sixteen.

She always honored the day, although she'd learned not to mention it at home because it always made her mother cry and her father leave the breakfast table earlier than usual. On this day, she had sneaked off during phys ed, cutting across the football field and into the woods skirting the edge of the school grounds. In a clearing, she had plopped down cross-legged in her gym shorts, closed her eyes and focused on an image of her little sister sitting in front of her fourth birthday cake, trying in vain to blow out all the candles.

She began to smile at the image. In a soft voice, she started singing "Happy Birthday" to a little sister who would never grow any older.

During the last line of the song, Addy had realized she wasn't singing alone.

Her eyes popped open. Across the clearing from her sat Danny Mayfield, also cross-legged and staring at her intently. She'd been embarrassed and, predictably, peeved.

"This is private. You had no business following me."

He had shrugged and looked sheepish. "I didn't follow you to spy."

She had given him a skeptical look. "Just because we've been out together a few times doesn't mean you own me."

"I know. I... You just...looked funny. Like something was bothering you. I wanted to make sure you were, you know, okay."

The notion that someone might look out for her had been a foreign one to Addy. Her petulant anger had subsided.

"Nona, that was your sister? The one who...died?"

Addy nodded.

"I guess you miss her?"

Addy nodded.

"I think it's nice you sing her 'Happy Birthday.'"

"You do? You don't think it's a little bizarro?"

He grinned. "No."

They had walked back, and as they came out of the woods onto the football field, she had said, "Thanks for singing with me."

And Addy thought that a guy who would help you sing to your little sister who wasn't even around anymore must be really special.

The next year, Danny had remembered the date himself, as he had every year since. But no matter how many times he'd tried to reassure her over the years, there had remained at least one person who had blamed Addy. She, herself.

But for the moment, at least, something felt different. She felt, as Gabby clutched her hand and pointed at a nest of young robins in a nearby tree, that some kind of healing had begun.

The moment would have been perfect had she not longed so for Danny. It seemed that no moment, no matter how special, felt complete without Danny. She felt the sharp, sweet reminder of a love that had been building for sixteen years.

She sat by the creek while Gabby found a twig to plant in the mud. In her mind, Addy watched a parade of all the Dannys she had known over the years. The reluctant high school hero, a running back who liked to fade right off the field without a single roar from the crowd. The painfully uncertain college student who had no doubt he was in over his head, even as his coaches and professors encouraged him and his adoring young wife nudged him ever forward, ever upward. The young husband who only wanted to please, who claimed he didn't know how to act like a father to their foster children because he'd never seen a good father at work.

He'd been a fast learner, Addy thought now. Or had known in his gut all along, maybe.

For the first time in sixteen years, Addy wondered if she would be growing old with him, the way she'd planned all these years. That uncertainty was a sharper pain, even, than the wound of her childlessness.

But what could she do? When he said the children always came first and left no room for them as a couple, he was right. But so was she. The children had no one else. So where did that leave them?

Gabby slipped her muddy hand into Addy's and led her back to the house.

CHAPTER TWELVE

DANNY HADN'T KNOWN there were so many solitary places in the world.

"Never knew a bar could make you feel so... alone," he said as he watched Tony lock up the front door of the tavern and shut off the neon sign outside.

Tony nodded as he made his way back across the room, all the while stuffing empty beer cans into a bag for recycling. "Yes, sure. This is why I say stay, finish up your beer. I can use the company while I make things cleaned."

Danny stared into his flat, room-temperature beer and contemplated all the lonely places he had discovered this past month. The den at his mother-in-law's house, for example. His office at the plant, even though he was surrounded by dozens of workers and millions of dollars' worth of racket-making equipment. The cab of his pickup. Sunday morning, anywhere and everywhere.

Even the Holy Spirits Tavern, Danny was learning, was powerful lonely when you knew that just a few miles away a woman with cinnamon-and-spice hair was crawling into a bed with a familiar hollow right in the middle of the mattress where two bodies were accustomed to cuddling close.

Danny wondered if all single men were lonely, or just the ones who knew how good being married could be.

"I wouldn't think a single guy like you'd have much trouble finding company," Danny said.

Tony shrugged and tossed the bag of aluminum cans toward the back door. He took a bar towel from behind the counter and started another round of the room, wiping as he went. "I don't see so many women who make me interested."

With his dark good looks and exotic accent, Tony made plenty of single women in Sweetbranch interested. Danny knew that much. But he recalled that Tony rarely flirted back when women made their interest known.

"Why not?" Danny asked, getting up and walking around to pour out the rest of his beer and swish his mug in the sinkful of sudsy water. "You carrying a torch for somebody?"

"Carry a torch?" Tony looked at him blankly.

"You know? Some woman steal your heart sometime?"

Tony gave a half nod and grinned. "Ah. No, I still have my own heart. But—" He began gathering the ashtrays. "I have the old-fashioned feelings, you know? I don't want the woman who comes to the tavern looking for a man."

Danny thought of Addy and knew exactly the kind of woman his new friend must long for.

"And I believe that many women here do not want a man from Cuba who doesn't speak such good English and runs a tavern. Maybe this man is not such good husband material. Not good father material. You know?''

Danny almost protested, but he realized he didn't really have a very good notion about how women thought. Here he'd thought all these years that he understood Addy. And now he wondered if it had all been a sham, if maybe he hadn't been as happily married as he'd always thought.

And at the heart of his discontent was the gnawing suspicion that he was just another one of Addy's reclamation projects. Just another kid she had saved, someone else to boss around and tell what to eat for breakfast. Not a partner for life.

Better to leave Tony to make his own mistakes.

"So," Tony said, snapping his damp bar towel over his shoulder and walking over with an armload of stacked ashtrays, "I think I want to find another business."

"Another business?"

"Yes. To be an entrepreneur. A business tycoon."

"In Sweetbranch?"

"*Sí.* I have this plan in my mind to buy the old drive-in theater. Fix it up like the old days."

"You want to buy the Dixie Drive-In?" Danny didn't catch himself in time to keep the disbelief out of his voice as the vision of the old Dixie filled his head. The weed-infested field sprouting its rusting speakers. The crumbling board fence, a perfect partner for the crumbling concession stand that had never seen a brush stroke of paint in its life.

From the look in his eyes, it was clear that Tony saw something entirely different when he peered down the end of Main Street at the Dixie Drive-In.

"Already I have talked to the attorney and I can get this property not expensive. Cheap. Yes, cheap. And I save away many profits from the tavern. Then I can have an old-fashioned drive-in. Families in Sweetbranch will love this, yes?"

Actually, as he listened to the enthusiasm in Tony's voice, Danny did discover that his own vision of the drive-in began to change. He, too, could see it revived. He, too, could see the families lined up on a summer night to watch a Disney double feature.

Other families. Not his.

Misery snapped at Danny's heels like the scrawny old hound who had kept an eye on his grandpa's moonshine stills twenty-five years ago.

"Then," Tony continued, his voice growing brighter as Danny's soul grew bleaker, "I will be respectable, and I, too, will have the wife and family. And maybe I will call my mother. Maybe she will come then, if her son is successful entrepreneur. What do you think?"

Danny thought he was a heckuva person for Tony to be asking for advice on working out problem relationships. He continued swishing mugs through the sudsy water. "I think that's a swell idea, Tony."

Tony grinned. "Yes. I have a place for my mother, you know." He pointed overhead. "In the loft is nice apartment, just for one."

Danny looked up through the high ceiling. "An apartment? Up there?"

Tony kept talking, but Danny heard next to nothing about the mother and father who had brought Tony and his three sisters over from Cuba in a homemade boat in the early 1980s. Heard only the vaguest of details about the woman from Sweetbranch that Tony had met somewhere in California, years ago, and how he had longed to make a place for himself in the idyllic little town she described. Danny murmured an appropriate response here and there, but his thoughts kept drifting up, to the choir loft.

There, at least, he wouldn't feel guilty when his mother-in-law looked across the bowl of mashed potatoes every night at supper. There, at least, he could crawl into bed with his misery without his wife's mother there to witness it.

"Say, Tony," he asked when they had stacked all the mugs in place and emptied every ashtray, "what do you do with that apartment now? I mean, is it something you'd be willing to rent out?"

ADDY'S HEART DID a happy flip-flop Saturday morning when she rode her bike into the driveway at her mother's house and saw Danny loading boxes of his clothes into his pickup.

He's coming home!

As she propped her bike onto its kickstand, she made her face blank and prayed her cheeks wouldn't turn the color of ripe strawberries. She wouldn't let on how she felt. She'd keep it light.

"Running away from home again?" she asked when she sauntered up alongside the bed of his truck, hoping she sounded casual.

He glanced up, then lowered his eyes as he tucked another cardboard box into the truck. "Figure I've imposed on Eulainie long enough."

"You *can* be a tad of trouble," she said, feeling cheeky.

"So I got my own place."

Addy's stomach plummeted, shot straight to her knees, which right now felt about as sturdy as the stuffed dolls she made.

"You what?"

"Over the tavern. Tony's got an apartment in the old choir loft. He said I could rent it for as long as I need it."

Dizzy with fear and anger, Addy wasn't about to be fooled by the picture he painted. Apartment in the old choir loft, indeed! Her husband was moving into a bachelor pad over the local tavern. She couldn't decide whether to throw up or throw something at Danny.

The dizziness cleared long enough for her to see one thing distinctly: she couldn't let him know how upset she was. That meant no anger, no tears, no reaction of any kind. If Danny Mayfield wanted to believe he could fool her on this one, just let him.

Addy tightened her jaw and shoved her shaking hands into the pockets of her seersucker split skirt. She had chosen the soft blue-and-white outfit this morning because she remembered how much Danny liked her in it.

It's all I can do to keep my hands off you when you wear that. She could hear him saying it. Could see the wicked gleam in his eyes.

She might just go straight home and burn the darned thing.

"Well, good for you, Danny Mayfield," she said with as much dignity as she could manage.

She might have to go back to bed before she could manage to set fire to this skirt. She suddenly felt as if every bit of energy had drained right out through the soles of the new white canvas sneakers she'd bought the night before last when she took the kids to Wal-Mart for flip-flops and shorts.

"You're glad?"

She decided to ignore that because she knew she hadn't a prayer of lying about it convincingly. "But just don't think this means you can cut back on what we need to keep the house running."

He looked exasperated. "Addy, you know damn well I won't let you and the kids do without."

"Darn right you won't."

She whirled around and headed for the house, wondering if she could manage to look her mother in the eye without bursting into tears.

Darn right she could, because she darn sure wasn't going to let Danny see her that way.

"You might try not being so quick to fly off the handle," he called out after her.

She sucked in her breath, pursed her lips tightly, kept her fists clenched in her pockets. When she had herself under control, she turned and gazed at him in what she hoped was a cool, unconcerned manner.

"I'm hot-blooded," she announced. "Not much chance that's going to change at this late date."

He grinned at that and it nearly broke her heart. She loved that grin.

"How's David's broken arm?" he said.

"It's not giving him any problem," she said.

"Good. Have they, uh, started softball practice yet?"

"Next week."

He nodded. "Guess there's been no word on Gabby yet?"

"Not yet."

"Well, guess I'd better get on with this. When I finish, I'll be over and work on the house."

Addy wondered where she could spend the rest of her afternoon. "Is that addition almost done?"

"Almost. Another two weekends, maybe."

Then there would be nothing to bring him back around to the house. It was all she could do to draw a breath. "Good."

She turned and walked back to her bike, completely forgetting her plans to visit with her mother. In two weeks, Danny would have no more excuse for hanging around the house on weekends. In two weeks, he could spend all his free time in his bachelor pad. And what, pray tell, did a married man need with a bachelor pad when he ought to be coming home to his family?

Could it be, she wondered, that the gossips were right about Heather, after all?

ADDY WANTED TO DIG A HOLE and crawl into it. So for the next week, she did just that. She stayed home whenever possible. She only answered the telephone during school hours, when the kids were away and she feared being out of contact. Once, she even hid behind the living room curtains until Susan Hutchins quit pounding on the door and left. Guilt-ridden, she watched while Susan made her laborious way back toward her house, leaning heavily on her walking stick. Addy shook her head and dropped the edge of the curtain.

You're losing it, kid. She turned away from the window, right into the reproachful gaze of Gabby, who sat in the orange rocker with her angel doll.

"I know, I know. I just can't," Addy said, knowing it must be one more sign of craziness to imagine that this little girl could understand what she was talking about. "I can't face anybody right now. Not until..."

And that was the problem that haunted her. She couldn't imagine what it was going to take to straighten this mess out. A compromise? An apology? Going to Danny on her hands and knees, begging him to come home so she could feel safe and loved and wanted again?

That was the point when the anger always reared its ugly head. The point when that vengeful voice in her head rose up.

"Danny can darn well do a little compromising of his own," she said now, yanking up the afghan Reno had spread on the floor the night before, when all the children were watching an animated movie about a baby dragon.

Gabby frowned.

"Well, he can," Addy continued, folding the afghan and resisting the other thoughts that warred in her ever-more-confused mind. "And if anybody around here deserves an apology, it's me."

Gabby's frown intensified as her fingers tightened around her angel doll.

"A little begging wouldn't hurt, either."

With that, Gabby slid down from the chair, turned and marched right out of the room. With the little girl's departure, Addy dropped onto the edge of the couch, balling up the folded afghan and holding it against her chest like a security blanket.

"Am I *that* wrong?" she whispered.

The answer came to her loud and clear, in a voice her heart told her was Gabby's, if Gabby had only had a voice. Addy didn't like what she heard.

Unwilling to give in to the threat of tears, she dragged herself off the couch and continued tidying the room. These days, the house was neater than ever because Addy couldn't seem to concentrate on her work. If it weren't for all the help Susan had given her since the wedding, Addy wouldn't be keeping up with Bunny's requests for the Country Bumpkin. She told herself that as soon as she shoved another load of T-shirts into the washer, she would pull out her project basket. If she worked faithfully this afternoon, she could finish the crib quilt she'd started last week.

But first, her guilty conscience prodded her, she would go next door and set things right with Susan.

Well, maybe she could do that second, she told herself as she set the water level on the washer.

She didn't get to Susan first *or* second, because as soon as the washer sloshed into action, she heard her mother's voice calling to her from the kitchen. Squeezing her eyes shut, she wondered if it would really be all that wrong to ease the laundry room door shut and crouch here in the corner until her mother went away.

Before Addy had a chance to discover just how crazy she was becoming, Eulainie stuck her head around the half-open bi-fold door. She smiled, with less greeting than gotcha in her smile.

"Gabby said I'd find you here," she said, then paused, a puzzled expression flickering across her face. "Well, of course, she didn't actually *say* anything. But I knew that's what she meant."

That explanation seemed to satisfy Eulainie, and oddly enough it satisfied Addy, too. She'd had the same kind of experience with Gabby too often to question it. She supposed it was something like the way blind people sometimes developed acute hearing. Gabby couldn't speak, so she'd developed other ways of communicating with others.

Addy didn't dwell on the fact that this, too, was a pretty screwy notion. Her head was full of screwy notions today. She shoved the box of laundry detergent back on the shelf over the washer and followed her mother back to the kitchen.

"Well," Eulainie said, settling onto the bench and propping her elbows on the picnic table. "You gonna offer me a cup of coffee or am I going to have to get it myself?"

Addy automatically reached for a cup, then remembered. "There isn't any coffee."

Eulainie looked incredulous. "No coffee?"

"I'm out." She opened the refrigerator door and studied the contents, as much to avoid looking at her mother as to fulfill the slim hope of finding something to offer her.

"I hear they got in a fresh supply at the Winn-Dixie just yesterday," Eulainie said, her tone tinged with a little more sarcasm than Addy had ever heard there before. "From the looks of that icebox, I'd say you're out of a lot of things."

Without an answer for that, Addy quickly shut the refrigerator door and shrugged. "I've been busy."

"Sit down."

Addy darted a startled glance at Eulainie, forgetting for the moment that she didn't want to risk real eye contact with her. Eulainie had a look about her Addy couldn't remember seeing since high school, a look that brooked no opposition. She sat.

"I never thought I'd have to say this," Eulainie told her, "but you're acting like a damn fool."

"Mother!" In all her thirty-two years, Addy couldn't remember ever having heard her mother swear. Southern ladies of Eulainie's era left the swearing to the menfolk.

"You're as hotheaded as my mother was and as mule-headed as me," Eulainie continued. "That's a dangerous combination, and I'm afraid you've let it get away with you."

"But I'm—"

"Just let me speak my piece first, young lady." Eulainie twisted her wedding ring, an inexpensive gold band whose ivy design had long since worn away. "You have a fine husband—none finer, if you want my humble opinion—and you're about to run him off with your stubborn pride."

"But—"

Eulainie held up a hand to quiet her daughter. "I know you've both been hotheaded in this. But I also know you were the one who put his clothes out."

Addy lowered her head, embarrassed at the memory.

"I also know you're the one who's placed an awful lot of demands on one man. And—" Eulainie hesitated and Addy looked up. She didn't like the worry she saw on her mother's face. "And I know that if you don't want a man like Danny, there are others who will."

Addy's shoulders gave under the weight of the words she hadn't wanted her mother, of all people, to verbalize.

"Now, I'm not saying Danny's done anything wrong," Eulainie hastened to add.

"I know," Addy said, as miserable as she'd ever been in her life.

"But I also know that no man is a saint. Just like no woman is an angel—including my own daughter."

Eulainie's sympathetic smile did next to nothing to lift Addy's spirits. "But what can I do? I don't know how to set things right anymore."

Eulainie reached over and patted her daughter's hand. "All I know is, somebody has to be willing to take the first step. Somebody has to be willing to give in just the least little bit.''

Rebellion rose up in Addy automatically at the suggestion that that somebody ought to be her. Eulainie saw the look, recognized it and shook her head.

"I guess you just have to ask yourself which is more important. Danny? Or that damn-fool pride of yours?''

The dilemma of her damn-fool pride haunted Addy the rest of the day. After Eulainie left, she swallowed part of her pride to call Susan with an apology.

"Don't beat yourself up over it," Susan said after Addy's halfhearted explanation. "Just don't think you can crawl in a hole and it'll all go away. It won't.''

Then she borrowed her mother's station wagon and faced the ordeal of the weekly trip to the supermarket. She was almost past being able to keep smiling and pretend nothing was wrong as she passed neighbors in the aisles. Addy saw curiosity and pity in their eyes, and by the time she and Gabby hit the bread-and-dairy aisle at the far end of the Winn-Dixie, Addy had very little left in the way of emotional reserves.

That was when Heather came through, one of those little red plastic baskets on her arm. Addy noticed she had a bottle of wine, some snack crackers and a six-pack of the brand of beer Danny liked to drink sometimes during TV baseball games. Addy's heart turned into a lump of pain in her chest as the young woman selected cheese to go with her crackers.

Head down, Addy walked swiftly past the redhead. And right into another cart. She looked up into the speculative gaze of Betsy Foster, Susan's mother and the most notorious gossip in Sweetbranch.

"You aren't watching where you're going, Addy Mayfield," Betsy snapped. "I'd say you'd best keep your eyes open."

"Excuse me, Mrs. Foster. You're right. I wasn't being very careful."

Betsy looked over Addy's shoulder, and Addy knew what she was seeing. Heather. "Mmm-hmm. So I see."

Addy turned her cart, hoping to get around her neighbor without further comment.

Betsy Foster was too adept a gossip to let Addy get away with that. She leaned closer and lowered her voice. "Don't you think it's time you saw an attorney?"

"A what?"

"You heard me. You call Ragan Hammond. He knows a good sight more than you do about errant husbands and grasping young girls." Betsy nodded in Heather's direction. "You'd best protect yourself. And all those young 'uns of yours. Unless you want to wake up one morning to find that one there moving into your house, buying all new furniture. Happens. Happens all the time. Men get to a dangerous age, you know. You call Ragan, Addy. You call him today."

Addy stopped breathing, couldn't even move. She barely registered the fact that Betsy Foster had departed. She jumped when she felt a hand on her shoulder. She looked up into the sympathetic eyes of Malorie Roberts.

"Don't pay a bit of attention to anything my grandmother says," Mal said.

Through dry lips, Addy said, "Maybe she's right."

"My grandmother has built a lifetime on squeezing guilt and misery out of people. Don't let her suck you in."

"Everybody in town's probably thinking the same thing," Addy whispered.

"What anybody else has to say doesn't matter. I know. All that matters is what your heart tells you."

Sighing, Addy looked into the confident young woman's eyes. She realized for the first time how difficult it must have been for Susan's daughter to endure all the gossip when she'd revealed the truth about her out-of-wedlock son. But from the looks of her, Malorie had weathered it well.

Still, Addy thought, surely her case was different. "Sometimes I'm not sure what my heart is telling me."

Malorie gave her a hug and said, "Keep listening."

A few minutes later, Addy was standing in line, still numb and cold from Betsy Foster's haunting words, when Heather went through the express lane with her cheese and wine and beer. She smiled and laughed with the cashier, a shy, naive smile that tied knots in Addy's stomach. Addy watched as Heather sashayed out, well-worn jeans clinging to her heart-shaped bottom.

Looking down at her loose denim skirt, Addy was aware as never before how frumpy she must look compared to a well-rounded nymph like Heather. If it came down to her versus Heather, Addy knew it was no contest as surely as if it were printed in the front-page headlines of one of the tabloids racked neatly beside her.

Young Girl Beats Out House Frump.

CHAPTER THIRTEEN

As soon as Heather heard her little sister begging their mother to take her to the PTA meeting so she could sing with all the other sixth-grade Spanish students, Heather knew where she would find Danny Mayfield that night.

A good family man like him, he'd be headed for the elementary school right after supper.

"I'll give you a ride, kid," she had said, eliciting a suspicious glance from eleven-year-old Tracy. Heather felt a fleeting pang. Apparently she wasn't the only Yates who knew better than to count on anyone else in the family.

"That old car of yours won't make it," Tracy had grumbled.

"Suit yourself. I'm going, anyway."

But as they drove toward the school, Heather had a better idea than her original plan, triggered by Tracy's doubts about the reliability of her sister's car. Even Danny Mayfield knew Heather's car couldn't be depended on. Hadn't he helped her out the last time it broke down?

"Wendy Kistler says her mother says you're making a fool out of yourself chasing after a married man," Tracy prattled as they rattled along in silence.

The car radio had gasped its last breath three days earlier.

"Wendy Kistler's mother can kiss my rear end," Heather replied. Even though she'd been responsible for starting the gossip herself, she still hated the idea of all the Goody Two Shoes in Sweetbranch looking down their noses at her.

They wouldn't do that when she moved into Danny Mayfield's house. She'd driven down Mimosa Lane last week, just to take a look at the house. It was prettier than anything she'd ever dreamed of. The way she had it planned, Addy could move back home with her mother and take all those brats with her. It would just be her and Danny. She would be the perfect housewife. She would learn to cook. She would—

"Mama says you dress like a slut these days," Tracy said.

Heather braked to an abrupt halt in front of the school. Like it mattered to her what their rotten excuse for a mother thought.

Tracy looked at her. "Aren't you coming in?"

Heather told herself that wasn't disappointment in her little sister's voice. Why should Tracy care if anybody in the family heard her dumb song, anyway? "I'll be back. I need to run to the store for a minute."

"Are you smoking again? Mama said she'd skin you if you started smoking again."

"It's none of her business. Or yours. I'm grown now."

Thirty minutes later, she was waiting by the side of the road, hood raised, when Danny passed. She'd already refused help from four other families. The distributor was safely hidden in her glove compartment. A strategic smudge of grease lightly touched her turned-up nose. She figured she looked helpless and adorable.

"Oh, Danny, I don't know what I would have done if you hadn't shown up," she said, scurrying to him as he jumped down from the cab of his truck. "I was so afraid it would get dark and I'd be stuck out here all by myself."

"What's the problem?"

She shrugged and tried to look confused. "I don't know. It just stopped. I've been looking and looking, trying to see what went wrong, but..."

She smiled at him, to show him how much faith she had in his ability to set things right. Danny glanced at his watch, frowning.

"Maybe I ought to give you a lift to that mechanic whose been working on this for you. Then he could come back with you and—"

She took him by the arm. It felt so strong it made her dizzy. "Oh, Danny, please don't do that. He tries to rip me off every time. If you just looked at it, I bet you could tell what's wrong. Then you could tell him yourself and he wouldn't try to take advantage of me. You know?"

Danny glanced at his watch again, then nodded. "Okay. A quick look."

Heather relaxed. She knew the mechanic she usually went to had made a run to Tuscumbia for parts this evening. She and Danny would have a long wait, sitting in those rockers underneath the trees beside the auto shop.

Anyway, those kids at the school didn't really belong to Danny. No reason why he ought to be there to see them in their silly PTA programs. No reason to feel guilty about that. Or Tracy, either, for that matter.

She leaned under the hood, her arm brushing Danny's. "Whatever it is, I just know you can fix it."

THE PLEDGE OF ALLEGIANCE was finished. The treasurer's report had been made. The minutes of the last PTA meeting had been read and approved as read. And still no sign of Danny.

Addy sat in the uncomfortable folding chair, Gabby on one side, the three boys on the other, separated by a solemn Reno. Brook was somewhere backstage, waiting with the other children in her class to recite a poem about springtime. Of course, Addy had already heard it so many times these past three weeks that she, too, knew it by heart. But she wouldn't have missed hearing it for the world. Neither would Danny, she'd have thought.

But here they were, twenty minutes into the spring PTA meeting and no sign of him.

Addy turned to look toward the door. Reno did the same. Where could he be? What could be wrong?

So miserable was she in her disappointment that she completely missed the report from the Beautification Committee. Addy realized now how much she'd looked forward to seeing Danny tonight. She'd pictured how he would tease the girls, giving them one of his infectious grins, crinkling up those dark blue eyes of his that warmed and lit the spirit. She knew how his smile dared you to resist smiling back.

She'd pictured how he would swing Brook into his strong arms after the program and tell her how proud he was of her. She'd pictured . . .

Enough of that.

She pointed her eyes on the recitation by a class of kindergartners. Darn Danny Mayfield. She *would* not think of him.

Brook's class came out and still no Danny. Addy paid close attention to the gangly, dark-haired girl with the excited smile. She applauded with the rest of the audience, her pride almost overcoming her disappointment.

As the sixth-grade Spanish class filed onto the stage, Addy heard a rustling behind her. Hopeful once again, she forced herself to keep her eyes focused on the stage. Then she heard the murmurs and realized it wasn't Danny. The murmurs continued right through the performance. As the song drew to a close, the whispers behind her were suddenly loud enough for her to understand in the momentary lull.

"... Who I saw riding down the road together on my way in. Danny Mayfield and that young Yates girl."

"No! Surely not!"

"Well, I reckon I'm not blind yet."

Addy felt the disappointment she'd been nursing turn to despair. Hadn't Rose warned her? Hadn't her mother? Hadn't she said herself that she couldn't compete with someone like Heather?

Just look at her tonight in her simple print dress, the bare feet she had slipped into canvas sneaks. She couldn't even remember if she'd bothered with any makeup. It had been all she could manage to get the kids fed and their faces wiped and troop them down to her mother's so they could borrow the station wagon.

At that moment, Gabby reached over and squeezed her hand. Addy squeezed back and looked down at Gabby's big, dimpled smile. *You're the prettiest mommy in town.*

Hearing the thought so clearly in her head startled Addy at first, until she remembered that Reno had said that just two nights ago, when Addy was staring at her closet wishing for something special to wear to the final PTA meeting of the school year.

The words had given Addy a momentary lift at the time. But right now, with Danny doing Lord knows what, Addy knew that even if she had been the prettiest mommy, that did nothing but compound the problem. Danny Mayfield wanted a *wife*. And Addy sometimes feared she'd given up everything else about being a woman for the sake of being a mommy.

At that moment, Addy would have given anything she possessed to have him look at her the way a man looked at a woman he lusted after, but she was probably going to have to settle for being considered the prettiest mommy in town by six young castoffs.

DANNY SPOTTED SOMETHING familiar about the woman the instant she walked into the Holy Spirits Tavern later that night.

She walked in hesitantly, as if taken aback by the honky-tonk music filling the air or the smoke that snaked in her direction. The fact that people turned to look at her seemed to give her pause, and Danny's re-action to her vulnerability shocked him.

That kind of yearning had no place in a married man's thoughts.

He turned back to his beer, trying not to notice that Tony's eyes, too, were drawn to the woman. But looking away didn't seem to help. It was as if he could feel her presence in the room and could no more keep himself from watching her than he could stop breathing.

He turned toward her again as casually as he could. She wasn't even his type, in her tight jeans and moussed hair, her lips a slash of tomato red in her pale face. Although, he had to admit, she had that slim-hipped, reedy build he loved. But he loved it best in soft skirts that slipped and slid over the sparse curves, loose shirts that slipped off the shoulder. Preferably a freckled shoulder partly hidden by cinnamon-colored curls that fell loose and soft, not moussed and sprayed and ...

Addy!

He laughed out loud when it sank in. The skintight jeans and the big hair belonged to Addy. He was so delighted with the discovery that he kept right on laughing. Right up to the moment when all the voices in the Holy Spirits died down and he realized that all eyes were on him and Addy.

His laughter froze in his throat. He'd made a big mistake. He knew that from the silence. And from the red-hot fury on Addy's face.

He stood. He would just walk over, take her by the elbow, get her out the door and explain that—

He was too late. She had already turned away with that little chin-up gesture she had when she wanted him to know she had no intention whatsoever of listening to him, much less forgiving him, in this lifetime. He opened his mouth but was so astonished by the way she was walking he couldn't have said a word if fire had broken out at his feet. He couldn't think what to call it. Sashaying, his mother-in-law would have said, with a certain amount of disdain in her voice. Butt-twitching, he'd heard from the guys at the bar, a spectator sport they apparently delighted in rating.

Danny didn't like it nearly as well as her usual walk, an unselfconscious sway that suited her a lot better than this forced provocation.

Still, forced or not, he had to admit she put on a pretty good show. Of course, he'd known that about Addy all along. This was the act she saved for him when they were alone at night or first thing in the morning or in the middle of the afternoon on those rare occasions when the kids were off with Eulainie or their cousins.

Danny grew a little hot under the collar thinking of her flaunting it right in front of God and everybody at the Holy Spirits Tavern.

She made it to the pool table, and that was when Danny's attention shifted away from her hips. He watched as she leaned against the table, one narrow hip jutting out at a provocative angle. Tibby Barker, who'd been chalking the end of his pool cue in preparation for a shot, kept chalking. His eyes were sliding up and down the length of Addy's tight jeans.

Danny moved in Tibby's direction, catching the auto-body repairman's eye. Danny made sure there was no mistaking the look he gave Tibby.

Tibby finished chalking and lowered his cue to the balls on the table.

Addy said something then, low enough that Danny didn't catch it. All he heard was her voice, and he would have sworn she was using the same voice she sometimes used first thing in the morning, when the early-morning sun filtered through the dotted swiss curtains and bathed them both in golden shadows.

The last month of celibacy was taking its toll on Danny. So was watching the unmistakable signs that his wife was trying to flirt with someone else.

Trying, hell! She was doing a pretty damned good job of it, judging from the look on Tibby Barker's face.

Danny made another threatening move toward the pool table. Tibby looked over Addy's shoulder, stud-ied Danny's face for a few seconds. Then, with an al-most imperceptible shrug, he turned his attention back to his shot and said, "Addy, I reckon you're blocking my light, if you wouldn't mind moving on."

Danny saw Addy stiffen as she moved away from the pool table. Seeing nothing but her back, Danny still knew exactly what was going on in her head, on her face. She was struggling with anger and humilia-tion and pride.

Anger won. It usually did, with pride a close sec-ond. Danny smiled, warmed by the knowledge that he knew her so well. Unfortunately, Addy whirled to leave at exactly the instant he smiled. The smile was all she saw. Her cheeks went up in flames. If she'd been a cat, she would have been hissing and spitting.

She was out the door before Danny could move.

Danny didn't know which to do first, give Tibby Barker a piece of his mind or chase after Addy. He paused on the way to the door only long enough to grab the nine ball just before it fell into the corner pocket.

Fingers clutched tightly around the striped ball, Danny shook his fist at Tibby and said, "The next time my wife flirts with you, you better act interested, you hear?"

Tibby yanked his Miracle-Gro cap off his head and punched it with his fist. "Aw, heck, Danny—"

"And *then* you stay the hell away from her. Am I making myself clear?"

Tibby shook his head. "About as clear as milk gravy. Now, dang it, Danny—"

Danny had no more time to waste listening to Tibby's excuses. He stalked out the tavern door. He had a wife who needed calming down—and straightening out.

ADDY STUMBLED AROUND the parking lot in a blind rage, looking for her mother's station wagon and finding only Danny's pickup. Grunting out her fury, she kicked the tires of the old truck and discovered the action brought no satisfaction whatsoever.

"I hope your muffler falls off!" she shouted at the familiar vehicle. "Especially if you *ever* let him cart around some other woman."

Tears stung her eyes at the very thought, but she wasn't about to let herself get distracted by *that* notion. She had other wounds to nurse tonight. And as soon as she could remember where she'd parked the station wagon, she planned to go home, huddle in bed and torture herself with thoughts of her own husband laughing at the sight of her and another man. Tibby Barker, for heaven's sake! He had his nerve, with that receding hairline of his, telling her to get lost. Right there in plain view of everyone in town.

By morning, she would be the laughingstock of Sweetbranch.

"By morning, you'll still be wandering around this godforsaken parking lot if you don't get your head screwed back on," she muttered to herself.

Okay. Parking lot. Station wagon. She had driven her mother's car, hadn't she? She dug in the front pocket of her jeans—and that was no easy feat; what were girls today thinking, cutting off all circulation to the lower extremities this way?—and found the keys. Yep, the wagon was definitely here somewhere.

In the back. She remembered now, driving around to the back in the hope that none of her rational friends would see the car and realize what she was doing.

What *was* she doing? she asked herself as she rounded the building and spotted the wagon beside a flight of wooden stairs zigzagging up the side of the building. Gussying herself up like some barely-out-of-adolescence bimbo to win back her own husband.

"You're nuts," she told herself as she slipped into the front seat and stared at herself in the rearview mirror. "Posi-lutely nuts!"

Even quoting one of Brook's favorite exclamations didn't draw a smile from the boldly made-up woman in the mirror. How different this woman looked from the woman Addy thought she had faced in her bathroom mirror just an hour earlier. Now, the smoky eyeshadow made her look more like she'd barely survived a round in the ring with a heavyweight champ than creating the sultry effect she'd wanted. The mascara had clumped up and looked cheap, and the mauve blush on her cheekbones stood out in livid contrast to the embarrassed color staining the rest of her face. Even her hair looked as if it would break in two if somebody came after her with a comb.

"If he doesn't love me the way I am," she told herself, "the way I *really* am, then to heck with him."

She had already backed the car up when she spotted the water hose coiled against the back of the building. At least she didn't have to run the risk of anybody else seeing her this way. She turned off the engine, got out of the car and stalked over to the faucet.

The water was cold and spurted unsteadily out of the nozzle. Addy knew water was dribbling onto her clingy T-shirt as she sprayed her face and hair, but it hardly seemed to matter. At least she would be rid of some of the evidence of her foolishness.

"For the love of Pete, what are you doing now?"

Addy started at the sound of Danny's voice. Her first instinct was to lash out at him. Her second was to

turn the water on him. She almost smiled at that. She
decided to count to ten first and see what that did for
her state of mind. If nothing else, it would catch him
off guard. She kept rinsing, feeling her hair stream
loose and wet down her back.

One. Two.

He put his hand on her shoulder and she jerked
away from his touch. It felt too right, and she couldn't
afford to think of that right now. Couldn't afford to
remember how her blood had started pumping when
she headed over here tonight, how her heart had raced
in anticipation. She wiped the unfamiliar color off her
face.

Three. Four.

"Addy, I didn't mean to laugh. I mean, I wasn't
laughing because I thought you were funny. For trying to be sexy. No, that's not what I mean, either. I
mean, you are sexy. To me. And... Damn, Addy.
None of this is coming out right."

He faltered. She wanted to glare at him. Five. Six.
The water continued to come out in spurts. Her face
felt clean, and she couldn't help but think how satisfying it would be to leave him standing here soaking
wet.

Less satisfying when she contemplated the fact that
she was the one who needed the cold shower, not
Danny.

Seven. Eight.

"What I mean, Addy, is that I love you the way you
are and I don't want you fixing up the way some girls
think men want women to look."

She heard something heartfelt in his voice this time and knew it would be an especially dangerous time to look at him. Nine. She kept the nozzle over her head instead. Goodbye, ultralashes. Goodbye, super-hold styling gel.

Goodbye, self-respect.

"Besides which, I think you've carried this wounded-wife routine far enough."

Addy forgot which number came after nine. Wet hair dripping to her shoulders, soaked T-shirt clinging to her chest, she whirled on him.

"Wounded-wife routine?" She waved the dribbling nozzle. Danny dodged. "You ain't seen nothing yet, Danny Mayfield."

She gave the hose another good shake in his direction. "The courts don't take well to husbands who fool around, Danny. Not even in the nineties. So—"

He closed a fist around the wrist of the hand that held the hose. Water dribbled down her arm, over the big hand that fit so easily around her wrist. She barely noticed. Danny's eyes had her full attention. They were, as he would have said during less serious moments, as serious as a heart attack.

"Addy Mayfield, in sixteen years I've never cheated on you. I sure don't plan to start now."

The water hose fell from her fingers. "You haven't?"

"No, ma'am."

"You don't...plan to?"

"No, ma'am."

Addy wasn't sure how she'd know if Danny was lying to her, because to her knowledge he never had. He wasn't even one of those men who sometimes indulged in little white ones, like shaving a few dollars off what he spent on a fishing rod. As long as she'd known him, Danny had been as true as blue eyes on a baby. Right now, the look in his eyes was as dead honest as any she had ever seen.

She didn't stop to listen to the mean little voice in her head that wanted to know if she was seeing only what she wanted to see.

"You mean that, Danny?" The fingers of their damp hands intertwined, and she took a half step that brought her close to him.

"With all my heart." He grinned, a gentle grin that took nothing away from the seriousness of what they'd just said. "And a few other significant body parts, as well."

She chuckled, then forced a frown. "Danny, this is serious."

"As a heart attack," he replied.

So delighted with the friendly feel of familiarity, she couldn't stop herself. Addy laughed. "Has anybody ever told you you're predictable?"

"Predictable? Me? Never!"

Then, before she had a chance to harrumph her disbelief, he had shut off the water, swept her into his arms and headed for the steep wooden staircase snaking up the back of the old building. "Danny, what are you doing?"

"Playing Rhett Butler." He paused and gazed up the unpainted wooden steps. "Not exactly a sweeping staircase, I know. But it won't hurt us to use our imaginations a little."

He started up the stairs.

"You think I was mad before, Danny Mayfield," she whispered against his neck, "just imagine how mad I'm going to be if you throw your back out before we get to the..."

"The what?"

He didn't seem to be having a bit of trouble breathing. Less trouble than Addy was having, actually.

"The climactic scene."

He chuckled, and she felt the familiar rumble in his chest. She smiled and rested a cheek against his collarbone, felt the funny bump where he had broken the bone in the final game of his junior year at Auburn. She remembered how frantic she'd been with him in an emergency room in Jackson, Mississippi, and her trying to ring up groceries in Auburn.

But the broken bone had healed, as most things do if given the proper care and enough time.

"Considering what you weigh," Danny said, giving the door at the top of the stairs a kick, "there isn't much chance of hurting myself. If you lose another pound, Addy, I swear—"

"Nobody likes a nagging husband, Danny."

"You better," he said, tossing her into the middle of a lumpy bed in the darkness. "You've got one."

The only light in the long, narrow room came through the stained-glass window overlooking Main Street. A street lamp shone into the room, casting red, yellow and blue glimmers on the room's meager furnishings.

But Addy wasn't looking at the furnishings. Danny was the only thing she saw as he took his shirt off.

She thought she had remembered everything about him. How could she forget fourteen years' worth of showers and bedtimes and wake-up calls? Especially all those wake-ups. But seeing him like this was like seeing him new all over again. The tiny dark nipples, barely visible in the dark mat of hair curling over his chest. His stomach, harder and flatter than she remembered. And his arms, stronger than she remembered as he fingered the snap of his jeans.

She watched until his jeans and briefs dropped to the floor. Then her throat closed up for a moment. He wanted her. As badly as she wanted him.

With one finger, she reached out and touched the tip of his erection. She found him moist, way past merely aroused. He groaned and she lowered her hand and ran her nails lightly along his hair-rough maleness, cupping him, feeling his weight, then moving her fingers back to caress the hard smoothness of him.

He trembled at her touch. She felt his response and ached with it.

"I've missed you like crazy," he whispered, leaning over to kiss her.

As hungry for the words as for the kiss, Addy clutched his head to her, winding her fingers through his hair while his lips closed over hers. The kiss was gentle only for a few seconds. Then Danny answered her hunger with his own. They couldn't kiss deeply enough, couldn't explore wildly enough. She pulled his bare chest to her, felt for the solidness of his muscle and found it with all the relish and reverence of the dying arriving at heaven's gates.

Still kissing her, Danny struggled with her skintight jeans, tugged at the hem of her T-shirt.

"If I ever get these off," he murmured against her lips, "I'm getting rid of them. For good."

She smiled and touched his upper lip with the tip of her tongue as he flung the jeans over his shoulder. "I thought tight jeans were sexy."

"Long skirts are sexy," he said, letting his lips drop lower, to trail along her neck. "Long, loose skirts that I can throw over your head to get right to the good stuff."

Addy's laugh turned into a gasp as he got to the good stuff. His tongue teased at her nipple while one hand feathered over the dark copper triangle where her thighs met.

"Animal," she whispered.

He touched her and kissed her in all the ways she would like to have said she'd forgotten. Except that the memories had haunted her the entire month he'd been away. The only things she'd forgotten were the intensity of her feelings, the sweetness of feeling one with him, the utter peace of losing herself in the sensations of loving and being loved.

When he entered her, they both grew still for an instant. His eyes sought hers.

"I love you, my sweet Adeline."

She ran her hand along his back, reaching the taut swell of his buttocks. "I love you, Danny-Boy."

"Forever and ever."

"Forever and ever."

They began to move together in the rhythm they had learned together half a lifetime ago. Slow and steady. Fast and hard. Faster. Harder. Until they reached the crest. Together.

CHAPTER FOURTEEN

ADDY WATCHED DANNY cross the room, shadowy light playing on his bare backside. He opened the pint-size refrigerator to retrieve a soft drink, casting equally interesting shadows on his bare front.

She wanted him again already.

"Where are we?" she asked as he popped open the soft drink, brought it back to the bed and handed it to her.

"The old choir loft."

She almost choked on the soft drink. "The choir loft? Of the old church?"

He grinned and stole the can for a swallow of his own. "Where'd you think we were?"

Addy settled into the crook of his arm and put a hand on his thigh. "Frankly, I wasn't thinking about it much."

They sat in companionable silence, passing the soft drink back and forth. Addy studied the room for the first time. The bed took up most of the space, although it was merely a mattress and springs atop a metal frame. A rag rug Addy knew had been relegated to the attic at her mother's added a frayed and faded look that she supposed was intended to be warm and homey. A vinyl recliner was the only other real furniture, unless you counted the bar stool pulled up to the foot-long kitchen counter. The stove had two burners, on one of which sat a shiny new teakettle.

"I had no idea bachelor pads were so stylish," she said, and wished right away she hadn't brought it up. She felt him stiffen beside her.

"It's got a few advantages."

"Oh?"

"The peace and quiet."

"Oh."

She shifted, trying to put a few inches of space between them without getting caught at it.

"Is that what you think this is, Addy? My bachelor pad?"

She gave up pretense and scooted to one side so she could face him. "What am I supposed to think?"

He bent the aluminum can and dropped it into the wicker basket beside the bed. "That I was tired of sleeping on my mother-in-law's couch?"

Addy pulled the sheet up to cover her nudity. "Then you should have come home."

"You haven't exactly welcomed me with open arms."

Addy wondered if it would do any good to try counting to ten again. The results had been superb an hour ago. She tried to recapture the feeling of closeness between them. She tried to remember Danny saying he loved her.

That he'd never cheated on her and never would.

The memory did nothing but make her more emotional. She swallowed her feelings. And her pride. What good was pride? It was cold comfort compared to having the man she loved lying beside her through the night once again.

"You know I want you home," she said, glancing up only long enough to confirm that Danny, too, looked disturbed.

"And you know that's where I want to be."

She heard the "but" in his voice and glanced up again. This time he was the one who looked away. Addy spoke, barely loud enough to be heard. "You might as well speak your mind."

He sighed heavily, picked at a worn place on the sheet. "Coming home without...reaching some kind of understanding... Aren't we just asking for more trouble down the road?"

Addy's heart began to thud heavily in her chest. She didn't want to talk about this. She wanted to have the rest of the night without fighting. She wanted Danny to come home. They might argue again, sure. But at least he would be home, where he belonged.

"Danny, we don't have to do this now."

"Yes, we do, Addy. Just because we don't agree on everything doesn't mean we're on the verge of...of..."

"Stop it, Danny." She knew what he was about to say, and she was terrified at the idea of either of them putting it into words.

"I can't. We have to reach some kind of understanding. You can't keep expecting me to go along with whatever it is you want just because you're the mommy."

Addy shot up in the bed. "What's that supposed to mean?"

Danny sighed. "You see, Addy. We can't even talk about this. You aren't willing to discuss making changes."

"I'm willing to talk."

"But are you willing to listen?"

She jumped up, dragging the sheet with her while she searched around the floor for her clothes. She yanked the wet T-shirt down over her chest, then snatched the jeans off the floor. "I'm listening. Now, tell me what it is you're getting at, Danny."

"What I'm getting at is, sometimes you treat me like I'm one of the kids. Like my opinion doesn't count."

She whipped the zipper into place and felt for the keys in the front pocket. "Oh, really?"

"Yeah. That's how I feel. Sometimes."

Addy began to tremble. "And I don't suppose Heather Yates makes you feel that way, does she?"

"Aw, Addy, I thought we settled that."

"And I thought you loved our kids. But sometimes things aren't exactly what they seem."

Danny dragged himself off the bed and began scrambling for his own clothes. "Of course I love them. I just think it would be better if we talked about a few changes. Surely you can—"

"You want changes? I'll make changes. How's this for changes?" She was backing toward the door now. She told herself it was time to shut her mouth, time to leave before she said something she would regret. But she couldn't quite manage it. "I want us to adopt two more of the children. Give them a permanent home. And if I ever again hear that you've been carting Heather Yates around town in your truck, I'll drive it off the Willow Creek bridge. How's that, Danny Mayfield?"

"Now, Addy, be reasonable about this. If you'd asked me about Heather, I could have told you—"

"I don't want to hear your excuses, Danny. I've made my offer. Take it or leave it. But I want your answer. You've got two weeks to decide."

"Addy—"

"Two weeks, Danny. I want your decision by our anniversary."

Danny stared at her, and for the first time in all the years she'd known him, Addy couldn't read what she saw in his face. He had that cool, stony expression she thought men only had on the movie screen.

"Sounds like we've both got some decisions to make," he said.

Addy felt her head begin to spin. Her mother's proclamation whirled around up there, making it hard for her to think. But she told herself to nod and she nodded. Then she told herself to leave and she left.

The cool spring night had turned stifling as she walked down the wooden steps, wondering if anniversaries counted when your marriage had hit the rocks.

DANNY LAY IN THE DARK after she left, listening to the station wagon pull out of the parking lot and inhaling the lingering scents of their lovemaking.

He stared at the ceiling, but all he could see was Addy's face, eyes half-closed, lips parted, cheeks flushed. The way she looked when she reached a climax. Just thinking about it, he grew hard on the outside and soft on the inside.

Every word he'd said, he'd meant. But damn if he knew what to do about it. He covered his eyes with his hands to shut out the visions in his head. The way things were turning out, Danny thought more and more that both of them were dead wrong. But knowing that didn't give him a clue what to do about it.

He got up and turned on the old black-and-white TV his mother-in-law had loaned him. He watched reruns of "I Love Lucy" until the station went off the air. Then he watched the blank, humming screen until he fell asleep and dreamed he was back home.

MAXINE HAMMOND'S FIRST impulse when she saw Addy Mayfield sitting in a swing at the park was to turn away and go home. People had overwhelmed this troubled young couple with advice, and she thought they needed space to work out their own problems.

As soon as she drew closer to Addy, Maxine was glad she had overcome her first, cowardly impulse. Addy was watching listlessly as Gabrielle, the mystery child with the golden ringlets, played on the sliding board with Jake McKenzie and Cody Roberts. Addy's shoulders drooped forward and a frown creased her forehead. Even her usually bouncy hair looked lifeless. Maxine's heart went out to the young woman.

"A lovely day, is it not?" She spoke softly and was uncertain, at first, that Addy had heard.

When Addy did acknowledge Maxine's presence, her nod was halfhearted and her voice had no spirit in it. "Real pretty."

Maxine sat in a swing beside Addy. "You are well?"

"Sure. Just fine."

Maxine kept silent. She pushed with her toe and the swing began to move, slowly. The only sounds in the park were the robins of spring and the little boys a hundred yards away. Gabrielle remained as silent as her guardian. But Maxine sensed the serenity in Gabrielle's silence, something she did not sense in Addy.

"Your young charge still does not speak."

Addy shook her head.

"And still you know nothing? Have no way of helping her?"

Addy sighed. "The sheriff says it's the strangest case he's ever seen. A little girl like that, and nobody in the whole country looking for her. We have an appointment for her to see a specialist in Birmingham about her speech, but until then . . ."

"A sad situation. And if only she would speak," Maxine said pointedly, "perhaps we could find a way to help."

"Sometimes," Addy countered, "nobody can help."

"Perhaps you are right. For myself, however, I believe *someone* can always help. It is for that reason alone that we are here." She saw Addy's head slant in her direction. "To help one another through the heartbreaks in this life."

"Really?"

Maxine shrugged. "That is my belief, but each of us must find her own path."

The robins' songs and the children's laughter took center stage again while Addy nudged the swing into motion with her toe.

"I was wondering," Addy began. She drew a long, clearly audible breath. "Wondering whether I ought to have some kind of... legal..." Her voice broke on the word. "You know. Some kind of written agreement. With Danny."

Maxine nodded, sad that Addy had reached the point of discussing a legal separation. This happened to so many couples, but she would never have thought it would happen to Addy and Danny. "To protect yourself and the children."

"That's right." Addy's voice was barely audible. "Just in case."

"You do not foresee a reconciliation?"

Addy fidgeted with something in the pocket of her denim skirt. "I don't know, Maxine. I gave him a deadline. He has to decide something by next week." The words trembled from her lips. "That's our anniversary."

"I see." Maxine stood and walked over to take one of Addy's hands in hers. The hand was cold and thin, and Maxine noted again how pale and fragile Addy looked. "You do not feel well."

Addy's smile was rueful. "I look that bad, huh?"

Maxine tried to make her own smile reassuring. "A little tired, a little pale, a little thin. That is all."

Addy shrugged. "I know. I don't know what's wrong with me. I don't have any energy at all. I keep thinking I'm coming down with something, but I never quite get sick. But I don't get any better, either."

"Stress wears us down." Maxine squeezed her hand, then raised Addy's chin to look her in the eye. "I will speak with my husband about legal matters. But you must speak with the doctor about health matters. Do we have a deal?"

They made the deal and Maxine walked back toward the heart of Main Street, wondering if she should talk with her friend Rose about this dilemma. Perhaps Rose would have ideas about this upcoming anniversary and the possibilities of reconciliation.

THE AFTERNOONS WERE longer now, but the highway that twisted its way through stands of tall pines and hovering slopes grew dark in a hurry under a gray, rainy sky.

"We should have waited until the weekend," Danny said, wishing he hadn't let Addy convince him they could make the trip to Birmingham and back after work.

"No, we shouldn't," Addy said.

Danny saw no reason to argue with her. But his already tense shoulders grew tighter as he fought back the urge to remind her that he was a grown-up, too, and perfectly capable of making his own decisions.

"I told you before," Addy continued, "it's Reno's birthday Saturday, and the party was already planned before the hospital called."

"I know. And Sunday is out of the question because...you said so."

"Watch that car coming up behind you, Danny. If he tries to pass on this curve, you'll want to slow down."

Just to be contrary, he said, "Maybe I'll want to speed up so he can't get around."

She darted a sharp look in his direction, crossed her arms and leaned against the door. "Fine. Have it your way."

"I've been driving seventeen years, Addy, and I've never had a wreck yet." He tried to let up on the gas pedal so slowly she wouldn't notice that he'd done exactly what she suggested when the car behind sped around them on the rain-slick highway. "I don't need a . . . anyone telling me what to do."

A stony silence filled the car. Danny was glad, because he knew he needed to keep his own mouth shut. He'd almost told her he didn't need a mother telling him what to do. And that, he knew, would have prompted a noisy disagreement that would have been a lot less pleasant than the chill of her cold shoulder.

Danny glanced in the rearview mirror of his mother-in-law's station wagon. Casey was strapped in and slumped to one side in the back seat, sound asleep. He didn't know they were going to see his mother, because Addy had been afraid he would be too excited during the trip to the hospital in Birmingham. Danny supposed she was right, although he was inclined right now to disagree with whatever Addy said simply for the sake of staking out a claim to his own decisions. Right or wrong, he figured, at least those decisions would be his.

The four days since they made love had been torture. As ridiculous as he knew it was, he swore his one-room apartment still carried her scent. He stayed away except to sleep, and then he tossed and turned. Even an extra spin through the Laundromat hadn't been enough to wash away the essence of Addy clinging to the worn sheets. It had occurred to Danny that her scent wasn't in the sheets, but in his head, in his soul. But that was too scary to contemplate because it meant he'd never be able to wash it away.

With her ultimatum looming just a week and a half away, that was a fate he couldn't face. What would he do if he had to spend the rest of his days wanting a woman who was too stubborn to give an inch?

"Do you think we're doing the right thing?"

Her quiet question came on the outskirts of Birmingham, where the reflection of red taillights and neon of all colors ran together on his rain-streaked windshield. He wasn't sure of anything anymore.

"About Casey?" he asked.

"After all these months of treatments, she's bound to look...different. I don't want him to be upset."

"She's his mother, Addy. She wants to see him. What choice do we have?"

The rest of it lay between them, unspoken. When Casey's great-aunt had called to say that his mother wanted to see her little boy, she had also said things that neither of them wanted Casey to hear. The intensive treatments weren't working. This might be Shoshonna Johnson's last chance to see her son.

Everywhere he turned these days, Danny seemed to run into another last chance.

Heather had been waiting in the cab of his pickup after work the afternoon before. One booted foot was propped on the dash, the other was hanging out the open window. Her jeans were so tight Danny didn't see how she could contort her body that way. But there were a lot of things Danny didn't understand about Heather.

That's why he'd done a little nosing around after that night she shanghaied him on the way to the PTA. He'd driven past her house and found it depressingly familiar. Weather-beaten and in desperate need of repairs, it reminded him of the house where he'd grown up. He remembered how he used to think he would do anything—*anything*—to get away from that life.

Despite his better understanding, Danny still wasn't eager for anyone to see him sitting in his truck with Heather. He had walked to the passenger window and peered inside. She smiled at him, that uncertain little-girl smile she specialized in.

"You gonna kick me out?" she said, catching her pinky finger in the corner of her mouth.

"If I don't, Ben'll fire us both, Heather."

"Mr. McKenzie wouldn't do that."

Danny didn't think so, either. But he figured in this particular instance, misrepresenting the truth was the lesser of two evils. "He told me to stay away from you."

That much was certainly true. Heather looked pleased with the news. She looped a long curl over her pinky and dragged that to the corner of her mouth. "I don't want to get you in trouble. We could sneak off someplace."

"I'm a married man, Heather."

"Oh, Danny, she treats you mean." The fingers that weren't playing with her hair traveled down the front of her western shirt. Her breasts strained against the denim. She toyed with the top snap. "I wouldn't do that if you were my man. I'll love you more than she does, Danny. I swear it."

Danny had felt sad for whatever had happened to a girl as young as Heather to make her believe the best she could do was throw herself at a married man who'd never given her the least encouragement. He gave her none that afternoon, either, and when she finally got out of the truck and stood on the edge of the parking lot, watching him pull away, she had called out, "You'll be sorry when I find somebody else. This is your last chance, you know."

The pleading in her threat had tugged at his heart so he hadn't even been able to look at her.

The next day, it had started all over again. This time, Heather's tact was that she would always look up to him, would always let him make all the decisions.

"It'll be like you saved my life," she had said softly after catching him alone in the break room. And from the look in her eyes, he could tell she needed saving from something. "You'll be my hero forever. I'll owe everything I ever am to you."

The words had struck some chord deep in Danny, and now, as he circled the parking deck at the medical center looking for an empty space, he thought he knew what chord that was. For as long as he had known Addy, he had regarded her as his savior. She had encouraged him when no one else—least of all himself—had believed in him, and made it possible for him to make something of himself.

How long had he felt like little more than another of the children Addy had rescued? Had he ever been the hero in her life, someone *she* needed? He watched Addy as she roused Casey and unbuckled his seat belt. Her long waves were dark in the parking deck lights. Her arms were slender, graceful. He would have given anything to be her hero. But this entire month they had been separated, it was clear she saw him as little more than a stubborn child, trying to get his way.

Well, it was time she learned he was an adult with some ideas of his own. He'd been thinking about this for days now, and it seemed, as he watched her caring for someone who needed her help, that surely she would understand.

"Addy, I've been thinking."

Casey rubbed his eyes with his fists, whined when she set him on the ground. "Sleep some more," he insisted, and held up his arms to be carried.

Danny saw the weariness in Addy's face and reached down to pick the boy up himself. Casey's pudgy cheek nestled into the crook of Danny's neck and shoulder. Danny leaned his cheek against the boy's soft curls as they waited for the elevator.

"About what?" Addy asked at last.

"About the way you help people."

She stiffened. "What about it?"

His heart was picking up speed. This *was* a good idea, wasn't it? "About this business with Heather and how the thing about it is, she's just a kid who needs a break.''

He waited for some kind of confirmation from Addy that she understood where he was going. None came.

''I was thinking maybe you and I could do something for her.'' He was thinking of the way Addy had talked to him about a scholarship all those years ago, had helped him with the applications, convinced him he could make a better life for himself. Why couldn't he and Addy do that for Heather now? ''You know, the way—''

''Are you telling me—'' The elevator lurched to a stop on the ninth floor. Addy didn't move as the door whirred open. Danny held it open and looked at her. He didn't like what he saw in her face. ''Are you saying that you expect me to... to...''

''It's just an idea. We could do it together and—''

She stepped past him into the oncology wing. He followed. ''Addy?''

''Danny, I don't even want to talk about it. I'm going to try to forget you even said anything. Okay?''

Danny didn't have time to answer. The family waiting room was directly across from the elevator, and a tall, ebony-skinned woman came forward to greet them. Danny paid scant attention to the conversation between Addy and the little boy's great-aunt. His thoughts were too caught up in the sinking realization that he somehow hadn't explained himself well enough, that somehow Addy had entirely the wrong idea about his suggestion.

He couldn't keep his mind on his own problems for long, however. Here in the hospital, with the smell of sickness around him, he began to wonder what would happen to Casey if it weren't for Addy. Besides his mother, who might be dying—his only relative was this great-aunt, a plant worker in Atlanta. Danny recalled Shoshonna Johnson's desperation when she had asked Addy to look after her son.

What, indeed, would happen to Casey without Addy?

Danny stood by the door in the hospital room, Addy by his side. Casey hung back at first. He didn't recognize the woman with the thin face and the dull, heavy-lidded eyes. When he was at last persuaded this woman was his mother, he took a few tentative steps to the side of the bed. Addy slipped out the door when the boy and his mother started talking, and Danny followed her.

She stood, stiff-backed, against the hospital corridor wall, her lower lip caught between her teeth. Danny knew the look and took her in his arms.

She didn't cry. But when he felt her narrow shoulders give way in his embrace, Danny thought he might cry instead. He held her like that until Casey came bounding out of the room a half hour later, all smiles.

"My mama, she's tired now," he announced. "But she's coming home soon. She said so."

Addy exchanged a glance with the boy's great-aunt, who nodded. "I do believe she'll be going home soon."

The three adults knew what the older woman meant by that, but it was clear the exuberant little boy had other ideas entirely.

"She won't be sick anymore. Real soon. I knew that already."

Addy took his small hand in hers, and they started down the corridor for the long drive home. "You did?"

Casey nodded. "Gabby said so. The angels told her."

CHAPTER FIFTEEN

ADDY PLAYED OUTFIELD, because the only time the outfielder saw much action was when David came up to bat.

Bump Finley pitched, Addy's mother played catcher, and all the kids lined up for batting practice. All the kids except Gabby, who merely shook her bouncy curls, plopped down in the sparse grass beneath the pine tree in the front yard and would not be moved.

Gabby made a fairly quiet cheering squad, so Addy pitched in with loud encouragement to go along with Gabby's clapping every time one of the kids scraped the bat against the stitching on the softball.

"Way to go, Reno!"

Addy made all the noise she could as the ball hit the ground about six inches in front of the girl. Reno stared forlornly at the ball, then turned and shoved the bat at Terrell.

Both Bump and Eulainie added their encouragement to Addy's, but Reno still hung her head as she went back to the front porch step that was doing duty as the home team dugout.

Terrell wasn't much better. He refused to wear his glasses when he batted, and Addy harbored strong suspicions that he couldn't see the ball until it was six inches from his nose. A development that always startled him into ducking and forgetting to swing the bat.

Addy gave the twice-weekly practice everything she had. The problem was, everything she had wasn't much. She still didn't feel good, and she hadn't liked the odd look in Doc Newman's eyes when he'd run his tests yesterday afternoon. But he had refused to speculate on the cause for her fatigue and her fever and her nausea.

"Soon as I know somethin', you'll know somethin'" was all he would say.

But her physical symptoms were the least of her problems. What really robbed her of her spirit was Danny.

Their fourteenth wedding anniversary loomed less than a week away. Neither of them had mentioned it since the night in his apartment. But Addy knew that neither had forgotten that her ultimatum came due soon and Addy had kicked herself a dozen times for being such a fool.

With Maxine's help, she had scheduled an appointment with Ragan Hammond the Monday morning after their anniversary. Every night, she prayed she would have reason to cancel that appointment at the last minute. And every night, a little voice told her all she had to do was be the least bit willing to compromise.

She came close, more than once.

She came close the Saturday after their visit to the hospital in Birmingham, when Danny had spent hours cleaning up after he let Casey "help" him paint the walls in the newly completed addition to the house.

She came close when Danny remembered how much Reno loved memorabilia from Las Vegas—where it was rumored her mother had moved when she left Reno behind—and for her birthday brought her a glittery vest with the city name spelled out in rhine-stones on the back and five playing cards fanned out beneath the words. Addy could tell the twelve-year-old felt glamorous and grown-up in the garish vest.

Then she heard the rumor that Danny had asked Ben McKenzie about a scholarship for Heather Yates, and her heart did a nosedive.

That made it easier to coach the softball practice without him. Nevertheless, her spirits were drooping when Bump and Eulainie and Krissy McKenzie and all six of the Mayfield brood spilled into the front yard. Acutely aware that Danny was the one who had started this tradition, Addy ran back into the house to re-trieve a pair of sunglasses so no one would notice the tears welling up in her eyes.

"Outfielders never cry," she had muttered through a clenched jaw.

The only one who seemed to notice that Addy's heart wasn't in the game was Gabby, who stared into the outfield at Addy as often as she stared at the pitchers.

About the only thing that occupied Addy's thoughts for long, besides Danny and the looming deadline, was Gabby. State and local authorities remained baffled by the child who had apparently appeared from no-where. Confronted with law enforcement's bafflement, Addy had just about given up on ever finding the little girl's parents. The idea had broken her heart for weeks, but the notion grew less distressing to her all the time. Gabby felt like such a part of her, in a way that none of the other children ever had, that a life without her was almost as hard to picture as a life without Danny.

What she hadn't given up on, however, was helping Gabby find her voice, even though Gabby continued to mystify the specialists.

"Want to tell me why you don't talk?" Addy had coaxed the little girl during the car ride back to Sweetbranch, after her first appointment with the doctors in Birmingham.

Gabby shook her head.

"I've got an idea," Addy had said, pulling her shopping list notebook out of the purse that sat beside her on the front seat of the car. She put the pad and pencil in Gabby's lap. "Draw me a picture."

From the corner of her eye, she saw Gabby's quizzical look. "Draw whatever you want. A picture of where you lived before. A picture about why you don't talk to me. Whatever you want."

Gabby sat with the pad in her lap and the pencil in her fist for a long time, her eyes on the passing scenery. Then, slowly and laboriously, she began to draw. Addy studiously feigned disinterest.

When Gabby at last laid the pencil and pad on top of Addy's purse, the little girl almost instantaneously nestled her cheek against her angel doll, leaned against the car door and closed her eyes. Despite her curiosity, Addy waited until she found a tree-shaded picnic area before she pulled off the highway. She left the car running, then picked up the sketch pad.

Hand trembling, Addy thanked her lucky stars she had pulled off the road before looking at what Gabby had drawn.

The drawing was of two little girls, astonishingly realistic for the artwork of a five-year-old. But it wasn't the level of Gabby's talent that had Addy trembling. It was the eerie familiarity of the two children.

The larger of the little girls wore overalls and cowboy boots—Addy's uniform of preference during much of her early childhood. The other child was smaller, with a headful of wild, curly hair. She clutched a rag doll in one fist.

Addy had shivered. She looked at the little girl in the seat beside her, smiling gently in her sleep. She had asked herself if Gabby could really have intended for her drawing to look so much like a young Addy and her long-dead sister.

She was so caught up in the memory that Addy almost missed the ground ball David shot at her feet. She absently tossed the ball back to Bump Finley and looked across the yard at Gabby. The little girl stared at her angelically, as if she knew exactly what was on her substitute mother's mind.

BUMP FIGURED HE WASN'T such an old dog that he couldn't learn a few new tricks. So, although he never had been one for old-fashioned Southern-gent-style chivalry, he offered to walk Eulainie Cook home after the softball practice.

"Good for the bursitis," he claimed, when she protested. Leastways, he reckoned that wasn't far from accurate.

So they walked down Mimosa Lane together in the first soft light of springtime dusk. Bump kept his face carefully averted when they passed Betsy Foster's big house. Not that he wasn't perfectly within his rights to have a little walk with whomever he wanted, especially when Krissy had already raced home ahead of him. Not that sharp-tongued Betsy Foster had any say-so, anyway.

Still and all, he and Betsy had spent a lot of time together these past few months since her stroke. Bump wondered how a woman like Betsy would interpret that. He had assumed, her being such a no-nonsense type, that she wouldn't read anything into it.

But she *was* a woman, after all. And women didn't always think the way menfolk thought. That was for sure. And Betsy was pricklier than most.

Eulainie Cook, now, she was a different story altogether.

"Never realized how much fun young 'uns was," he said, shoving his hands deep into the pockets of his trousers, putting a strain on his blue-striped suspenders. Strip-straps, Krissy and Jake had called them when they handed him the package for Grandparents' Day. Imagine, an old coot like him getting packages for Grandparents' Day.

"Indeed they are."

Eulainie's voice had a pleasant, soft ring to it. Bump couldn't help but contrast it with the sharp bite in every word Betsy Foster spit out.

"Reckon it'll keep me in shape, running around out there a few days a week. Unless my bursitis acts up." He rolled his trick shoulder and found it surprisingly limber.

"Maybe I'll *get* in shape," Eulainie said, looking down at her loose warm-up suit.

"Shoot-fire, Eulainie, you're in fine shape," Bump ventured, knowing she would assume his comment was more polite malarky.

"Oh, hush up, Bump Finley," she said, growing a little pink in the cheek. "I heard your lady-charming days were over, but I reckon that was just another one of Sweetbranch's wild rumors."

Bump laughed, wondering if that wasn't the least bit of flirty teasing he heard. Truth was, he'd never noticed what a fine-looking woman Eulainie Cook was until he watched her back there behind home plate, trotting after wild pitches and leaning over to demonstrate a good grip for inexperienced young batters. Underneath that pink-and-white warm-up suit she looked right womanly to him. And those fluffy curls framing her cheeks looked as soft as the snow white peonies Rose fussed over along the side of the house.

Yes, Bump was glad for the opportunity to realize what a fine figure of a woman Miz Eulainie Cook represented. And sweet-natured, to boot.

As they reached the end of Mimosa Lane and turned toward Eulainie's house at the end of Dixie Belle, a familiar pickup slowed at the corner and turned in the direction they had just come from.

"Oh, dear," Eulainie said under her breath.

"Danny?"

Eulainie nodded and directed a troubled look at the truck. "I swear, I would have thought they were both too old to be acting so foolish."

"I expect the heart leaves room for all kinds of foolishness, no matter how old it gets."

She glanced at him. "Why, I suppose you're right. Love makes fools of the best of us, doesn't it?"

Bump nodded, hoping he looked wise. "Yep. Reckon it does. Say, Rose tells me those two have a wedding anniversary coming up."

Eulainie sighed. "That's right. The end of the week. I don't know if I can bear it if they let that day come and go without so much as a nod."

"Rose was thinking... That is, the womenfolk down at The Picture Perfect were talking... Wonder how those two young folks would take to a little meddling?"

Eulainie looked at him, and he saw a twinkle in her honey brown eyes that he liked right away. Yep, this was a fine figure of a woman, any way you sliced the pie.

"Meddling?"

He took her hand and pulled it through the crook of his arm, drawing her a cat's whisker closer. "Just a little something to give them a nudge. What do you think?"

Eulainie laughed and gave his arm a squeeze. "I think all those folks saying you're not a rogue any longer haven't taken a close look. Now, what do you have in mind?"

DANNY HAD DONE A LITTLE coaching of his own that day—coaching himself on how to behave when he dropped by after work to see his wife and kids.

No wild-pitch displays of temper. No out-in-left-field accusations. He would be all smiles and batting a thousand. In fact, he planned to hit a home run. He was tired of being alone.

The smell of Addy's meat loaf drifted out the kitchen window to greet him when he parked the pickup behind the house. The addition looked great if he did say so himself. He could see through the windows that Addy had already hung the curtains with the appliquéd trains and boats she had been working on before... before.

Anyway, a few finishing touches on the trim, which he had planned for the next two weekends—assuming he could figure out some way to keep his little assistants otherwise occupied—was all it lacked.

His satisfaction with the thought was short-lived. Once the addition was completed, he would have no more excuses for hanging around the house on weekends.

Definitely time to hit that home run.

He walked through the back door without knocking. The kitchen was in its usual chaos. Tonight, it made him smile. Night after night of walking upstairs to an empty one-room apartment could do that to a guy. Reno stood at the table, whipping butter and pepper and milk into a bowl of potatoes. Terrell laid out the plates under Reno's meticulous guidance—"Not that way! Forks on the left! The *left!*"

Gabby dribbled tea into glasses, leaving amber puddles beside each one. David sat on the counter making airplanes out of paper napkins and shooting them at Casey, who giggled as he in turn shot them onto plates. When Reno wasn't delivering instructions to Terrell, she was barking futile orders to the unruly boys. Brook carefully sliced the meat loaf with a butter knife. Danny felt certain a ladle would be needed to get the results onto each plate.

Addy was nowhere to be seen.

"Daddy!" Brook spotted him first and almost flung a chunk of the evening meal across the table in her eagerness to run up and hug him around the middle. "We're having meat loaf. You want some, too?"

"I made it," David boasted as he scrambled down from the counter.

"Did not!" said Reno.

"I killed onions with my pocketknife!"

Danny forced himself not to dwell on what else David might have vanquished recently with his pocketknife. "What are you doing with a pocketknife, anyway?"

"We all helped," Reno said, giving David the chance to duck out of the kitchen without an explanation. "Gabby lined up ingredients and Brook measured and—"

"And I squooshed it up with my fingers!" Casey said, wiggling the instruments in question in the air.

Reno nodded approvingly. "I made him wash first."

"With *soap*."

Danny shared a sympathetic look with the little boy, whose disgusted expression said plenty about his attitude toward such unsavory practices as washing with soap. Then, into the temporary lull in the chatter, he asked, "Where's Addy?"

Reno lowered her voice. "Lying down."

A shot of anxiety hit Danny squarely in the gut. He'd never known Addy to lie down in the middle of the day.

"She was tired 'cause she said old ladies who play outfield get that way," Brook volunteered.

"So we said we'd make supper," Terrell said as he walked around the table studying the alignment of his forks and spoons, making an adjustment here and there.

"Why don't I go tell her it's on the table?" Danny said, heading for the bedroom without waiting for the okay from Drill Sergeant Reno.

The bedroom was dark, and Danny's heart thumped unpleasantly as he peered at his wife's slight form curled up on his side of the bed. What if something was wrong with her? Could he ever forgive himself?

Although he wanted nothing more than to curl up behind Addy, wrap his arms around her middle and hug her to him, he made himself stay in the doorway and call her name.

She stirred, sleepily mumbling his name.

"Can I come in?" Asking permission jabbed another little puncture wound in his heart. But he was determined tonight not to set her off again.

"I'd better get up," she said, her voice still drowsy. She swung her legs off the side of the bed and sat there rubbing her eyes. Danny fought the good fight to stay away from her.

"Are you okay?"

She yawned a "yes" but still didn't move.

"You're sure?"

"Posi-lutely."

He smiled at the inside joke and edged a step farther into the bedroom where he ought, by rights, to be sleeping. He was far from convinced there was nothing wrong with finding his invincible wife napping while the kids fixed dinner. But he knew an immovable object when he heard one yawning. "I've been thinking."

"You sure that's a good idea?"

"About Friday night."

She choked off the yawn she had been just about to launch. But instead of saying anything, she leaned over to fish her tennis shoes out from under the bed.

"What I was thinking was, Friday night might be a good night for a date."

"A date?" She sounded incredulous. That made Danny's smile deepen. He liked the idea he could still surprise her.

"To celebrate."

She was down on her knees now, fanny in the air, sweeping an arm under the bed for her shoes. He doubted they were there. She'd probably abandoned them under a tree in the front yard, but he'd let her figure that out for herself.

"Do we have something to celebrate?" she asked, coming up for air at last.

"If you keep waving your backside at me, we might have to do a little celebrating right now."

She had a tennis shoe in her right hand and turned to throw it at him. He ducked and caught the shoe as it whizzed past his ear.

"That's my curve shoe," she said.

"I like your low slider better."

"You're a dog, Danny Mayfield." She stood slowly and faced him, hands on her hips.

"Is that a yes on Friday night."

"That's a maybe."

Reno's voice summoned them to the dinner table and Addy slipped past him, barely brushing his arm.

"What'll it take to turn that maybe into a yes?"

She stopped in the doorway, so close he could smell the fresh spring air in her hair. He felt himself stir and cursed the idea of waiting until Friday.

"I'll tell you what it'll take, Danny. It'll take a real good excuse for that rumor about you setting up Heather Yates for a scholarship."

Danny barely had time to open his mouth in self-defense—after all, he *had* tried to discuss it with her first, even tried to solicit her help—before she was gone, breezing down the hall toward the kitchen. Which was just as well. He'd known from her reaction that she wouldn't be happy that he'd gone ahead and done it, anyway. Nothing he could say would go far toward making peace with Addy.

Damn this town all the way to hell and back for the way gossip spread!

He should have known better, he told himself as he followed Addy back to the kitchen. He didn't even debate the wisdom of staying for supper. He was past being able to figure out what was going to tick Addy off and what wasn't. All he knew was, he was lonely as hell. Thinking about his kids working on their softball game without him this afternoon had nearly driven him nuts.

Besides, the meat loaf smelled better than anything he'd eaten since leaving his mother-in-law's house. The Clock was fine in a pinch, and it beat eating alone. But nobody came close to Addy when it came to putting supper on the table.

Nobody came close to Addy when it came to lots of things.

He was going to tell her that, too, come Friday night. She could kick and scream all she wanted, but one way or the other, he would get her alone for their anniversary.

CHAPTER SIXTEEN

ADDY HAD HEARD, of course, about Krissy Mc-Kenzie's real mother being in town.

But Addy had her own true-life soap opera going on, and she didn't think much about the stories. She didn't even pay much attention the afternoon the big, silver car lurched to a stop in front of her house, its shiny hood pointed crookedly toward the house and its trunk jutting crazily into the street. Because right at that moment, she was having another fight with Danny, under the oak tree on the edge of the yard, farthest away from where the kids were practicing softball. At least, she was *trying* to have a fight with him. He wasn't cooperating.

When he showed up this afternoon, she hadn't been able to help herself. After vowing to keep her mouth shut, she'd asked him about Heather Yates and that darned scholarship. The more she'd thought about that whole situation, the greater its hold on her. Now it wouldn't let her go. So she'd decided maybe she could make *him* worry about it instead, punish *him* with it instead of punishing herself.

It wasn't working.

"Do you know how I felt, Danny Mayfield, when Betsy Foster spoke right up in front of every single soul at The Picture Perfect and asked me what I thought about you asking Ben McKenzie to help that...that...woman...get a college education! Why, nobody's even talking about Malorie Roberts and her little boy anymore. They're all talking about us!''

Addy shoved her glasses back to the bridge of her nose so she could get the best possible look at him. But he wasn't even squirming, so what was the point? He just stood there, thumbs hanging from the empty belt loops on his jeans.

"I've tried to tell you how I thought it would be better for everybody if—"

Addy didn't want to hear any more about how he'd gotten so worried about Heather Yates's low self-esteem that he thought he'd try to help before she got herself into real trouble with some married man with a few less scruples than Danny had. That didn't ease her humiliation. All in all, she was glad for the intrusion of the big car.

Softball practice came to a halt in the Mayfield front yard at the same time Danny's explanation did— when the door of the unfamiliar car opened and a tall, polished-looking blonde slithered out of the front seat.

Addy had never seen Cybil Richert before, but she knew right away who this city woman with the slightly unsteady walk must be. From the "Oh, Lord" he murmured, Danny must have known, too.

"Mommy?" Krissy's voice was small and confused.

"Hey, baby!" Cybil Richert's voice was slightly too loud and a little bit slurred around the edges.

Addy glanced at Krissy, who had dropped her bat and was walking slowly toward her mother. Then she looked at Bump Finley, who had taken a couple of steps in Krissy's direction. He looked as uncertain as Krissy.

Even in the little bit she'd been out and about in the community these past weeks, Addy had heard all the talk. Had heard that Krissy's mother had taken to hanging out at the Holy Spirits Tavern. The woman's presence had stirred up all the talk about Ben McKenzie's arrival in town a few years back, and Sweetbranch had closed ranks around Krissy and her father, Jake and Rose.

Addy wasn't quite sure what she was supposed to do now that this woman had all but driven into her front yard. She did remember that her mother always said to give people the benefit of the doubt. She looked at Eulainie and saw that she looked as uncertain as the rest of them.

"What now?" she whispered to Danny.

"No reason for a scene," he whispered back. "As far as I know, she's within her rights to see her daughter."

Cybil didn't bend down to give her daughter a hug, and Addy wasn't able to banish the thought that it was because she would have fallen flat on her face if she'd tried. Instead, Cybil ruffled the little girl's silky dark hair.

"You playin' baseball, baby?"

Krissy squirmed away from the hair-mussing. "Softball, Mommy."

"You ought to be learning ballet, baby. Not out here getting your knees scraped."

"I like softball, Mommy. I can hit real good."

Cybil looked around the front yard, her suspicious gaze landing on Addy, who decided the only thing to do was be as gracious as her upbringing had taught her. "She's right, Ms. Richert. She's going to be a real slugger come Little League season."

"Is that so?"

"Krissy," Bump called out. "Come on back over here and we'll have a demonstration."

His ploy didn't work exactly as he'd planned, because Cybil followed her daughter back toward home plate, pausing once to take off the four-inch heels that kept sinking into the ground. When Krissy and Cybil reached home plate, Cybil stood directly behind her daughter, swaying.

Addy's heart began to thump. Danny put his hand on her wrist and said, "Go call Ben. Find out what he wants us to do."

She nodded and started edging toward the house. Danny was moving slowly toward home plate. As Addy passed the pine tree where Gabby usually watched the practice, she noticed that the little girl had stood up.

"You stay put," Addy whispered as she passed the little girl.

Krissy missed the first ball Bump Finley threw.

"Come on, baby." Cybil's encouragement sounded slurred. "Knock it outta the park."

The second ball limped across home plate. Krissy swung at it, anyway, a hard swing that threw her off balance.

Danny, Addy noticed, had run into a roadblock of children. Brook clung to his waist; Casey tugged on his pants to point out the new softball glove his mother had sent in the mail the day before; and Reno tried to get them out of his way, which merely added to the confusion.

Addy was almost to the front porch when she heard her mother's murmur of distress.

Gabby was no longer under the tree, but heading purposefully toward home plate. As was the softball, just released from Bump Finley's gnarled hand. At the last minute, Cybil leaned forward and wrapped her arms around Krissy's to guide the little girl's swing. But Cybil was unsteady and leaned too far. Krissy stumbled under her weight. Directly into the path of the ball.

Addy started running. Bump called out a warning. Danny picked up Brook and set her aside, running, as well. Eulainie reached for Krissy. But before anyone could reach her, Gabby stepped right in front of Krissy.

The softball that had been heading straight for Krissy's forehead caught Gabby on the shoulder with a dull thud.

The next few seconds were mayhem.

An avalanche of children landed on home plate. David shoved Terrell to get closest to the action. Terrell squealed indignantly. Reno shouted orders at everyone. Danny shouted orders at everyone. Cybil shrieked over her torn stockings and grass-stained skirt, as well as her wounded dignity.

And Krissy just shrieked.

The only one who made no sound was Gabby, who sat calmly at the center of the madness.

Elbowing her way to the middle of the bickering and noise, Addy knelt beside Gabby and tenderly touched one of the little girl's pale cheeks.

"Sweetheart, are you okay?"

Gabby smiled then, her brighter-than-sunshine smile. Color came back to her cheeks at the same time the dimples arrived. Gabby nodded, one quick affirmative dip of her head. Then, with tears stinging her eyes, Addy pulled the child into her arms and said, "What a brave little girl you were."

About that time, Addy felt a shuffling movement at her elbow and looked down into Casey's shy smile. "She's a guarding angel, that's why. Guarding angels have to be brave."

Giving up her battle against the tears in her eyes, Addy used her free arm to pull Casey against her chest, too. Guardian angel, indeed. Wasn't Addy herself supposed to be the guardian angel of this brood?

If so, she seemed to be falling down on the job these days.

DANNY TRIED TO MAKE himself indispensable until the ruckus died down. He called Ben, who came to usher Cybil out of the way. Rose came, too, to comfort Krissy, who was nearly hysterical over the crisis she felt certain she had caused. He recruited Bump and Eulainie to stay with the rest of the kids. Then he put

Addy and Gabby into the pickup and hightailed it to
Doc Newman's office to make sure Gabby was all
right.

Nothing, the Doc said. Just a tap with a softball.

"You tell Bump Finley it's a good thing he's got no
power in those wild pitches of his," Doc said, sending them on their way with his friendly smile and gentle eyes.

The thud the softball had made when it struck
Gabby kept echoing in Danny's head, telling him Doc
Newman must be wrong. But he'd never known the
Doc to be wrong yet. So he tried to soothe Addy's
fretful concerns and put his own out of his mind, as
well.

"Somebody was looking over us this time," he said,
handing Gabby up into Addy's lap once Addy was
settled in the cab of the truck. "That's all."

Addy frowned and gave him a sharp look.

She was shaken, he could see, and looked as tired
and washed out as she had looked the day before. So
when they got back to the house, he put her to bed,
took the kids out for burgers and ice-cream cones,
then brought them home and put them to bed, too.

When he finished, he looked in on Addy. She was
sound asleep, moonlight throwing a stream of soft
light across her cheek and shoulder. Danny couldn't
help himself. He tiptoed into the room, leaned over
and kissed her forehead. She stirred, murmured
something, then sighed and settled back into sleep.

At lunchtime the next day, he came back to check
on Addy and Gabby. Gabby, who was creating mas-
terpieces with a box of sixty-four colors and a color-

ing book of favorite bedtime stories, was all bouncy little girl. Addy, in her rocker with her quilting spread in her lap, looked like the one who had been whacked with a softball. Her cheeks were wan, her smile forced.

"How is she?" he asked, even though he could see for himself.

"Still no bruising. No swelling." She sounded skeptical, as if certain someone was hiding something from her.

"That's good. How about you?"

"Me?" Now she looked guilty, Danny thought. "Nothing wrong with me."

"You always said fibbing to each other was a bad example to set for the kids."

She didn't seem to have the energy even to glare at him. He was about to say more when the phone rang. It was on the table at his elbow, so he answered it. Doc Newman was on the other end. Danny was instantly on edge.

"What is it? Something wrong after all?"

"No, no. Nothing wrong with Gabby. All the X rays look good."

"Then what *is* wrong?"

"I, uh— Is Addy there, Danny?"

"Yes, but—"

"Fine. I think I'd better speak with her if you don't mind."

He did mind. He minded one hell of a lot. But he took the phone to Addy. "I expect to know what this is all about."

She snatched the phone from him with the glare she hadn't been able to muster a few moments earlier. He watched as she talked, staying close by on the off chance he could overhear some of what the doctor said. He couldn't. And Addy's responses told him absolutely nothing, although it did seem to him that her pale cheeks grew even paler for a moment.

"I see." She was very still. "All right." Then she began to fidget with the corner of the pot holder she had been working on. "Yes, I can do that."

She hung up then, set the phone on the table beside her and picked up her needle.

"Well?"

"Well what?" She kept her eyes on her work.

"Don't play games with me, Addy. What's wrong?"

"Nothing's wrong. Everything is... perfectly normal."

"What did he say?"

"He said I should start taking vitamins." Then she smiled, a baffling, mysterious kind of smile that needled him coming from this woman he used to think he knew so well.

She wouldn't budge an inch, of course, and when he went back to the plant he knew no more than he had when he'd first picked up the phone and heard Doc Newman's voice. He had known in his heart that Addy wasn't well, and he fantasized about ways to find out whatever it was Addy didn't want him to know, from bribing Doc Newman's nurse to breaking into the office after hours and rifling through the files.

"I could call my mother-in-law and ask her," he said to Tony as they went about their nightly closing-up ritual.

Tony shook his head and gave the stack of dirty ashtrays on the bar a deep, dark frown. "No. No, this is not a good plan, to get behind your woman's back. No, I think the break-and-entrance, she is the best idea."

"You think I'm joking."

A twinkle sparked to life in Tony's dark eyes. "One only can hope, *mi amigo*."

Danny sighed heavily and leaned against a bar stool. "Okay. Maybe I am a little out of control on this thing. I just know one thing: thinking something might be wrong with Addy, well, it makes me realize something."

"Yes?"

Danny's hands were splayed on the bar and his eyes were drawn to his wedding band. "I can't imagine life without her."

"Then things are suddenly much easier, yes?"

Staring at the gold-and-silver ring, Danny remembered the day they had gone to pick out the bands. The task had taken two days and involved trips to Tuscaloosa and Birmingham because Addy knew what she wanted and wouldn't settle for anything else.

He smiled and closed his fist so the ring disappeared from view. "You don't know Addy."

D DAY MINUS ONE and Addy had worked at a fever pitch to keep from thinking. Now every scrap of fabric in the house had been used, her monthly quota of angels had been completed and delivered to Bunny's Country Bumpkin Boutique and she had nothing but housework to keep her from thinking about her fourteenth anniversary the next evening.

Some anniversary. What should be a real celebration was reduced to Danny coming for dinner. Danny and six noisy children. Somehow it seemed safer that way, with her worrying that Danny's answer to her ultimatum might not be what she'd bargained for. With her worrying, period, but not wanting to influence his decision. She wanted him back because he wanted to come back. She would keep her worries—and her news—to herself until she knew.

She took the bucket out of the laundry room, poured in a generous amount of ammonia cleaner and realized right away that scrubbing the floors was not going to agree with her unsettled tummy. Leaving the bucket on the kitchen counter, she went out the back door and sat in one of the lawn chairs. In two hours, the children would start pouring in from school, Gabby would come home from playing with the neighbors, and it would be time to start supper. Maybe she would just sit for a few minutes, try to rest.

So weary that even her fears of losing Danny and facing an uncertain future couldn't keep her awake, Addy had just dozed off when she heard a voice from the driveway.

"Mrs. Mayfield?"

Addy's eyes popped open. Her glasses were halfway down her nose, and she reached up to straighten them, smudging them in the process. When she looked up at the voice, she was startled by the difference between this Cybil Richert and the one who had all but staggered into her front yard the afternoon before.

Both were turned out like a magazine spread on New York fashions. But this one had none of the brashness and bravado of the one from the day before. This one looked and sounded unsure of herself. This one looked troubled. This one's hands shook. This one made it easy to see the wisdom in Eulainie Cook's admonition to give everyone the benefit of the doubt.

Addy smiled and pointed to the other lawn chair. "Have a seat."

Cybil looked doubtful. "I came to apologize."

"That was real thoughtful of you."

"I know I created a real mess here yesterday, and I just had to come by and say how sorry I am. And to make sure the little girl is okay."

"Gabby is fine. Please, have a seat. Can I get you something cold to drink?"

Anxiety flashed over Cybil's face, and she dropped into the chair as if her legs had been knocked out from under her. "Oh, no. No, I don't want anything to drink."

All the sympathy in Addy's heart went out to the woman. She'd never been around heavy drinkers enough to understand what drove them to keep creating havoc in their lives, but she had seen the results in the lives of some of her children—and Danny—enough to know what an insidious problem it could be. Looking into Cybil's face, it was clear to Addy that Cybil was as much her own victim as anyone else was.

"I was thinking a tall glass of iced tea would be nice," she said gently. "Sure you won't join me?"

Cybil nodded and Addy went after the tea. When she came back and handed her visitor a frosty glass, she realized Cybil's hands still shook.

"This is awfully nice of you, Mrs. Mayfield."

"Sometimes things get turned upside-down when we didn't even mean them to," Addy said softly.

"It's because I...I drink too much. I quit for a while, but when your daughter's been taken away and..." Cybil's hands shook so hard the tea in her glass was in danger of sloshing out. Clasping it carefully with both hands, she set the glass on the metal table between their chairs. "Anyway, I'm not going to make any more mistakes. I know what I need to do now and...I'm going to do it."

Mixed with Addy's sympathy was a touch of uneasiness. "What is it you need to do now?"

Cybil kept her eyes trained on the edge of the woods. "I won't keep you any longer. I just wanted you to know I'm sorry. And I hope your little girl's okay."

Cybil Richert left right after that. Addy told herself at least she had something to worry over besides the wreckage of her own life. She could worry over whether or not to tell Rose or Ben about her visit from Cybil. But what could she tell them, really? That she had come to apologize? That she'd said she wouldn't make any more mistakes?

That her sixth sense had kicked in and told her Cybil was convinced that getting Krissy back—no matter what she had to do—would solve all her problems?

That thought resolved the dilemma, and she went into the house and dialed Rose's number.

As she listened to the ringing, however, she wondered how much her foreboding had to do with recognizing how much her own thinking mirrored Cybil Richert's. Hadn't she always thought that getting Danny back—even with all the same old disagreements—would solve all her problems?

Maybe it wasn't meant to be, she thought as Rose answered and she launched into a halting explanation. Maybe no woman was supposed to be given *all* her dreams. But losing Danny was more than she had ever expected to have to pay.

CHAPTER SEVENTEEN

BETSY FOSTER WATCHED the comings and goings across the street, peeking cautiously between the snugly closed curtains in her bedroom window. No one could see her even if they did happen to look up. Which seemed highly unlikely, considering the fact that everybody in Sweetbranch seemed completely focused on those young Mayfields.

She, of course, had stayed out of it. None of her business whether they celebrated their anniversary or not.

Betsy was about to drop the corner of the curtain and shut off her view of the Mayfield house when she saw Jacob Finley sneaking around the side of the house in the deepening dusk like some arthritic old cat burglar.

Her own daughter had started off the parade of busybodies about an hour ago. No sooner had Danny Mayfield's pickup pulled up behind the house than Susan and Tag were on the doorstep. Minutes later they left, everyone waving goodbye at the door. Reno, the oldest girl, was with them. Betsy had spoken to Susan earlier, so she knew their ploy: they had asked if the twelve-year-old could help them baby-sit Susan's young grandson, Cody.

"As if a twelve-year-old is going to be one whit of help with a little scamp like Cody," Betsy muttered into the empty, echoing house.

But no one had asked her opinion. No one had asked what she thought when her granddaughter had decided to admit she was actually Cody's mother. Or when Susan married that ne'er-do-well Tag Hutchins. No, nobody seemed to want Betsy's opinion anymore, especially since her stroke. If they did, she would have been glad to tell them to stay out of the Mayfields' lives.

That much she was beginning to learn herself.

After Susan came two strangers, tall, attractive African-American women, and they left a few minutes later with the youngest boy who stayed with the Mayfields. He carried a suitcase and waved interminably, and everyone seemed overjoyed with *that* departure.

Then Ben and Rose McKenzie showed up and took off with a carful of children. Miniature golf in Muscle Shoals was their destination, Jacob Finley had told her. Then the children would sleep over with their grandmother.

With a disapproving sniff, Betsy saw the lights go off in the Mayfield house and knew Jacob had completed his assignment at the fuse box.

"Adolescent fiddle-faddle," she snapped, at last dropping the curtain and starting down the stairs. She'd told him so, too, when the scheming started making the rounds in town.

"Those two can work out their own problems with no help from the rest of this town," she'd said the day she ran into him leaving the pharmacy.

He'd chuckled. "And here I thought you believed the world wouldn't keep revolving if you didn't get in your two cents' worth."

"I've a good mind to tell them what's going on."

"I wouldn't do that if I were you, Betsy." And for once there was no hint of a twinkle in his eyes. "Lots of people are trying to do a good turn here. Why, even Mellie over at the diner pitched in with the supper."

"And what bit of nonsense are you pitching in?"

The twinkle was back. "Me? Why, I'm going to see to it they eat by candlelight."

And so he had.

Betsy walked downstairs and sat in her own dark living room, which was not lit by candles. She thought about her daughter and great-grandson, who were right across the street but wouldn't be coming over because she'd made it clear she had little use for her new son-in-law. She sat in the darkness and stewed about the town that had rallied to give her neighbors a night of romance.

The one thing she wouldn't stew about was where Jacob Finley had gone after he removed the fuses at the Mayfield house. If he traipsed off like some young fool to keep that featherheaded Eulainie Cook company, it was certainly none of her affair. After all, at her age, Betsy was hardly looking for a beau. Especially one who had already deserted her once.

SOMEHOW, ALTHOUGH everything had gone wrong tonight, things couldn't have been more perfect.

Addy told herself that might be a silly way to look at things, but as she dished beef burgundy and new potatoes out of the chafing dishes Mellie had brought from the diner and set the good china plates on the candlelit table, she couldn't help but feel that some guardian angel had been looking over things tonight.

"Lucky thing you had candles," Danny said, pouring glasses of the fancy French wine he'd said Tony insisted on giving them.

"I wouldn't have if it weren't for Bunny." She sat at the seldom-used dining room table and took in the romantic setting. "When I took some things over to the boutique yesterday, she insisted I bring some home. Said they were scented and she wanted my opinion."

Danny had his hand on the stem of one of the goblets they were using as wineglasses, and she thought for a moment he would propose some kind of toast. But the moment passed and she told herself there was no reason to feel disappointed as they started the meal.

He'd looked wonderful to her the minute he showed up, but she had to admit the candlelight did exciting things to his appearance. His dark hair seemed to shine and the shadows accentuated his dimples, made his jaw look even stronger and more determined. His hands looked especially appealing in the dim light. She kept hoping he would touch her. Take her hand in his, maybe. Kiss her lightly. The way they kissed in movies while dining by candlelight. Lips barely brushing, while everybody in the audience knew their hearts were racing out of control.

The way hers was.

She wondered whether Danny felt that way. Whether he was sorry all the kids were gone. Whether he had places he would rather be tonight.

She couldn't think that way. Things had happened this way for a reason. Things had happened this way to give them a chance. Maybe, she thought, the candlelight would make everything a little softer, a little easier, tonight. Even sharing her news.

Her hand gave an involuntary quiver and she set her goblet down quickly. They were going to be parents. Right now, deep inside her, their very own baby was growing. After all these years, she was pregnant.

Strong feelings fluttered through her and she had to restrain herself to keep from putting a hand on her erratic heart.

"I still can't believe the turnaround in Casey's mother," he said.

"I know. It's like a miracle." As was the baby she nurtured inside herself.

And she thought of what Casey had said, about the angels telling Gabby his mother would get well soon. The call had come early today. Shoshonna Johnson was in complete remission. She and her aunt were coming for Casey, to take him home.

"Do you believe in miracles?" she asked.

"I don't know," he said. "Ask me later."

"I do."

He stared at her over his glass of wine. "Do you?"

She nodded, but still couldn't bring herself to tell him about her miracle.

"You look especially pretty tonight," he said.

She smiled, surprised she could feel this shy around the man she had been married to forever. "It's the candles. They hide all the flaws."

He shook his head. "No. I noticed it before. You have a glow. It seems to come right from the center of you, lighting you up all over."

She knew what it was. This was the moment she had wanted ever since he finished college, the moment she had begun to believe would never happen. The excitement and wonder of it had left her feeling charged, electrified. But how to tell Danny? How to even know if telling him was the right thing? If she told him now and they reconciled, could she ever be sure he had come back because he loved her? Or would she always wonder if his sense of responsibility had brought him home?

No, she had to wait for the right moment.

And hope she didn't explode first.

THE STEPS CREAKED BIG TIME. David stopped dead. Maybe this wasn't such a hot idea, after all. Holy moley, if he got caught at this, he'd be in deep you-know-what.

He took another creaky step, then another. He heard some guy laughing real loud, coming around from the front of the bar to the parking lot in the back. He ran the rest of the way up the steps. He was already in trouble, anyway, because before the night was over everybody would know he had sneaked out of the car when the McKenzies stopped for gas. That alone would buy him a major grounding, even if nobody ever figured out he was the one who went up to Danny's apartment.

The door was unlocked, which was lucky because he couldn't have broken the glass without the guy in the parking lot hearing. So he walked right in.

He wrinkled his nose as he walked around looking at Danny's pad. It was nothing like he'd expected. Sort of dumpy, really. He couldn't figure out why Danny would rather live here than back at the house, which always smelled like something good—cookies or bread or beef stew or something—and had this neat family room where you could flop around and watch TV and nobody yelled at you about putting your feet on the couch.

Actually, he figured he knew the reason. He was pretty good at math, even though he never turned in his homework so his grades always made it look like he was pretty much a meat head. But David knew how things added up. And it was like this: his own old man left after his mom died because he couldn't stand his own kid. Now Danny plus David equaled adios.

David shivered, although it was actually pretty warm up here. He didn't know where to start. All of a sudden, it didn't seem like as much fun as he'd thought it would be. Still, it was a good plan and he was sticking to it.

First he wrecked all the stuff in the kitchen. Poured stuff all over the place, taking care not to get any gross junk on his cast. Catsup and sugar and even a bowl of leftover chili beans he found in the tiny refrigerator. All in all, it was pretty cool.

He grinned at the thought of old Danny walking into this. Who wouldn't move out after finding all this glop? Anything would be better than having to clean it up.

Next, he took out his pocketknife and shredded the sheets and stabbed the feather pillows. Those feathers flew everywhere, and for a few minutes David forgot he was on a mission and just swatted them all over the place. *Awesome!*

The last thing he did was smash the TV. That was pretty cool. He looked down at all the broken glass and smiled. That ought to cinch it, because who could stay up here without a TV?

Yep, with no place else to go, Danny would have to come home.

And when he did, David would take off. 'Cause he knew how sad Addy had been without Danny. So he would fix everything he'd screwed up, then blow this joint so it didn't get screwed up again.

Satisfied, he folded up his pocketknife and headed for the door. But before he could step over the pile of junk that used to be a TV, someone stepped through the door he'd left standing wide open.

It was that girl. The one everybody said was Danny's new girlfriend. Anger and fear welled up in David.

"What are you doing here?"

She started at his voice. "Who are you?"

"You're not supposed to be here," he said, stepping in her direction and wishing he were just a little bit taller.

"Where's Danny?"

"He's at home. And you better leave him alone."

"Are you one of those kids? One of the ones his wife keeps taking in?"

"No. I'm nobody. Okay? Now, get out of here."

"Listen, I'm not—"

A third voice floated into the room from the bottom of the stairs. "Danny? Why do you have so much noise tonight? Is anything wrong?"

David groaned. He'd been caught for sure.

Worst of all, so had this bimbo with the mall bangs. Addy wasn't going to like this at all.

DANNY KNEW HE HAD TO GET his announcement out of the way, but he hated to spoil things.

This night was turning out so perfect. And deep down in the part of him that had learned in childhood that things were bound to go wrong whenever things seemed most right, he feared telling Addy what he'd decided. He had the words all lined up in his head, had tried them out in the lonely silence of his apartment the night before. But what if he told her he would agree to the adoptions she wanted only to discover she now had some other reason for telling him he couldn't come home? The what-ifs were driving him nuts, so he just kept holding her close while they moved to the music on the old stereo.

"I can't remember the last time we danced," she murmured.

"The beach, 1991," he said, wondering how long he could hold her this way without carting her off to bed. She was soft and delicate beneath his hands, and her thighs whispered against his like the voice of temptation. A man would be crazy to let a woman who still made him feel this way slip through his fingers. "The summer we had the twins."

"You remember?"

"I remember perfectly. Maggie and Maddie were sleeping on the porch, and you were wearing a sundress."

"And you were counting the freckles on my shoulders."

"I always liked those freckles." A man would be crazy to let a woman who had been his best friend for sixteen years slip through his fingers.

"That was the night we decided to adopt Brook." The music stopped, but they didn't. "You...you aren't sorry, are you? That we adopted her?"

"Never for a minute." He looked into her eyes. There it was, everything he loved about her. Her soft heart and her hard head, her temper and her tenderness. A man would have to be crazy... "I love Brook. I love all the kids."

Now, he told himself. Now tell her. But another impulse seemed more imperative.

"Danny, there's something I want to—"

"Later," he said, and lowered his lips to hers.

"But this is import—"

His lips brushed over hers, and her protest died on a breath of surrender, the way he'd hoped it would. "Not this important."

He explored her mouth in detail. The fullness of her lips, the smooth, damp, sweet recesses. Her playful tongue, the teeth that nipped and tugged at his lower

lip. Being home again, that's what he wanted. All he
wanted. And he would tell her that. Soon.

But not right this minute.

Right this minute, he was rediscovering the soft
planes of her body. The gentle slope of her hip and the
way it fit perfectly in the curve of his hand. The way
her waist dipped in. And her breasts, rising to his
touch, the moan in her throat speaking to him. Telling him a man would have to be crazy. Telling him—

The phone was ringing.

He ignored it.

Addy didn't. "What if something's happened?"

To one of the children. It could go unsaid because
it was one of the constants he'd been living with for
years. Only this time, he didn't mind. This time, he
realized that the strength of Addy's love for her children was part of what he loved about her. Without
that, she wouldn't be the woman who had kept him
happy and delighted and on his toes for so long.

She was about to pick up the phone, but he reached
around her and closed his fist around it first. In response to her look, he said, "In case it's somebody we
can hang up on."

She smiled, snuggling against his side as he spoke.

The solemnity in Tony's voice made him tense immediately. "*Mi amigo,* we have a slight problem."

"What?"

"One of your young boys, David, he has...ah, paid
you visit."

Danny knew there was more. "And?"

"I think the term is vandals."

"What!"

Addy jumped at the bite in his voice. "What's wrong?"

"Is real mess."

"Look, do me a favor and—"

Addy tugged on his sleeve. "Is it one of the children? It is, isn't it?"

"I am afraid you will have to come, Danny. Sheriff Baylow was downstairs when we hear the noise and..."

"Listen, just ask Mikah if he could—"

Addy's grip on his sleeve tightened. "The sheriff's there? Danny, what's going on?"

"There is one more thing, *mi amigo*."

"Okay. Let me have it."

"The girl, Heather. She is here, too."

"What do you mean?"

"In your apartment. I don't think this is going to straighten out so easy."

The sick feeling settled into the pit of Danny's gut. Just as he had known, the good stuff couldn't last. The bad stuff was always lurking, waiting to happen. "I'll be right there."

Addy was all over him as he hung up. "What, Danny? Tell me what happened? It's one of the kids, isn't it?"

He put his hands on her shoulders and faced with resignation the fact that white-lying his way out of a tough spot wouldn't work in Sweetbranch. The headline news network had nothing on the gossips in this town. Hell, he probably wouldn't get to Main Street before one of them would be on the phone to Addy.

"Nobody's hurt," he said. "But David's stirred up a little trouble."

"I'll get my purse."

Danny almost groaned. "There's no need for—"

She already had her purse in hand and was headed for the door. "What did he do?"

"I think he trashed my apartment."

"What?"

He caught her by the wrist. "I wish you'd stay here."

"Why?" she asked, sounding suddenly suspicious. "He's hurt, isn't he? There's something you don't want me to know."

"Well . . . He . . ." Danny sighed heavily. Better him than someone else, he supposed. "When Tony and Mikah went up to see what all the ruckus was about . . . David wasn't alone."

"Not Terrell? If Terrell was there, I don't believe for one minute that—"

"Not Terrell."

"Who, then?"

"Heather."

"Heather *Yates?*"

He nodded.

"She was *in your apartment?*"

"Don't you think it would be better if you stayed here, Addy?"

She slipped her wrist out of his grasp. "I'm going with you."

What scared him most was her voice. She didn't even sound angry. And if there was one thing he didn't know how to handle, it was an Addy who didn't get angry.

CHAPTER EIGHTEEN

HER ANNIVERSARY celebration in pieces at her feet, Addy walked numbly through the rest of the evening.

David was belligerent and refused to discuss why he had vandalized Danny's apartment. "Go ahead and lock me up," he kept saying.

David's tough comment brought a smile to Sheriff Baylow's lips. But Addy didn't find much that was funny about the situation. Her hands were cold, and her heart had squeezed itself into a tight, thumping, painful ball in her chest. Her face, luckily for her, had frozen in place. She hoped it looked stern but unmoved.

She couldn't bear it if all the people milling around in the Holy Spirits parking lot when she arrived had been able to read a bunch of feelings she didn't even know about herself. Because they had to be there. She had to be hurting. She had to be angry. She just couldn't feel it right now.

Not even with Heather Yates pouting and slumped against the closet door.

Danny was grim-faced and angry and seemed to think that hurrying everybody out of his apartment was the best solution to the evening's problems.

"Let's make it quick, Mikah," he said to the sheriff. "We know what happened here. Do we really have to have a federal inquisition?"

Mikah Baylow just looked at Danny, shook his head and said to David, "Now, son, I know this was some kind of fun and games to you. But it's serious business, and I got to say, we're gonna find out one way or the other if somebody else was in on this thing. You hear?"

"I already told you. It was just me."

Mikah sighed and directed a question at Tony.

Addy's head was spinning. If she didn't sit down, she might fall down. But the only place to sit was on the bed, and she wasn't about to sit there, or on the steps outside, either. As far as she knew, the deputy's car was still in the parking lot with its red light flashing and the rest of the lot was still filled with gawkers.

"Now, one more time," said the sheriff, who was obviously enjoying his shot at a big-time crime-scene investigation. "What exactly were you doing here, Heather?"

Heather mumbled something, so low Addy couldn't hear it. Apparently neither could anyone else. Mikah asked her to repeat her answer.

"I wanted to talk to Danny."

"Were you in the habit of visiting Danny up here?"

"Oh, for— Mikah!"

Danny's vehement protest drove something sharp and painful through Addy's chest. She shouldn't have come. She should have done exactly what Danny told her to do and stayed home. She might be sitting there making herself crazy imagining stuff, but at least she wouldn't be making herself crazy right here in front of the whole world.

"Danny, it's nothing personal," Mikah said. "I've got an official report to file, that's all, and I need all the facts."

Addy's world was coming to an end, and all anybody could think to do about it was file a report with the sheriff's department. She couldn't think of a soul she had ever hated in her life, but right now she might hate Mikah Baylow for the glee with which he was checking and double-checking the facts. And for the relish with which he would no doubt repeat all those facts over breakfast at the Clock the next morning.

"I've never been up here before," Heather said as Mikah continued. "You can put me under oath and I'd say the same thing."

Heather's timid protest didn't do much for Addy's confidence in the girl's story, either.

Addy didn't look at Danny, because it hurt too much. And she couldn't look at Heather, although she wanted to glare a big hole right through her, because she guessed she didn't want to see whatever was in the girl's face. So she finally did the only thing that came naturally.

She went over to David and pulled him close. He remained stiff in her embrace, but she kept her arm around him, anyway. He needed somebody, even if he didn't know how to admit it. "Mikah, nobody here is going to file charges against this boy, so I'd like to take him home. It's late and he needs to be in bed."

"Well, now, Miz Mayfield..."

"She's right, Mikah." Danny edged closer to her, and she thought if he put a hand on her, he might somehow manage to penetrate the barrier of numbness that was keeping her from making a fool of herself in front of the whole darned town. "Let me get her and the boy home. You and I can take care of anything else you need after that."

"I want Mikah to take us home," she said, putting all the determination she had into her voice.

"Now, Addy..."

"Will that be all right, Mikah?"

The sheriff looked at Danny. Then the direction of his gaze slid ever so slightly toward Heather. "Yes, ma'am. I reckon that'll be just fine."

The one idea Addy didn't want to entertain for long was the thought that her husband would be left alone here with Heather Yates. So she marched out the door and down the stairs, refusing to think, her arm around David's narrow shoulders, which slumped in a way that perfectly matched her own frame of mind. She, however, went down to the sheriff's car with her shoulders back and her chin up.

She was in the back seat with David, about to shut the door, when someone stopped her. She looked up into Heather's face. It was filled with sympathy, and Addy wanted to crawl under something.

"Honest, Miz Mayfield, I truly do regret making this worse than it had to be. I...I know I've caused everybody a lot of trouble. I...I just came tonight to thank Danny for putting in a good word for me with Mr. McKenzie. That's all."

Addy's mouth was so dry she could barely form words. "Don't worry about it, Heather. You didn't do anything wrong."

At least, she hoped not.

The car pulled out of the parking lot, lights still flashing. The last thing Addy saw was Danny standing at the top of the steps, looking forlorn.

Addy wanted to cry, but darn if she would. She had wanted so badly to tell him her news. Wanted to see his face when she told him they were going to be parents. Wanted, even, to make love with that knowledge between them. Would it have been as sweet as she had imagined?

But now a part of her had to be glad she hadn't said anything. Because if he knew, he would come home. And if she had learned one thing tonight, it was that she didn't want him with any doubts between them— his or hers. She wanted him not because he felt obligated, but because he wanted her, too. And she wanted him only if she could trust him wholeheartedly.

Right now she was too confused and too hurt to sort out whether that was possible.

As the sheriff's department car turned down Mimosa Lane, David whispered, "Isn't he going to arrest me?"

Addy tried for a reassuring smile. "No. You might get sentenced to cleaning up tomorrow. But you won't have to be a jailbird."

They got out of the car and walked toward the house, where the lights that had been out earlier in the evening now blazed. As if someone knew there was no longer any need for a touch of romance. Addy ignored the hurt as she sent David off to get ready for bed.

When she went in to tuck him in, he had already pulled the covers up tightly under his chin. His usual irrepressible smile hadn't surfaced all night. "I guess you guys'll hate me for sure now."

Addy sat on the edge of the bed and smoothed the carrot-colored cowlick at his forehead. "We still love you just as much as we always did."

David looked away.

"What is it, David?"

"I thought if he had nowhere else to go, maybe he'd come home. 'Cause I know how much you miss him."

Addy certainly didn't have the heart to tell the little boy that, if anything, he had simply reinforced Danny's conviction that there were too many children in the Mayfield house. "I do miss him. But we can't force him to come home."

It crossed her mind that she had, however, forced him to stay away on more than one occasion when he had wanted to come home.

She kissed David on the forehead. "Sweet dreams."

When she turned out the light, he called, "You really think I'll have to clean up all that glop?"

THE REVEREND WESTON SISKE hated to be critical, but he had expected better of his first dinner on the grounds as new pastor of the Sweetbranch First Freewill Baptist Church.

Oh, the food was glorious, as he'd heard it would be. Betsy Foster's famous coconut cake rose high and light, a cloud of temptation on one of the several folding tables that lined the churchyard. Bump Finley's fried chicken, according to more than one veteran observer, was close to perfect, and the potato salad Bump's niece, Rose McKenzie, brought was highly sought after by connoisseurs. Susan and Tag Hutchins had contributed fresh-baked yeast rolls, and Susan's daughter, Malorie, and her young husband, Sam, had signed up for iced tea duty. The Reverend Siske smiled at that; newlywed couples had better things to perfect than the family recipe for squash casserole. Pecan pie and collard greens and corn bread and pickled okra, all that and more were certainly enough to tempt even a saint.

But something else about the day troubled the Reverend Siske, something he couldn't quite put his finger on. He was new and he was young—small-town parishioners still thought of forty-six as young, he had learned, even if you'd been a widower for five years—but he still knew people well enough to sense when something wasn't quite right.

And today, the people of the Sweetbranch First Freewill Baptist Church were covering up some things that definitely weren't quite right.

The Reverend Siske mingled, tasting everything and complimenting all the cooks and urging his new parishioners to call him Wes.

Betsy Foster gave him a hard look when he said that. Harder than her usual hard look. "Well, I'm not sure I'll be able to manage that, Reverend Siske."

He smiled, anyway, and nodded toward the table, where Betsy's coconut cake was disappearing faster than anything else. "Mighty fine cake, Mrs. Foster."

"It's a God-given talent, I'm sure," she announced with pleased piousness.

Wes Siske wondered that she didn't seem more grateful for the God-given blessing of her family. She hadn't exchanged a word with any of them all day long. In fact, Betsy Foster's disapproval and disappointment in them were written all over her face.

"I only made it because my son-in-law once said coconut is his favorite," she continued.

"What a nice thought." But it didn't explain the way she had snubbed Tag Hutchins when he came by to fill a plate for his wife and himself. "Have you let him know you made this gesture just for him?"

"Well, certainly not."

The gravelly voice of Bump Finley squeezed its way into their conversation. "She's got a reputation to protect, Rev. Doesn't want the townsfolk thinking she's gone soft since that little stroke she had. Right, Bets?"

"Jacob, you're an old fool."

Wes tried not to smile, even when Bump Finley cackled and retorted, "Reckon I'm in good company, then."

Betsy flushed and chose to ignore Bump Finley, speaking directly to Reverend Siske. "My son-in-law and I are not on the best of terms. He drove his mother—my best friend—to an early grave. I tried to give him the benefit of the doubt, but I fear I am not yet charitable enough to forgive him. Or bless his union with my daughter. She is vulnerable, you know."

He took her hand in his and squeezed it, "I suggest you pray for him, Mrs. Foster. He doubtless needs it."

Everyone he sought out seemed troubled, and it occurred to him he had his work cut out for him here in Sweetbranch. Ben and Rose McKenzie seemed tense, more watchful of young Krissy and Jake than seemed warranted here in such a small town. And he couldn't help but notice that they pulled their two out of the herd of children who had congregated after dessert to play Red Rover and Mother, May I in the side of the yard not taken up by tombstones. If he wasn't mistaken, they kept casting nervous glances in the direction of a woman who seemed to be alone. An outsider, Wes would have guessed, because she didn't dress like most of the other people here. Tall and slender and coolly blond in the way of a Hitchcock movie star, she piqued Wes's interest. Everyone else, however, seemed as suspicious of her as the McKenzies.

Wes made up his mind to speak to her, to offer his welcome even if no one else did. But before he could make his way across the lawn, she had disappeared.

The only one busier than Wes was Bump Finley, whose stiff-kneed stride took him first to Betsy Foster, then to Eulainie Cook and back again. Back and forth he went all afternoon. By the time the coconut cake had been reduced to crumbs and every bite of Eulainie's sweet potato soufflé had been scraped from the side of the dish, Bump Finley looked as if he needed something for his game knee and something for his indigestion, as well.

"I ain't much cut out for this Don Juan stuff anymore," he grumbled when Wes passed close by.

"It's been my experience," Wes replied, "that one good woman is more than most of us mortal men can handle."

"I 'spect that's the gospel truth. It's just figuring out which one's the *right* one. Now *that's* the trick. And I ain't found the man upstairs any too eager to give me the benefit of his wisdom, either. He ain't talking."

Wes laughed. "Maybe you aren't listening."

Bump thought about that a moment, then laughed. "That's what Rose says is my biggest problem. I tell 'er I'm hard of hearing, but she says I hear whatever I want to hear."

"I suppose the man upstairs finds that's true of many of us."

Bump shook his head ruefully and rubbed his knee. "Maybe I'll see if I can manage to listen a mite closer next time He's talking to me about womenfolk."

At least Bump Finley appeared to take everything in good humor, which was more than Wes could say for anyone else.

The saddest case, of course, was the Mayfield family. Wes, like everyone else in town, had heard about what happened Friday night. But both Danny and Addy showed up, children in tow.

"So glad to see the two of you," he said as Addy examined a scraped knee on one of the little girls and sent her back for another round of Red Rover. She had coaxed the dark-haired little girl with the gap-toothed smile back into a good mood in seconds while Danny looked on. Wes knew of only one way to describe the look on the young man's face.

Lovesick.

Unfortunately, the young couple didn't look at each other, and they didn't look directly at him, either.

"The children really didn't want to miss it," Addy said, and Wes knew that was the only reason they had shown up.

"But Addy's tired," Danny said, putting his hand on her shoulder. "I don't think we'll stay long."

Wes saw the instantaneous look of comfort that came unbidden into Addy's face with Danny's touch. She banished it just as quickly. But it was there long enough for Wes to realize that she loved her husband as desperately as he loved her. Wes knew love when he saw it.

"I understand," he said. "We make many sacrifices for our children. But it's important to remember to care for ourselves, too. Please, if there's anything I can do, anytime, I hope you'll let me know."

Danny looked hopeful; Addy looked doubtful. Both of them looked to be hurting. Wes wasn't surprised when they rounded up the children and left shortly thereafter. As he watched them go, he couldn't resist sending up a silent plea for help in healing their relationship.

When he finished his prayer, the smallest of the five children turned back and looked at him, flashing a dimpled grin and nodding her bouncy golden curls in his direction. Almost as if she had heard his thoughts and agreed wholeheartedly. He smiled at her and felt better without understanding why.

AFTER ADDY AND THE KIDS went home, Danny knew he had to do something besides go back to that empty, lonely apartment. He thanked his lucky stars that David had been over all day on Saturday, cleaning up the mess he'd made. At least he hadn't been alone, going stir-crazy.

So instead of spending the rest of his Sunday alone and brooding, Danny decided to go to the plant. He could catch up on paperwork, get a head start on payroll. Something. Anything.

He was slumped in his chair and staring at the blank wall across from his desk when the phone rang hours later. Unable to imagine who would call here on a Sunday, he was startled by the sound of Addy's breathless voice.

"Danny, thank God! I've been looking all over for you."

He bolted upright in his chair. "What's wrong? Are you okay?"

"It's Gabby." Her voice cracked and Danny heard the terror beneath her breathlessness. "Danny, she's disappeared!"

CHAPTER NINETEEN

ADDY WANTED TO BE STRONG, but all she could do was tremble.

Oh, Danny, hurry!

This was all too familiar—the house full of murmuring, solemn-faced townspeople, the quiet that had settled over even the children, the forceful bark of men in the yard as they marshaled forces and planned their strategy.

She remembered how it turned out, too. She had never again seen her little sister.

What if I never see Gabby again?

There was no one she dared say that to. No one, despite the fact the house was full—her mother, Rose, Susan and Maxine, plus a half dozen others who had come over with coolers full of soft drinks and pots of coffee for the searchers.

Where is Danny? It had been ages since she called him. She glanced at her watch. Four minutes, actually.

She jumped when a hand came down gently on her shoulder, and she looked up into Rose McKenzie's comforting face. "Can I get you anything?"

"No. No, I'm fine."

Rose would know it was a lie, but Addy knew that admitting otherwise would mean losing control completely.

Hurry, Danny. Hurry!

The children, her own and the neighbor children who had come with their parents, were watching a video in the family room. Addy longed for the comfort of her favorite, ratty orange rocker. But she couldn't bear to see the children, because none of them had a headful of golden curls.

She heard a familiar engine screech to a halt in the driveway and dashed outside. She threw herself into Danny's arms and felt him absorb her trembling.

"I don't know what happened," she said, her voice thick with tears. "One minute they were all playing in the backyard. Then a stray puppy came through and everybody got distracted, and the next thing we knew... Oh, Danny, if something's wrong, she can't even call out to let us know where she is!"

He rocked her gently in his arms and murmured the comforting nonsense that only husbands are allowed to say. She wanted to stay right there, but he backed away gently, still holding her shoulders in his big, capable hands.

"It's going to be all right, Addy. I promise. I'll find her."

She nodded. A hundred men in town might be looking, but now that Danny was here, she could believe everything would be all right, just the way he said it would be.

He gave her a quick, hard kiss, then turned to the clutch of men gathered at the end of the driveway. She heard them explain that the woods—and that meant the creek—were already saturated with searchers. So Danny agreed to join the smaller numbers of men who were fanning out toward town.

As he moved off, giving Addy a quick, reassuring wave, David burst through the door, whizzed past Addy and caught up with Danny.

"I'm going, too."

Danny looked down at the redheaded boy who had caused so much trouble less than forty-eight hours earlier. Addy moved toward them, knowing Danny wouldn't want a child tagging along, slowing him down.

"You'll have to keep up," Danny said, putting a hand on the boy's shoulder.

The face of the young-man-to-be appeared for a fleeting moment in the buck-toothed, freckled face of the boy. And Addy knew another level of love for the man who had brought it out.

"I won't hold you back," David said.

Danny nodded at him, man to man, and they started off together down Mimosa Lane.

This time, the arm around Addy's shoulders belonged to her mother. "Don't worry. She'll turn up soon. All children wander off."

"It's getting dark."

Eulainie looked up. In another hour, Addy knew, dusk would descend on Sweetbranch. It had been nearing dusk the other time, too.

"Mother?"

"Yes?"

"I'm sorry. About Wynona."

Surprise and dismay and a hint of twenty-year-old grief swept over Eulainie's face. "Why, honey, you've got no reason to be sorry about that."

"But I was supposed to be watching out for her. I was the big sister. I should have ... done something."

Eulainie wrapped her arm more tightly around Addy. "None of us could have done anything. And none of us can know why things like this happen. All I know is, we aren't meant to blame ourselves."

"Didn't you blame me?"

Tears misted Eulainie's eyes. "Not for a second."

"I did."

"Ah, Addy, no wonder you're always trying to save the world." Eulainie sighed. "Come back in the house. Maxine Hammond brought this wonderful coffee. Chocolate flavored. You and I are going to have a cup, and I'm going to tell you all about how Wynona couldn't have had a better big sister."

"You don't have to do that," Addy protested, her voice thick with tears she refused to shed. But she followed her mother, anyway.

"Then I'm going to tell you all about what you're going to do to be a better wife once all this is over."

"You are?"

"Mmm-hmm. And you're going to listen. For a change."

DAVID AND DANNY STUCK their heads inside sheds and garages, peered under porches and checked out a giant cardboard box the Lingerfelts had just brought home with their new microwave. David climbed up for a peek into the tree house behind the McKenzie house on Dixie Belle Lane.

"She could be there," the boy said, pointing to a peaked doghouse guarded by a none-too-friendly-looking pit bull.

"I hope not," Danny muttered.

"I'll go see."

"David, that dog might be—" Too late. David hadn't waited for the majority to rule on his hunch. "Mean."

The dog growled and looked menacing, but the boy crooned at him and moved slowly and came back to Danny's side all in one piece.

"The doghouse is clean, Chief."

Danny smiled, careful not to let the boy see it. "Good. Next time, wait for your backup."

David turned that impish, irresistible smile on him. "Oh. Sure."

They waved to other searchers, called out updates, studied the sky. Darkness was approaching far too quickly to suit Danny.

They went to the park. They went to the old drive-in theater with its garish For Sale sign and its jungle of weeds. They stopped at a pay phone to call the house and learned no one else was having any luck, either.

"Maybe I ought to take you back to the house before it gets any darker," Danny said, trying not to sound as discouraged as he felt. He could still see the despair in Addy's face. He knew its source. And he couldn't bear the thought of what she would put herself through if something happened to Gabby.

"I'm not afraid of the dark."

"I know. But Addy might worry if you're out late."

David grinned, but Danny could see it was forced. "Sure. I understand. A kid like me, I'll just be in the way." He kicked at the gravel in the driveway they were crossing. "Probably Addy'll need me, anyway. To help with the rest of the kids."

For the first time in the months David had lived with them, Danny truly heard the need in the little boy's voice. The need to be wanted. Valued. The need to know he wouldn't be abandoned again. He thought, now, about all the times that need had been there, in David's rambunctious actions, his never-failing smile. He thought, too, about how often he had managed not to see or hear that need.

That's what Addy did so well, so effortlessly. That was Addy's gift, and in that moment he knew an even greater love for the woman who wanted to heal so many hurts with nothing more than her own caring.

"Tell you what," he said. "I know Addy could use your help. But she's got lots of people with her back at the house. And I'm sort of on my own without you. If you're up for staying at this awhile, *I* could sure use you."

The smile, about a thousand watts' worth, flashed up at Danny. "Sure. I'm game."

It was David's idea, in fact, to go back to the church. "She didn't want to leave, 'cause we left early this afternoon," he said.

"She didn't?"

David shrugged. "Well, that's what Reno said. Reno acts like the little twerp is all the time talking to her. So Reno said Gabby wanted to stay and talk to the angels some more.''

And he rolled his bright blue eyes, as if such silly little-girl talk was more than he cared to recount and did so only because he knew it was his manly duty to pass on every clue.

"Then, let's go," Danny said, feeling a sudden excitement as he recalled that evening church services had been suspended for the day because of the town-wide search.

When Danny shoved on the heavy front door, however, his excitement dimmed. No little girl Gabby's size could have managed that door alone, even though it was unlocked. He called her name and headed for the soft light from the sanctuary.

"Come on out, twerp," David called out encouragingly. "You're not in real big trouble yet."

Danny walked into the sanctuary and peered around.

"I bet she'd go downstairs," David whispered. "There's lots of cool hallways and closets and stuff downstairs, where you could hide forever."

"We'll try there next," Danny said, drawn to the sanctuary as if being there might revive his hope.

What he saw first were the tufts of golden curls, wild and fuzzy and barely visible over the back of the front-row pew. Relief and disbelief flooded him. "Gabby!"

"Aw, cool, man! We found her!"

But Gabby didn't move, gave no indication she had heard them, and Danny had a moment of fear that something might yet be wrong with her. Pausing only momentarily to acknowledge David's gleeful high-five, he hurried to the front of the sanctuary.

She sat still and straight on the pew, pudgy hands clasped in the lap of the pink-and-white dress she had been wearing the day she appeared in the park. Her eyes were closed, and a small smile brought the barest hint of dimples to her cheeks.

"Gabby, you twerp, wake up!"

She opened her eyes then, slowly, and looked at them. Her smile widened, and Danny felt what Addy always said she felt, as if Gabby's smile bathed him in sunshine. He scooped her into his arms and hugged her to his chest.

"We were so worried about you, little one," he said, propping her on his hip. "Addy's going to be so glad to see you."

He looked down at David then. The smile was intact, but Danny could see the reticence in it, the uncertainty now that he was no longer a necessary part of the search team. Danny understood that what he saw was the little boy's belief that all the love and attention would now be showered on Gabby.

David was steeling himself against being left out in the cold.

He put his free hand on the boy's shoulder and said, "Man, I can't believe I was lucky enough to have you as my partner. You're the hero, man."

"Me?" The hope in David's eyes was tinged with mistrust.

"You were the one who thought of the church. If you hadn't been along, who knows what might have happened." Danny made up his mind at that moment. David was going to learn to trust again. He was going to have a family again. Addy was right. And he couldn't wait to tell her that David was going to be the first one they tried to adopt. "Addy's going to be so proud of you, David."

"She will?"

"You betcha. And so am I. Now, come on, gang. Let's head for home."

FROM HER POST at the kitchen table, Addy heard the cheer go up in the front yard. The sound was like fireworks, setting her asparkle.

"They found her!"

And without waiting for anyone else, she ran out the back door and down the driveway. Up ahead, she could see the procession, led by Danny, with Gabby sitting on his shoulders, grinning, and David striding alongside like the conquering hero.

After all the stoicism with which she'd faced the miserable six weeks just past, tears filled Addy's eyes. She blinked hard to keep them from spilling over, but it was a futile effort.

She rushed toward the trio, but found it hard to force her way through the crowd of searchers and neighbors and children and sheriff's deputies who now encircled Danny and the rest. Everyone was talking, laughing and crying. Addy waved over Sheriff Baylow's head and caught Danny's eye.

"You found her!"

"David knew right where to find her!" he called back, ignoring the hand that tugged on his sleeve. "He's the real hero."

That made the tears come heavier, and for a moment everything blurred out of focus.

"I love you," she said, but another shout drowned her out as the searchers from the woods began straggling back.

David bolted through a low-lying opening in the crowd and flung himself at Addy, encircling her waist with a hug. Her first hug from him, she was sure of it. "He said he couldn't have done it without me! 'Cause I remembered she might be in the church! And sure enough, there she was! It was so cool!"

She hugged him back and completely gave up trying to stem the flow of tears. "That's wonderful, David. I'm so proud of you."

Danny was closer now. He reached across the crowd and took her hand. "I'm coming home, Addy. Tonight. No argument."

For the first instant, she was thrilled. Then she remembered. He still didn't know about the baby. She had to tell him that before he came home. What if he changed his mind after he heard?

"But first—"

"No buts," he interrupted her, lifting Gabby off his shoulders and handing her over the sea of heads and shoulders into Addy's eager arms. "I'm going right now to get my things."

She kissed Gabby's cheek and said, "But if we could just—"

"I'll be back by the time this dies down," he said, already backing away. "We can talk then."

"But there's one thing you should—"

He blew her a kiss and was gone, swallowed up by the crowd.

It took an hour for everyone to clear out and leave Addy in peace with her excited but weary brood. She paced while they ate chicken noodle soup, and prayed that everything would work out when Danny came back. What if a new baby was the last straw?

When a vehicle pulled into the driveway, her heart started to thump with anticipation. Then she realized the vehicle wasn't the familiar old pickup, but the sheriff's patrol car. Sheriff Baylow was coming up the driveway with a woman Addy had never seen before. She peered out the window, reluctant somehow to greet him. One of the children passed her, and she looked down to see Gabby opening the front door.

"Mommy!"

Addy's heart almost stopped when Gabby shouted the greeting and headed right into the strange woman's arms.

CHAPTER TWENTY

THINGS HAPPENED SO FAST, Addy could hardly take it all in. One minute she was rejoicing that the little girl who had stolen her heart so completely was safely home. The next, she was grieving that that little girl was going away with a woman she called Mommy.

Sheriff Baylow looked apologetic as he explained that someone from the state bureau of missing people had been waiting when he got back to his office, with Mrs. Peterson. "She's got all the documentation we need, Addy."

"Yes, I see," Addy said, noting with a pain around her heart the way her Gabby clung to Mrs. Peterson. Mrs. Peterson called her Gabrielle. Both their faces shone with adoration, and Gabby's expression was strangely beatific.

"Strangest thing how this happened," Mikah said, launching into the details of Gabby's disappearance. "Apparently one day Gabby just wandered away. Mrs. Peterson said she knew she'd find her when it was time. Danged if I know what's going on."

Drawn by some childhood sixth sense, the other four children wandered out of the kitchen, wiping their milk mustaches and looking curiously at Gabby and the strange woman. They reacted quietly when they heard the news, especially David, and said their goodbyes with a calm acceptance that Addy envied.

Addy felt cheated.

She wanted to be angry with the woman who had come for this little girl who felt like part of the fiber of Addy's being. Angry that she hadn't come long before now, before Addy had a chance to love so much. Angry that the first time—the only time—she'd heard Gabby's voice it was to hear the child call someone else Mommy. But as she looked at the plump, motherly woman, Addy's anger and sense of betrayal simply evaporated. Mrs. Peterson radiated the same sense of serenity as Gabby.

Addy felt the peace of knowing that little Gabrielle had been with her only a short time, but had brought her so much. And that was the way it was meant to be.

When the others had said their goodbyes, Gabby came back to Addy and put her arms around Addy's neck and whispered, "It's all fixed now. Don't worry anymore."

DANNY SAW THE DISTRESS in Addy's face as soon as he walked back into the house. The children were in bed, and she sat in her orange rocker in the dark. But he could see.

He knelt beside her. "It's over now, Addy. There's nothing else to worry about."

Her smile was strange. "You don't know. She's gone, Danny. Gone for good."

"What do you mean?"

"Her mother came. She's gone."

He gathered her in his arms and let her talk it out. An emptiness in his heart answered what he heard in her voice. He knew that Addy was glad Gabby would be going home, where she belonged. And so was he. But he also understood the barren feeling that came with losing a child who had worked her way so thoroughly into your heart.

He would tell her about wanting to adopt David and the others later, when she wasn't grieving. He didn't want her to think he was offering this decision as some kind of consolation prize; it was something he'd decided long before now.

"I'm going to take you to bed now," he said softly, and started to pick her up.

"No!" She backed out of his arms. He'd known she was upset, but her vehemence startled him. "No. First I have to tell you."

He remembered, then, how impatient she had been to tell him something earlier in the day. "What?"

She studied him closely, warily. "I'm pregnant."

What struck Danny first about her message wasn't the content but the tone. She sounded belligerent, as if she expected him to protest. He was filled with disappointment when he realized she didn't know whether to fully trust him again. He could understand, but it still hurt.

She whirled and turned away. "I knew it. You're not happy about it."

Slowly, he stopped reacting to her mood and her message sank in. *Pregnant. A baby! Their baby!* Danny had to admit, the news had him in shock. After all this time, he'd thought it would never happen. And now, when everything was upside down—

He realized, too late, that she had needed enthusiastic, wholehearted joy from him.

"That's not it, Addy. I'm not unhappy. I'm just—"

"Yes, you are," she mumbled miserably, hugging herself tightly and refusing to look at him.

"Well, it might be a little scary but—"

"Don't worry. I know how you feel about children."

Somewhere in the back of his mind, he remembered Ben McKenzie talking about how emotional Rose used to get during her pregnancy. And if anybody had a right to be emotional—maybe even a touch irrational—it was Addy, after the day she had been through.

"Why don't you just go, Danny, before you get the kids all excited again."

Like a sailor sniffing bad weather, Danny knew exactly what would happen if he stayed. Another big fight. And he didn't want Addy going through that right now. So he did the hardest thing he'd done since the last time he'd taken his clothes and left.

He took his clothes and left.

ADDY KNEW SHE WAS WRONG and unreasonable and all kinds of other unpleasant things she didn't have a name for. But she would get the children off to school and cancel her appointment with Ragan Hammond and call Danny at the plant and do whatever she had to do to make sure that Gabby's last words to her were true.

It's all fixed now. Don't worry anymore.

The children ate their breakfast more quietly than usual, and she wandered through the house, making beds. She got to Gabby's bed, which hadn't been touched. There beneath the spread, she saw a funny lump and figured Gabby had forgotten her pajamas. She reached beneath the spread and pulled out the angel doll.

That almost brought the tears back. She touched the doll gently, remembering how much Gabby had loved it. She wondered if she should find out how to get in touch with Mrs. Peterson, see about getting the doll to Gabby.

Or maybe she should simply let it go.

Before she could decide, Brook came dashing back into the bedroom after her book bag.

"Oh, good! You found S'mantha." She wrinkled her nose and smiled sheepishly. "I forgot."

"What did you call her?" Addy shivered at the name, which just happened to be the name of another doll she knew she would never forget. Samantha. Her little sister's doll.

"S'mantha. Gabby wanted you to have it. I was s'posed to ask you to take care of S'mantha, but I forgot."

Addy touched the doll's whipstitched smile and felt a charge of energy. Like a touch.

"I'm sorry, Mommy."

Addy looked down at the sound of Brook's troubled voice. She smiled a bit uncertainly and said, "No, sweetheart. You did just fine."

Brook's beaming smile returned, and she darted out of the room as quickly as she had entered.

Addy touched the face of the doll Gabby had named Samantha, wondering at the coincidence. But the feeling from a moment ago was gone. Nevertheless, something remained. She felt light, as if she'd been freed of the burden she had carried so much of her life. She felt forgiven.

It's all fixed now. Don't worry anymore.

Hands trembling with the power of lingering sensations, Addy put the little doll inside her apron pocket. She couldn't explain what had just happened. But she accepted it for what it was—the grace of something greater than herself, bringing healing to her life. She headed for the kitchen; she wanted to give every child in the house a great big hug. Just to make sure they knew, as they went through the rest of the day, that they were loved.

She walked back into the kitchen at the same moment Danny came in through the back door, a big shopping bag in his hands, and a smile on his face. A smile just for her.

Gabby was right. Everything was fixed now. Addy smiled back at the man she loved, a smile promising she would do whatever she needed to do to preserve the gift of love they shared.

Suddenly the children spotted Danny, and the morning's quiet erupted into greetings and giggles.

Addy didn't even worry about the fact that they were overlapping into toothbrushing drill.

"Okay, everybody," Danny said with a ring of authority that gave her heart a boost. "Gather round. I've got some homecoming presents that need passing out."

"But you're the one coming home," Reno said. "We're supposed to give *you* presents."

Danny held up a hand. "Never fear. I've thought of everything."

With a flourish, he pulled a gold-and-purple baseball cap out of his bag. Across the front was written Manager. He pulled it on decisively and the children cheered and applauded. Addy just smiled.

"And, for the lady of the house..." He pulled another cap out of the bag and displayed its letters so everyone could see.

This cap read Coach. He pulled it down over Addy's mass of unruly curls, and again everyone cheered.

Then he started passing out softball shirts, one for each of the children. On the front of each shirt were the words Addy's Angels. Everyone liked that, but the squeals really began when Brook discovered that on the back of each shirt were the words Danny's Devils.

Terrell was already tugging his T-shirt on, and Reno was helping Brook with hers. David merely clutched his in his fist, staring at Danny as if the sun had suddenly risen over the breakfast table.

When Danny finished distributing the shirts, only one was left. This one he presented to Addy. As she held it up, the noisy brood of children grew quiet once again.

The one remaining shirt was a very, very tiny one—just right for a newborn.

"Oh, Danny."

"Now, Addy, you're not going to cry on me, are you?"

She nodded. "Uh-huh."

And she did. And all the while, there were more cheers and more hugs and more than one big, sloppy kiss as the Mayfield clan reunited.

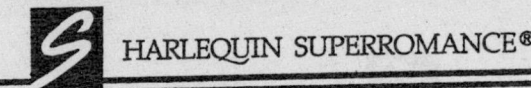

HARLEQUIN SUPERROMANCE®

An exciting new trilogy by *Peg Sutherland*

Welcome back to Sweetbranch, Alabama. Reintroduce yourself to old friends and make some new ones, too!

To an outsider, Sweetbranch may look like a sleepy small Southern town, but anyone who read Peg's outstanding Superromance novel *Late Bloomer* (#553) knows otherwise.

If you want to go back to the place where it all started, you can still order a copy of *Late Bloomer*. And don't forget to continue the adventure in

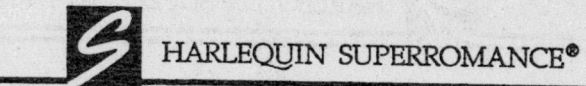

Emergency!

Dr. Stephanie Sheldon counseled pregnant teens. Now she was pregnant herself after a poignant one-night stand with Dr. Talbot Robichaux. How was she going to explain *that* one to her class?

Well, maybe it would be easier than she thought. Talbot proposed a marriage of convenience, and right now marriage would be very convenient indeed—if it wasn't for his resentful teenage daughter.

There were other complications too: her missing twin's daughter showed up at Stephanie's New Orleans clinic one day. How could she not offer *her* a home? Suddenly this makeshift family was growing faster every day—as were her feelings for Tal!

Look for this heartwarming story from Karen Young in February 1996 wherever Harlequin books are sold.

UNLOCK THE DOOR TO GREAT ROMANCE
AT BRIDE'S BAY RESORT

Join Harlequin's new across-the-lines series, set in an exclusive hotel on an island off the coast of South Carolina.

Seven of your favorite authors will bring you exciting stories about fascinating heroes and heroines discovering love at Bride's Bay Resort.

Look for these fabulous stories coming to a store near you beginning in January 1996.

Harlequin American Romance #613 in January
Matchmaking Baby by Cathy Gillen Thacker

Harlequin Presents #1794 in February
Indiscretions by Robyn Donald

Harlequin Intrigue #362 in March
Love and Lies by Dawn Stewardson

Harlequin Romance #3404 in April
Make Believe Engagement by Day Leclaire

Harlequin Temptation #588 in May
Stranger in the Night by Roseanne Williams

Harlequin Superromance #695 in June
Married to a Stranger by Connie Bennett

Harlequin Historicals #324 in July
Dulcie's Gift by Ruth Langan

Visit Bride's Bay Resort each month wherever
Harlequin books are sold.

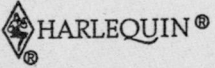

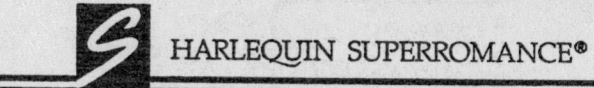

HARLEQUIN SUPERROMANCE®

From the bestselling author of
THE TAGGARTS OF TEXAS!
comes

THE CAMERONS OF COLORADO

Cupid, Colorado...

This is ranch country, cowboy country—a land of high mountains
and swift, cold rivers, of deer, elk and bear. The land is important
here—family and neighbors are, too. 'Course, you have the chance
to really get to know your neighbors in Cupid. Take the Camerons,
for instance. The first Cameron came to Cupid more than a hundred
years ago, and Camerons have owned and worked the Straight Arrow
Ranch—the largest spread in these parts—ever since.

For kids and kisses, tears and laughter, wild horses and wilder men—
come to the Straight Arrow Ranch, near Cupid, Colorado. Come meet
the Camerons.

THE CAMERONS OF COLORADO
by Ruth Jean Dale

Kids, Critters and Cupid (Superromance#678)
available in February 1996

The Cupid Conspiracy (Temptation #579)
available in March 1996

The Cupid Chronicles (Superromance #687)
available in April 1996

Let

 HARLEQUIN SUPERROMANCE®

welcome you home

Welcome to West Texas—and the Parker Ranch!

Long before the War Between the States, Parker sons and daughters ranched Parker land. Eighty-one-year-old Mae Parker aims to keep things that way. And as far as Mae—and almost everyone else on the ranch—is concerned, her word is law. Except to Rafe. And Rafe, thirty-five years old, iron-willed and *unmarried,* is Mae's favorite great-nephew. But he has no plans to buckle under to her by changing his marital status.

That's why Mae invites Shannon Bradley to the ranch. Something about Shannon—the only person other than Rafe who has ever stood up to Mae—gets under Rafe's skin. Still, after years of watching his great-aunt manipulate the rest of his family, he's damned if he'll fall in love to order!

Watch for *A Match Made In Texas* by Ginger Chambers
Available in February 1996
wherever Harlequin books are sold.

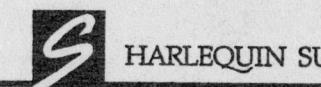

HARLEQUIN SUPERROMANCE®

a heartwarming trilogy by *Peg Sutherland*

Meet old friends and new ones on a trip to Sweetbranch, Alabama—where the most unexpected things can happen....

Queen of the Dixie Drive-In (Book 3)

Carson Delaney hasn't paid any particular attention to romance in years—not since she met Tony de Fuentes in California. Now she's back home in Sweetbranch to build a new life for herself and her sister. And the last person she expects to see there is Tony!

Look for *Queen of the Dixie Drive-In* this February wherever Harlequin Superromance novels are sold. And if you missed *Double Wedding Ring* (Book 1) and *Addy's Angels* (Book 2), it's still not too late to order them.